OWN THE EIGHTS GETS MARRIED

OWN THE EIGHTS: BOOK TWO

KRISTA SANDOR

CANDY CASTLE BOOKS

1

"Georgie Jensen, can you share with our viewers how it all began?"

Georgie smiled at the glossy-haired *Wake-Up Denver Morning Show* TV host then glanced at the cameras pointed in their direction. One would think after a whirlwind three months in the spotlight, she'd be used to the glaring lights and the bevy of how-did-you-get-here questions. She turned up the wattage on her grin, relying on her childhood days as a contestant on the beauty pageant circuit to get her through another interview when a gentle squeeze to her hand brought her back. Warmth traveled from her fingertips all the way to her chest as relief edged out anxiety and calmed her frayed nerves.

She dialed back her deranged prom queen expression, then tightened her grip on the hand holding hers.

"I think Jordan would agree that it all started with a dog."

"A dog? I thought you two met when you were paired up to compete in the CityBeat Battle of the Blogs contest back in June?" the shiny blonde replied, sharing a look with her equally shiny male counterpart.

"No, Georgie's right! It all started with a runaway mutt named Mr. Tuesday," came the deliciously sexy voice of her boyfriend and co-creator of their joint blog, More Than Just a Number, Jordan, no longer a perfect ten, Marks.

Jordan ran his thumb over her knuckles, and a tingle that wasn't made for morning TV traveled down her spine and landed squarely in her lady parts.

"The day we learned we were chosen to compete for a spot as a paid contributor on the CityBeat lifestyle blog site, I'd gone for a run, and Georgie was out chasing down her dog," Jordan added.

She chuckled. "I'd forgotten to attach the leash to Mr. Tuesday's collar, and he took off toward the park."

Jordan laced their fingers together, reigniting that zing of a tingle.

"Georgie was yelling at the top of her lungs and demanded I help her catch her dog."

She scoffed. "I didn't *demand* you help me."

"You did," he answered with a cocky smirk that damn near melted her panties.

Georgie held her boyfriend's gaze as the characters from her three favorite books, her imaginary literary trifecta, Lizzy Bennet, Jane Eyre, and Hermione Granger, swooned in her head.

Once upon a time, her CrossFit guru boyfriend blogged about striving to be a perfect ten in his Marks Perfect Ten Mindset blog.

But not anymore.

Jordan Marks had significantly veered away from the perfection-or-bust mantra he'd preached in his debunked philosophy.

Now, that didn't mean he'd abandoned his fitness regime and his goal of helping others follow a healthy lifestyle. Thanks to the prize money they'd won, he'd opened a gym right next door to her bookshop. Between him training clients and her spouting the genius of Jane Austen or reading aloud to children in the shop's newly added kids' section, they collaborated on their joint More Than Just a Number blog. Here, they offered a measured approach to relationships, fitness, and a myriad of other lifestyle topics. And to say the blog was a success would be the understatement of the century.

Every day, the offers rolled in.

Advertisers. Book deals. Speaking tours. Interviews. Product endorsements.

During the CityBeat Battle of the Blogs, she and Jordan had been splashed all over the internet's top blogging site. Millions of people across the globe had tuned in to watch them not only compete but go from being enemies to lovers in real-time.

She still maintained her Own the Eights blog. However, after joining forces with Jordan on their new endeavor, her blog had morphed into more of a book club only site where she chatted online with literary enthusiasts and led a monthly book discussion. To her surprise, in only a matter of months, she'd garnered nearly as many followers as Oprah's behemoth of a book club.

It was no joke. Their lives had completely changed the moment they'd learned the blog battle they thought they'd been competing in had been a giant ruse to catch two cheating fraudulent sibling bloggers, known on the CityBeat site as the Dannies.

In the end, she and Jordan were brought on as paid

contributors and were crowned the winners, and not just for the contest but in the game of love as well.

A romance fit to be made into a movie? Yep, they'd even received offers for that.

A naughty spark glinted in her boyfriend's eyes. "The day we met, I helped Georgie corral her pup and then we parted ways, but not before she called me an—"

Georgie pressed her hand to Jordan's lips, silencing him but not dampening the playful twinkle in his gaze.

"It's safe to say it wasn't love at first sight," she finished, feeling her cheeks heat with embarrassment.

She'd called him an asshat, which, at that point, he was. He'd grumbled about helping her, insulted her beloved Birkenstock sandals, and was a giant, well, asshat, when he spouted that dog leashes worked better when actually attached to dog collars.

But it wasn't just that. She remembered every second of their first encounter.

All bare-chested and glistening with sweat and looking like a photoshopped fitness god, Jordan Marks had been the epitome of everything she'd preached about avoiding.

A little over two years ago, after a date from hell when a handsome creep named Brice Casey told her he could only date a perfect ten and that she was an eight at best, she'd become a woman on a mission.

A mission to help others avoid the pitfalls of looks and status and focus on the attributes that really mattered. Substance. Character. Kindness. Intelligence. She'd deemed these the qualities of a solid, reliable eight. And thus, the Own the Eights blog was born.

The shiny male morning show host tapped his chin. "So, Georgie, when you learned you would have to team up with

Jordan to compete in the CityBeat Battle of the Blogs contest, I'm assuming you weren't excited."

Jordan chuckled. "She was the opposite of excited. That's when Georgie anointed me the Emperor of—"

Again, Georgie pressed her hand to Jordan's mouth.

The Emperor of Asshattery.

That's what she'd dubbed him.

And, again, it was a spot-on description in the beginning.

Georgie schooled her features, determined to get them back on track. "I was absolutely floored and completely mortified that I was going to have to team up with the *asshat* I'd met in the park a few hours earlier."

Jordan chuckled and shook his head.

She gasped and pressed her hand to her chest. "Did I just say *asshat*?"

"Yep, and now you've said it twice on a live morning show," Jordan answered, biting back a grin.

"That's the *Wake-Up Denver Morning Show*," the female host chirped as if on cue.

Georgie stared at the frozen perma-grins plastered across the hosts' faces as her trifecta cringed.

Would she ever be camera-ready? Would this life of fame and notoriety ever feel normal?

"Moving on," the male host replied, rustling a pile of papers. "It says here that you two are quite involved in the community and have an event coming up."

She breathed a sigh of relief. There was no chance of dropping another asshat bomb now.

"We sure do," Jordan answered, then gave her hand another gentle squeeze.

"Yes, we've partnered with area rec centers to put on an event combining literacy and physical fitness. Many Denver high schools require students to memorize and recite one of Shakespeare's sonnets or a passage from one of his plays. We asked the schools to give their students the option of signing up for our event. Here, they'll compete in a 5K run and then recite their piece to judges, stationed at tables past the finish line," she answered, sounding a little less moronic.

"We're calling it The Shakespeare Shuffle, and it's only a couple weeks away," Jordan finished.

Okay, now they were back on track.

They'd worked hard putting the event together, and, as their first major project with the More Than Just a Number blog, their reputations were resting on it being a success.

The shiny lady host turned to the camera and flashed her pearly whites. "Running and reciting Shakespeare! It sounds like the perfect combination. Stay close, and we'll be back after the break with more from your favorite blogger sweethearts, Jordan Marks and Georgie Jensen."

"And, we're clear," a producer called. "Two minutes and thirty seconds until we're back live, people."

Georgie slumped against the sofa and stared down at Jordan's hand still clasped around hers. "I think I'm getting better at these things," she teased.

Jordan lifted her hand to his lips and pressed a kiss to her palm. "You've certainly broadened the vocabulary of any kid listening."

She brightened up. "As a bookshop owner, I am all for increasing one's vocabulary."

"Then you've succeeded," Jordan answered with that smarty-pants grin she'd grown to love.

She took in the studio, bustling with activity. "And, we'll probably get emails."

"We always get emails," he answered.

"Not with *asshat* in the subject line," she replied.

"How about this? As the reigning Emperor of Asshattery, I'll personally field those messages."

And just like that, it was the two of them, cocooned in their love as a tornado of activity swirled around them.

"Have I told you how much I love you?" she asked.

He leaned in. "You were screaming my name this morning. So, I'd say you were pretty clear you like having me around."

Her slight blush from the asshat mishap deepened to a full crimson flush.

"Jordan, you can't say that here!" she whisper-shouted.

He stroked his thumb across her knuckles, then gestured with his chin as a production assistant zoomed past them.

"For once, we don't seem to be the center of attention. We should do the news more often."

She glanced over at the morning show hosts, surrounded by assistants and makeup people.

Jordan was right. No one seemed concerned with them at all.

A sly smile pulled at the corners of her mouth. "I distinctly remember you using some very colorful language yourself this morning."

His gaze grew carnal. "I am the reason you've got sex hair today."

She twisted a loose lock of hair that had fallen free of her messy bun. "I tried take a shower, but then this sex god joined me under the spray."

"Sex god, huh?" he said, his voice sending another tantalizing tingle down her spine.

"Oh, yes! You see, I'm a dirty, dirty girl, and I couldn't resist him. Before I knew it, I was down on my knees—"

"Miss Jensen!" someone called.

Her head whipped toward the sound as a young man

wearing a pair of headphones and carrying a clipboard sprinted over to the couch.

He pointed to her chest and blushed. "You're hot."

"What did you say to Georgie?" Jordan asked with a hardened expression.

The kid shifted his weight from foot to foot. "Hot! Miss Jensen is hot!"

"Who the hell are you?" Jordan pressed.

"I'm Cooper, sir."

Jordan held the man's gaze. "Do you have a death wish or like getting your ass kicked, Cooper?"

She was wondering the same thing. The poor guy looked barely old enough to get into a bar, let alone hit on her with her boyfriend right there.

The color drained from the man's face. "The mic she's wearing. Well, the mics that both of you are wearing. They're on. They're hot. Anyone with a headset can hear you."

Georgie cringed. "Wait a second. You heard me say the thing about the shower?"

He nodded. "Yeah, seventeen of us heard."

She turned to Jordan. "Oh, my God!"

"You've been saying that a lot this morning," he teased as his anger dissolved into amusement.

Georgie cupped her hand over Jordan's mic and pressed her other palm against her own. "What will they think?"

Jordan shrugged. "At least everyone here knows we like each other."

"Yes, but." She glanced up at Cooper, then scanned the studio, counting the number of people wearing headsets.

Yep, it was seventeen.

She took in the group, throwing quick glances their way.

"I think everyone is looking at my hair."

The production assistant nodded. "They are. We heard you mention sex hair and wondered if we should send hair and makeup over to you. We don't get a lot of sex hair on the morning show. We're mostly PG around here."

"Look at that, messy bun girl, you've sexed up morning TV," Jordan replied with that damned cocksure grin in place.

"It's *Wake-Up Denver*," came a chorus of startling voices.

"They can still hear me?" she asked, glancing wildly back and forth.

"The mics are really sensitive," Cooper offered apologetically.

"Thirty seconds, folks. If we're going to address the sex hair, it needs to happen now," the producer announced.

Holy hot mics!

Georgie sunk into the couch cushion, praying it would swallow her whole.

First, she dropped asshat on live TV. And now, the entire morning show crew knew she had dirty girl sex that had left her with sex hair.

A woman carrying a makeup bag crammed with brushes and beauty supplies rushed to the set.

Georgie touched her bun then tucked an errant lock of hair behind her ear. "I think I look all right," she said as the woman stared at her bun and frowned.

"Twenty seconds. Places, people."

The makeup lady skittered off the set as the hosts took their seats at the desk, looking even shinier than before.

Georgie tried to compose herself. All they had left to do was a segment where she would talk about the Own the Eights book of the month. Then, Jordan would take over and dole out a few tips on exercising outdoors.

She tucked another loose tendril of hair behind her ear as the producer started counting down.

"In ten, folks."

She turned to Jordan, who's expression had done a one-eighty.

His confident smirk had disappeared, and his knee bounced as if he were a naughty schoolboy, waiting to see the principal.

"Are you okay?" she whispered.

"Nine," the producer called.

Jordan nodded, then glanced off stage where Bobby Chen and Hector Garcia, the CityBeat lifestyle blog founders, now stood.

What were they doing here?

"Eight."

She and Jordan had grown close with the tech power couple over the last few months, but there was no need for them to show up for this interview.

And then Georgie's stomach dropped.

Hector and Bobby were known for adding a little twist or a touch of flair to any CityBeat related event. And they loved a good story. Especially something juicy for all the CityBeat subscribers to sink their virtual teeth into.

"Seven."

And it wasn't just Hector and Bobby waiting in the wings. Barry, one of the CityBeat producers, was with them. She shielded her face and caught his eye through the bright lights. He gave her a thumbs-up with one hand while holding his phone with the other, which was, most likely, livestreaming to the main CityBeat page.

"Six."

She patted Jordan's arm. "Bobby, Hector, and Barry are here."

Jordan swallowed hard and nodded.

"Five."

She turned to the hosts. "Are we getting punked? Is that even a thing anymore?" she asked the hosts, who, in return, greeted her with plastic camera-ready smiles.

"Four."

A series of rapid clattering clicks off set caught her attention. She did a double take as her friend and bookshop employee Becca Murphy joined the CityBeat trio and had Mr. Tuesday with her.

"Why is Becca here with our dog?" she whisper-shouted to her boyfriend, then glanced around. "And why the hell is everyone smiling at us like a bunch of creepy wax figures?"

"Three."

Georgie stared into the camera as the producer stopped voicing the countdown, held up two fingers, then one, then pointed at the female host.

"And we're back. For all those just tuning in to *Wake-Up Denver*, today, we've got the CityBeat Battle of the Blog winners, Georgie Jensen and Jordan Marks here in the studio with us. Let's take a peek at this montage of how they fell in love."

Georgie's jaw dropped.

What the heck? Nobody had said anything about a montage!

But she knew there was plenty of tape.

During the Battle of the Blogs, Barry, their assigned CityBeat producer, had recorded footage at several of the blog challenge events.

But nobody had told them they'd be doing a walk down memory lane this morning. She was all ready to introduce the book of the month and had emailed images to the morning show producer to use for her segment. Instead, the musical stylings of Michael Bolton singing "How Am I Supposed To Live Without You" blared as the screen behind them, seemingly the size of the side of a semi-truck trailer, flashed images.

First, a pic of Jordan feeding a baby goat after he'd conquered his fear of interacting with the tiny farm animal during a goat yoga session. Next, came a video clip of the two of them, sitting side by side in the grass, laughing while surrounded by a hoard of bleating animals.

So far, nothing terrible until, dark and grainy, another image flashed, and Georgie sucked in a tight breath. She could almost taste the six Jell-O shots that had preceded the night she'd lost her damn mind. There she was, super-sized on the enormous screen, strutting down a makeshift runway inside a seedy Denver bar as a wet T-shirt contest contestant in heels and Daisy Duke shorts.

"Here it comes," she whispered, watching herself trip and then fall into Jordan's arms.

"We really need to write a post about how, once something is on the internet, it never goes away," she murmured to Jordan, who barely nodded and was still acting like he was in some sort of half-comatose state.

More pictures of the two of them carouseled through before a clip of her running in the Denver 10K Trot splashed across the screen. Jordan took her hand as they watched him catch up with her with a tube of vegan cookie dough and then profess his love for her.

Nothing is worth winning if it means losing you.

She blinked back tears, remembering when Jordan had spoken those words.

The clip ended, and she exhaled a shaky breath. They were still on live TV, and she wasn't about to go full-on waterworks.

"What a story!" the male host offered.

"Yes, I love that moment when you're power-walking, Georgie, and Jordan catches up to you," the anchorwoman added, dabbing at her eyes with a tissue.

"I was actually running," she corrected.

The male host shared a look with his co-host. "It sure looked like a power walk to me."

Georgie sighed. This was simply not a battle she'd ever win. She glanced at Jordan, sure he'd have something to say about her glacial running pace and found him nodding toward Hector and Bobby.

Once this segment was over, she was bound and determined to figure out what the hell was going on.

"What does the next chapter hold for Georgie Jensen and Jordan Marks?" the female host asked.

Georgie looked from her tongue-tied boyfriend to her friends before realizing it was up to her to keep this crazy train from going off the rails.

She resurrected her beauty queen expression. "We're exploring all avenues and ways to expand the More Than Just a Number blog and brand. We wanted to start locally because the community is very important to us..." she answered but trailed off as Jordan released her hand and got down on one knee in front of her, and the penny dropped.

One knee.

A freaking falling in love montage.

She scanned the studio, filled with smiling faces and a cameraman now standing only a few feet behind her.

She lowered her voice. "Jordan, what are you doing?"

He looked up and met her gaze. "Hopefully, starting our next chapter."

2

He was doing it. He was really doing it.

Right here. Right now.

Down on one knee, he stared into Georgie's eyes. Not quite blue and not quite green, they weren't only beautiful. They were the color of his future. The last thing he wanted to see before he went to sleep, and the first thing he wanted to lay his eyes on each morning.

Georgiana Jensen, former Miss Cherry Pie, and the eternal love of his life.

This remarkable woman had made him question everything. She'd peeled past the layers he'd erected around his heart. With her messy bun and her librarian cardigans, she'd blasted through his guise of physical perfection.

It wasn't like there was anything wrong with working hard or, for that matter, caring for your appearance. But it wasn't everything. Not even close.

Before Georgie, he'd put so much energy into proving to himself that he was no longer the string bean high school weakling everyone had teased. They'd called him Straws back then, thanks to his long skinny legs. The jocks and the school jerks would stuff his locker full of the cafeteria staple just to laugh and gawk when he opened his locker, and they all tumbled out in a humiliating wave of white paper wrappers.

He'd tried to bury his past and forget that sad, skinny kid. And for nearly a decade, he'd almost done it, thanks to a chance encounter delivering food to a CrossFit gym when he was eighteen. His life changed after the gym owner, Deacon Perry, had taken a shine to him. Through dedication and damn hard work, the string bean boy morphed into a powerful man.

Fifty pounds of pure muscle can do that. And as his body changed, so did his mind. Many of the changes were positive, others were not.

With each pull-up and every deadlift, he endeavored to erase all the signs of his former self and took on a hyper-masculine edge to mask the bullied boy within. Instead of honoring the creative and introspective kid he used to be, he began equating bravery with brawn and toughness with physical tenacity. When he'd come up with the idea for the Marks Perfect Ten Mindset blog, he did want to help people reach their personal best. But he also used it to create another layer between himself and that skinny kid from the Colorado plains.

Thanks to Georgie, he could be both the ripped fitness trainer as well as the comic-loving, literature-reading man who wasn't defined by a number.

He glanced over his shoulder and nodded to Becca. She gave him a thumbs-up then unhooked Mr. Tuesday's collar.

This was really happening.

Black and white with one ear cocked up while the other drooped down, the dog he'd come to love bounded toward them with a ribbon tied around his neck.

"Jordan is this what I think it is?" Georgie asked as she scratched between the dog's ears.

"Well, it's not a segment on selecting the perfect pet for your lifestyle," he answered, untying the ribbon and sliding an engagement ring off the strip of satin.

"How did you arrange all this?" she asked wide-eyed.

"We can answer that!" Hector exclaimed, taking Bobby's hand and joining them on set.

Something he was absolutely not expecting as the couple took a seat, one on each side of Georgie.

"Jordan came to us and asked about how we got engaged, and then it snowballed from there," Hector, the more outspoken of the power couple, explained.

"We shared with Jordan how I had brought Hector to our favorite bench, hidden away in the Denver Botanic Gardens, and asked him to be my husband and partner for life, surrounded by tulips and the buzz of bees," Bobby answered softly.

"It was so romantic. So intimate," Hector gushed.

Jordan caught Georgie's gaze. "This is kind of the opposite of intimate."

Georgie leaned to the side as a cameraman pushed in and entered their personal space. "Yeah, you could say that."

"But a proposal on morning TV is completely apropos for CityBeat's most-watched and adored couple," Hector answered.

"That's *Wake-Up Denver*," the host injected with a grin so wide she looked as if she belonged in a scary clown movie.

Shit! This whole idea sounded perfect when he'd spoken with Bobby and Hector. Now, with the cameras and the lights, he couldn't help wondering if he'd made the wrong call.

He glanced between the men. "Do you guys mind if I," he began, then held up the ring.

Hector nodded. "The engagement ring! We can't forget that!"

"Yes, it's a vintage piece, dating back to the forties," Bobby added.

Inches from his hand, the cameraman angled in to get a better shot.

"We were there with Jordan when he picked it out, Georgie," Hector said, fanning his face, as the man grew emotional.

"We knew with your love of all things vintage, like those old, dusty Jane Austen volumes you adore, that a ring with history would be right up your alley," Bobby added softly as the TV host handed Hector a tissue.

The man blew his nose. "Georgie and Jordan, you two are like the children we never had," Hector blubbered.

Georgie patted the emotional man's back. "Hector, you're only like ten years older than me."

"You know what I mean. Our little wet T-shirt contest winner and our big strong man who overcame his goat phobia are getting engaged," the man replied, blotting tears.

Bobby, the more reserved of the two, pushed up his glasses. "You both are very important to the CityBeat family and to us."

"Without the Battle of the Blogs contest, you two may have never met. Bobby, we're like Georgie and Jordan's virtual fairy godfathers," Hector added while accepting another tissue from the *Wake-Up Denver* host.

Mr. Tuesday curled up on the floor, uninterested in the melee, then released a dog fart.

Everyone stilled as the pup, unbothered, yawned, then proceeded to fall asleep.

Georgie bit her lip, clearly holding back laughter as her cheeks grew pink.

This marriage proposal had not only gotten sidetracked. It had become an all-out circus.

He held up the ring. "Um, guys, would you mind if I proposed?"

"Let's ask the world!" Hector answered, waving Barry over.

"Our producer has been live streaming right to the City-Beat main page and monitoring the comments," Bobby added.

The male host perked up. "Let's get that up on the big screen for our *Wake-Up Denver* viewers at home."

A second later, there they were.

"Wow! We're on live TV while watching ourselves on live TV," Georgie murmured, craning her head toward the giant screen.

"Very trippy, right?" Hector replied with a nod.

Trippy.

That was an excellent description of their current situation. And bam, bam, bam! The screen flooded with comment bubbles, likes, and heart emojis as pandemonium exploded on CityBeat's main page.

"We're getting messages from all over. All across the US, India, Denmark, Tunisia, France, Canada, and more by the second. Jordan's proposal has ignited an outpouring of excitement from CityBeat subscribers across the globe," Barry offered.

Jordan's gaze bounced between the men. "Guys, I haven't proposed yet."

"And Georgie, look at that!" Barry exclaimed. "A Belgian princess posted that she wished you and Jordan a happy life together."

"A Belgian princess?" Georgie repeated.

Barry shook his head. "Oops, my bad! That's the *Belgian Waffle Princess*. She's got an amazing blog on all things waffles."

"I don't know about you, but I love a good Belgian waffle," the female host said, grinning into the camera.

"With some cut up strawberries, powdered sugar, and a drizzling of real maple syrup. That's the definition of delicious," the male host chimed as Bobby, Hector, and Barry began sharing their favorite ways to dress up a waffle.

Georgie pressed her hand to her lips.

They were way past shitshow at this point. The proposal he'd pictured in his head had turned into one hell of a waffle-house sized cluster.

"Hold on, everyone! The CityBeat subscriber Passion for Ponies commented that Jordan and Georgie aren't officially engaged yet."

Hector cocked his head to the side and frowned. "Well, what are you waiting for, Jordan? Are you going to make Passion for Ponies wait for a second longer?"

What was he waiting for?

A moment of sanity with his girl?

A waffle-free zone to propose?

A little less pressure from pony enthusiasts?

He turned to Georgie, and all the craziness melted away when he looked into her eyes. She smiled down at him, and all thoughts of ponies or waffles or baby goats—that he no longer feared—vanished. He glanced at the ring. It was perfect. Delicate and beautiful while also strong and enduring, he'd known this was the ring for Georgie even before Hector and Bobby had uttered a word about the sparkling gem.

He traced his thumb down her ring finger. "Georgiana

Jensen, messy bun girl and the woman who owns my heart, will you marry me?"

"Everyone! Stop the waffle talk! Jordan's proposing!" Barry called, waving for the group to quiet down.

"If I say yes, will it make me the Empress of Asshattery?" Georgie asked with a sly twist to her lips.

He met her teasing grin with one of his own. "We'd probably need to consult the Belgian Waffle Princess on matters of royal protocol to be sure, but I'd say there's an excellent chance of that happening. And by the way, you've said asshat or some form of it at least three times on morning TV."

"That's *Wake*—" the host began, but Jordan held up his hand, silencing the *Wake-Up Denver* plug.

"You've dropped it a few times yourself, mister," his hopefully soon-to-be fiancée parried back.

He brushed his thumb across her knuckles. "What do you say, Georgiana? Will you be mine forever?"

"Bobby, look at them," Hector clucked through a veil of tears.

Georgie's gaze traveled around the set.

"Yes or no, Georgiana? Denver and the entire world are watching," the male host coaxed in a made-for-TV purr. A sugary sound that made Jordan want to pick up the guy and toss him over the giant *Wake-Up Denver* jumbotron screen. But before he had time to go full CrossFit cretin on the man, Georgie cupped his face in her hand.

She stroked his cheek—something she'd done every day —but today, on the day of his proposal, it brought tears to his eyes. He was over six feet of pure muscle, but with the brush of her thumb, this wisp of a woman could bring him to his knees.

Her gaze grew glassy. "Yes, a thousand times, yes."

He chuckled, savoring the warmth of her touch. "You had to throw a little Jane Austen in there, didn't you?"

"What did you expect? You did just propose to a book-shop owner."

She gave him a sweet shrug as he tried to slide the ring onto her finger.

And it was too...

Hector gasped. "It's too big! It doesn't fit?"

Bobby scratched his head. "I would have sworn Georgie was a size six."

"It's fine, guys. We can get it resized. I'll wear it on my middle finger until we can get that done," Georgie answered, offering up the larger digit.

"What does it mean if the ring doesn't fit?" Hector questioned in a low whisper.

Jordan tried to hold it together as a wave of frustration washed over him.

Christ! First, the proposal from hell and now, the damn ring didn't fit.

"Georgie, I—" he began, wanting to apologize, scoop her up, throw her over his shoulder like a sack of potatoes, and get them the hell off that set. But he froze when the *Wake-Up Denver* producer signaled to wrap it up, and the host turned to the camera with her plastic smile blazing.

"Don't go away! We'll be back after this commercial break with seven ways to spice up Taco Tuesday."

"And, we're clear," the producer chimed.

Georgie sat back. "Wow, that was intense."

He took her hands into his. "Georgie, I'm sorry. When I planned this in my head, it looked a lot different."

"So, you weren't already in cahoots with the Belgian Waffle Princess?" she replied, gazing down at their hands and the ring sparkling on the wrong finger.

Jesus, this woman! He was one lucky man. The fact that she could see the humor in this mess said more than words ever could.

He shook his head and cringed. "No way. You know how I feel about empty calories in breakfast foods. The only way to eat a Belgian waffle is if it's made with buckwheat flour, and you've added ground chia seeds for an Omega punch."

"And speaking of buckwheat waffles!" Bobby said as he checked his phone. "We need to get you two into a car."

"A car?" he and Georgie repeated in unison.

"Yes, a car, so you can get to the champagne engagement party," Barry added, hammering out a text on his phone.

Jordan shared a look with Georgie. "A champagne, what?"

This was news to him.

Hector handed the Kleenex box to a passing production assistant. "You silly things, of course, we're going to celebrate. And what better way than to celebrate with champagne!"

"And CityBeat will be there to share in this happy day!" Bobby added.

"CityBeat will be there?" Jordan asked, coming to his feet.

Bobby held out his phone. "Yes, look at these stats. The world loves you guys. And with your More Than Just a Number blog growing, this is exactly the type of content you need to share with your subscribers."

Content?

His proposal was a hell of a lot more than merely content for their newsfeed. Sure, he loved their More Than Just a Number blog. He valued every person who chose to subscribe. It was their platform, their vision, and they wanted to help and inspire people. But their blog wasn't a voyeuristic site intent on broadcasting every facet of their lives.

He was about to set the record straight when the production assistant, who he'd almost punched into next week thanks to that whole *you're hot* mix-up, approached the group.

"Sorry, folks, but we need you off the set so we can set up for the Taco Tuesday segment."

"Jordan and I aren't doing our segments?" Georgie asked as two large men lifted the couch she'd been sitting on while another burly man rolled out a table on squeaky wheels.

The kid shifted his stance. "Sorry, your whole waffle wedding proposal took the place of it."

"Waffle wedding proposal?" Jordan repeated as Georgie's expression grew pained, which hit him like a punch to the gut.

Dammit! He'd shared the whole engagement idea with the *Wake-Up Denver* producer a couple of days ago. Still, the man hadn't mentioned anything about cutting the educational component of their time on-air.

Georgie produced a grin that didn't quite reach her eyes. "It's okay. I understand," she answered, then lifted a sleeping Mr. Tuesday off the ground and into her arms.

They followed the production assistant off the set as a woman buzzed past them, removing their mics then flitted away toward the chefs standing at the taco set.

Being in this place was starting to feel like a continual case of whiplash. He pressed his hand to the small of Georgie's back and followed the CityBeat wedding brigade off the set when Becca met them in the hallway.

"Congratulations! Let's see this ring!" Georgie's friend exclaimed.

"No time!" Hector called, waving them forward. "Do the doggie switcheroo, and then we need to be off."

Georgie looked from Mr. Tuesday to Becca. "Do you mind taking him home? I'm not exactly sure what's happening at the…"

"Why, we're all headed to the Denver Palace Hotel! The perfect place for the prince and princess of CityBeat!" Hector supplied.

Jordan looked between the blog site founders. "You guys can't be serious with this whole prince and princess thing?"

"That's what the Belgian Waffle Princess dubbed you guys, and it seems to be trending online along with Emperor of Asshattery," Barry said, tilting his phone for them to see the post.

"You know what that means," Hector said, rubbing his hands together.

Jordan shared a look with Georgie, who shook her head.

"No, we have no idea what it means," he answered.

"Tiaras!" Hector breathed with a wild glint in his eyes. "We need to start investigating tiaras, pronto, Bobby."

Georgie stiffened. "I think I'd like to skip the car ride over."

"Whatever for?" Bobby asked, concern etched on his face.

"The Palace Hotel isn't far from here, and I could use a meandering walk," she answered, and Jordan's heart jumped into his throat.

Georgiana Jensen's meandering walks meant she had something weighing on her mind, most likely due to the over-sized engagement ring sparkling on her go-fuck-your-self finger. But, truth be told, he could use a break from tissues, TV, and tiaras, too.

Georgie passed Mr. Tuesday over to Becca, and the

women began to talk dog logistics as he gestured for Bobby, Hector, and Barry to join him down the hall.

He schooled his features into his do-not-mess-with-me CrossFit angry-god expression. A little something he kept in his back pocket from his Marks Perfect Ten Mindset days.

He narrowed his gaze. "Georgie and I will meet you at the hotel, but you guys have to take it down a notch."

"Jordan," Bobby said with a placating expression. "You know my husband, Hector—make a big deal out of everything—Garcia. He could turn a trip to the podiatrist into a major event."

"Well, why wouldn't you? I have those gorgeous eco-friendly sandals I wear anytime my little piggies need attending to," Hector replied, then watched him closely. "You're not afraid of piglets, are you, Jordan?"

Jordan scrubbed his hands down his face, suddenly feeling insanely exhausted. "No, it was just baby goats, and I'm totally over that," he answered, not entirely telling the truth.

But close enough.

"Such a powerful moment for CityBeat," Barry chimed, pressing his hand to his heart.

Georgie came to his side. "Are you ready?"

He took her hand. "We'll meet you there," he said to the men as he led Georgie out of the building.

She exhaled an audible breath and leaned into him as they strolled down the sidewalk. It was the perfect early fall day in Denver. The trees were beginning to pop with splashes of gold and red, and all he wanted to do was take his fiancée over to a bench and sit.

No words.

No Belgian Waffle Princesses or *Wake-Up Denver* plugs.

Just the two of them with his arm wrapped around her shoulders.

"Are you contemplating our escape, too?" she asked, breaking into his thoughts.

He chuckled. "Not so much as an escape but a moment alone with you without some idiot trying to work-in the words, Wake-Up Denver."

She held out her hand with the sparkling diamond. "You mean a moment alone with your fiancée?"

He liked the sound of that.

He sighed. "I'm sorry the ring is the wrong size. Between myself and the wedding wonder twins, I thought I could have gotten that part right."

She wiggled her fingers as the diamond sparkled in the sunlight. "It's nothing a jeweler can't take care of. But I have to ask you, when did you start thinking about proposing? Don't get me wrong. I love you. I want to spend the rest of my life with you, but today was a huge surprise."

"I had to ask before you got another proposal," he replied, suppressing a grin.

She looked up at him, her eyes twinkling. "From who?"

"Remember when that little kid asked you to marry him a couple weeks ago?"

"Little Joey, the five-year-old from the bookstore?" she asked with a thread of incredulity.

He laughed. "It sounds crazy when you put it like that. But I have to admit, I was a little caught off guard by it. But the kid was right. What was I waiting for?"

She hummed a sweet chuckle. "You know there's no one I love more than you."

"I know," he answered gently, wrapping his arm around her.

"I can't wait to be your wife," she said, smiling up at him.

This—the two of them. This is who they were.

The hotel came into view, and Georgie stopped and stared at the building.

She turned to him with a slight crease to her brow. "We want this, don't we?"

He knew exactly what she was talking about and wrapped his arms around her, drawing her in close.

He ran his hand down her back. "We both want to help people live their best life. It's what we've wanted from the beginning."

She sighed, and her warm breath tickled his neck. "I wanted to talk more about the Shakespeare Shuffle. Do you think we'll be able to pull it off?"

"The high schools are all promoting it, and we post about it every day," he answered.

"It's our first big project. I don't want us to crash and burn," she whispered.

Neither did he.

"Hey, we've proven there's nothing the wet T-shirt girl and the goat guy can't do. With enough vegan cookie dough, we're unstoppable."

She grinned up at him with a smile that turned him to mush.

"But we do have one problem," he said, working to keep his features neutral.

"We do? What's that?" she asked.

His stony expression gave way to a wide grin. "I haven't kissed you as my fiancée yet."

"No, you have not," she replied, her gaze darkening.

He leaned in. "We need to change that."

"Why's that?" she purred.

"Because after we finish with whatever the hell kind of champagne party Hector and Bobby have up their sleeves,

I'm taking you home, and we're getting your sex hair back."

Georgie drew her fingertips down his torso. "Is that so?"

He nodded. "And there won't be enough hair conditioner in all of Denver to untangle it after I'm through with you, soon-to-be, Mrs. Marks."

He tilted her chin and stroked his thumb across her jawline. With a sexy as hell sigh, Georgie closed her eyes and melted into his touch when a sharp gasp and shrill yelp accompanied by the scent of perfume left them frozen.

"Pumpkin! Jordan! There's not going to be a soon-to-be-*anything* if you two don't stop playing kissy-face for all of the city to see and make an appearance at your party!"

Georgie cringed.

She'd know the haughty huff of the Denver socialite Lorraine Vanderdinkle, aka her mother, anywhere.

She squeezed her eyes shut. Maybe if she didn't officially see the woman, she and Jordan could take off running down the street.

"Georgiana? Pumpkin?" came the familiar chime of her mother's voice.

"You told my mother?" she whispered.

"Of course, I did! I went to see her and Howard to ask for their blessing. And I've got to tell you, Howard is a pretty great guy. I've never talked that much with him."

"Me neither, actually," she answered.

"It wasn't like I could go to Lizzy Bennet, Jane Eyre, or Hermione Granger and ask for their approval. But I did reread *Pride and Prejudice*. So, there's that," he whispered back.

Her trifecta shrugged.

Dammit! Going to her mother and stepfather was the honorable thing to do.

"But there's more," Jordan said, keeping his voice low.

More? What more could there possibly be than knowing her mother had probably already decided this wedding was going to be Denver's next big social event?

She squeezed her eyes shut even tighter. "What kind of more?"

"I'm pretty sure she's been in contact with Bobby and Hector."

"Oh, my God," Georgie whisper-shouted as her eyes fluttered open.

Jordan cringed apologetically, and she held his gaze, her eyes growing wider.

"It's like we've got our very own Hydra of Lerna."

Jordan cocked his head to the side. "What the hell is that?"

"It's from Greek mythology. It's—"

He gasped. "I remember. It's a three-headed monster."

Georgie risked a glance and found her mother flanked by Bobby and Hector.

"The Hydra of Denver," she said with a gulp, fearing the power of three.

"The Hydra of Denver? Is that a fancy cocktail or a new spa treatment at the Ritz, pumpkin?" her mother asked with a frown in her voice.

Knowing her mom, Lorraine Vanderdinkle probably thought she was frowning, but with the Botox, all that happened was a slight twitch to the corner of her mouth.

Muted frown or not, if she thought Hector and Bobby's involvement was bad, the addition of her mother to the wedding planning mix would be absolutely catastrophic.

Georgie caught Jordan's eye, expecting to find the same level of dread she was sure burned in her gaze when the man winked at her. He actually winked! The thing is, it was just what she needed. That tiny gesture helped ease the surge of frantic energy she experienced whenever her mother was in the vicinity.

"Come on, you two. You don't want to keep your guests waiting," Hector added, waving them toward the entrance.

Georgie shared a look with Jordan as they followed the wedding brigade into the hotel.

"I hope they didn't go too crazy on this champagne breakfast thing," she said, mustering courage.

"Would a champagne fountain the size of a skyscraper count as too crazy?" he asked.

"Why?" she questioned, as a wave of apprehension washed over her.

But Jordan didn't need to elaborate.

They entered a room that could only be described as Willy Wonka meets pretty, pretty princess. Square in the center of the grand space, a tower of champagne bottles and crystal flutes formed what looked like a Dom Pérignon monster Christmas tree.

But that wasn't all.

In each corner stood giant fountains, flowing with chocolate and littered with strawberries and other fondue delicacies.

Georgie gasped when she caught a glimpse of a man dressed in a pink chef's uniform. He stood behind a table teeming with polished silver chafing dishes. Brandishing two large knives, the man held them over his head like a culinary samurai before turning his attention and knife skills on a giant hunk of meat.

And the baby pink! It was inescapable. From the bouquets of flowers placed on every flat surface to the tablecloths to swaths of fabric draped between the chandeliers, they'd walked into a Pepto-Bismol champagne party prison.

"It's so pink," she uttered.

"But you like pink, pumpkin," her mother replied with her signature tinkling laugh.

"I like the color rose, Mom," she muttered.

"And there are a lot of people here," Jordan added, taking in the masses, mingling in the opulent room.

Her mother waved him off. "It's only family and friends. And, of course, everyone from the Country Club and Howard's venture capitalist chums. Oh, yes, and the media!"

"As well as CityBeat and all their subscribers," Barry added, holding up his phone.

Startled, Georgie shrieked. "When did you get here?"

"I was behind you the whole time."

Jordan tensed. "You followed us?"

Barry raised a hand in mock defense. "Only to get some shots of you two walking. I wasn't close enough to hear you."

She gestured to his phone. "And now?"

"Now, you should say hello to everyone at CityBeat. We're livestreaming."

Georgie resurrected her beauty queen grin. "Hey, everyone! Jordan and I are so happy to have you along with us today."

And she was. She really was. But they'd been engaged less than an hour, and all this fanfare and publicity around their pending nuptials was already snowballing into one behemoth of an event.

"Mom," she said, turning away from Barry. But before she could utter another word, Lorraine Vanderdinkle went into full-on socialite mode, plucking a flute of champagne from a passing waiter and calling for the crowds' attention.

"Dear friends and members of the Denver Country Club and global community! Our guests of honor have arrived!" she declared, flashing a Botox grin Barry's way.

The rapid snap of the photographers' cameras pelted the air in a clatter of clicks.

Jordan took her hand and leaned in, his lips millimeters from her earlobe. "Remember, Miss Sex Hair, after we get through this, I'm taking you home, and I'm not letting you out of bed until we've gone through the entire naughty section of the Kama Sutra."

She gestured to the bevy of men and women taking their picture, then lowered her voice. "It may take a couple of times through to get this out of my head."

He gave her a wolfish grin. "Thanks to following the More Than a Number exercise and healthy eating protocol, you know I'm up for it."

"Jordy! Georgie!" came the booming voice of Jordan's father, Dennis Marks, and her apprehension over the circus of an engagement party subsided.

Denny slung a zipped up faded garment bag over his shoulder as he shook his son's hand, then pressed a kiss to her cheek.

"Congratulations! You kids looked great on TV."

"I don't know if great's the word," she answered, but she was *grateful* to have him there.

Denny waved her off. "Nah, everybody loved it. I watched most of it with the guys from the shop. They all wanted me to wish you well. Even the crustiest of mechanics have a soft side."

"A crusty mechanic who also harbors a secret love of Michael Bolton ballads?" she teased, lowering her voice as the big guy blushed.

He'd come a long way from the sullen, angry man he'd become after his wife passed away when Jordan was a kid. But over the past few months, thanks to the father and the son making a real effort to talk *to* each other rather than *at* each other, the man had transformed.

And, as of a few weeks ago, he happened to be living down the block from them in Denver's quaint and eclectic Tennyson neighborhood. He'd sold his home on the Colorado plains and used some of the money to purchase an automotive shop from Jordan's friends, Ginger and Zeke, the old owners, who were leaving Colorado to be closer to their families on the West Coast.

"I'm glad you're here, Dad," Jordan said, throwing a mock punch at the man's arm.

Denny's gaze grew glassy. "I wouldn't miss it for the world, son."

"We are so happy you could join us, Dennis. Now, what is this monstrosity you've got hanging off your arm?" her mother asked, eyeing the bag suspiciously.

Denny's eyes lit up. "This here is a Marks family tradition."

Jordan paled. "Oh no, Dad! I don't think..."

"How lovely! Let's have a look!" Lorraine replied.

Suddenly, Georgie was thankful for her mother's Botox face as Denny proudly removed a wrinkled electric blue tuxedo with a ruffled dress shirt and matching trousers.

"Is that a vintage sharkskin tux?" Hector asked.

"Sure is. My dad married my mother in this suit, and I married my beautiful late wife in it. Son, it looks like you'll be wearing it soon, too."

Jordan's gaze bounced between his father and her mother. "Dad, I didn't even know you still had that."

"I'd never part with it!" he said, running his index finger tenderly over the ruffled shirt.

"Wow, Denny! That tux is unique," Georgie said, choosing her words carefully and trying to breathe through her mouth. She didn't want to hurt the man's feelings, but the suit was in awful shape and smelled terrible.

"Has that suit been stored in a chemical waste plant, or is that the mothballs I'm smelling?" her mother inquired, her face frozen in a muted state of surprise.

But the woman was right. The garment reeked.

"It's the mothballs. And there's more!" Denny answered, his features becoming more animated.

"More?" Lorraine Vanderdinkle repeated, drawing her hand delicately to her nose.

"Yes, ma'am! These are the very mothballs my grandfather used more than fifty years ago."

Hector demurely pressed his fingertips to his nose and turned to her mother. "You could call it a vintage piece of living history."

More like smelly history, but she was grateful Hector was trying to put a positive spin on the situation.

"Let's have Nicolette take it off your hands so you can enjoy the celebration, Dennis!" her mother said with a practiced grin.

Georgie looked around. "Who's Nicolette?"

"That would be me," a petite woman with her dark hair in a severe bun answered in a thick French accent.

"And you are?" Georgie asked.

"She's my personal assistant," her mother replied with a wave of her hand.

Georgie frowned. "Why would you need a personal assistant? You don't have a job."

"Georgiana!" her mother scoffed. "Are you going to stand there and tell me that being a mother isn't a job?"

"But I'm not a little kid. I'm twenty-seven years old."

"And don't I know it! Twenty-seven times more work!" her mother replied with an exaggerated sigh.

Georgie glanced at Jordan, who gave her a slight shake of the head. He was just as perplexed as she was with this Nicolette. Or perhaps it was the stench of the half-a-century-old mothballs.

"Nicolette, I need you to put this someplace *special* for Mr. Marks," Lorraine purred.

Denny gazed at the suit. "Shucks, I was thinking of putting it on and wearing it for the party—for old times' sake."

Botox be damned! With Jordan's father's declaration, her mother's eyebrows shot up to her hairline.

"No, no, no! We can't have that and risk this *heirloom* getting stained or torn."

"I guess you have a point," the man conceded as the petite Nicolette whisked the garment out of his arms and sailed out of the ballroom like a member of a seasoned hazmat response team.

"Now, if you don't mind, I should attend to the guests and check on the champagne fountain," Lorraine said as her gaze traveled to the CityBeat producer livestreaming to the internet.

Her mother smiled into the camera. "Bobby, Hector, and, dear Barry, will you sweet men accompany me? So much to do! And I think your subscribers would love a behind the scenes sneak peek at Georgiana and Jordan's party. As you all must know, it's a mother's duty to ensure the success of her baby's special day," the woman finished with yet another dramatic sigh.

Oh no!

A duty-bound Lorraine Vanderdinkle was never a good thing, but she sure as hell could use a brief respite from her mom and the CityBeat spotlight.

"And, Georgiana?" her mother said, gesturing to a lavish spread of pastries and petit fours.

"Yes, Mom?"

"That tray is off-limits—no sweets for you, pumpkin. The wedding diet starts now," she added over her shoulder as she flitted into the crowd with Hector, Bobby, and Barry close behind.

Georgie groaned, then stared longingly at a row of delectable eclairs before bristling at the sight of a pineapple display.

"What is it?" he asked.

"Pineapple," she said, the word alone nearly making her gag. "I've never liked it."

"I didn't know that," he answered.

She turned away from the yellow pile of tropical fruit. "Yeah, you don't even want to know about the pineapple incident of 1999."

"Why?" Jordan queried with a perplexed expression.

"Let's just say my mom made me eat a fruit cup containing the awful stuff before one of my pageants, and thanks to some impressive projectile vomiting, I'm no longer welcome at the Little Miss Pineapple Pageant in Honolulu."

"Forget about the pineapple," Jordan said, tucking a lock of hair behind her ear. "We've got three tubes of vegan cookie dough at home."

"This is why I love you," she answered, staring into the eyes of her future husband.

"Oh no! You guys aren't going to kiss, are you?"

Georgie chuckled, then hugged her favorite freckle-faced fifteen-year-old. "Simon! I wasn't expecting to see you here."

"I came with Mrs. Perry and the girls. My granny said it

was okay for me to miss a couple of hours of school to celebrate with my favorite bookshop owner and trainer."

"Did you get in your workout this morning?" Jordan
asked, crossing his arms.

The boy lifted his chin. "I sure did, Mr. Marks. And I did
ten extra push-ups."

"That's what I like to hear," Jordan answered, giving the
kid a high five.

"Dad, this is Simon Bacon. He's one of my most dedi-
cated students," Jordan said, introducing the kid to his
father.

"How are you doing on the Shakespeare Shuffle prep?"
Georgie asked the teen.

Simon had been the first student to sign up for the
competition.

"Thanks to Mr. Marks, I've shaved thirty seconds off my
mile, so I'm not too worried about the race part."

"And the sonnet recitation? Are you sticking with the
one Jordan and I suggested?" she pressed.

"Oh yeah! It's sonnet one-sixteen every day after school,
isn't it, Simon?" Jordan said, clapping the kid's shoulder.

The teen nodded. "Mr. Marks has me reciting it, over
and over—no matter what exercise he's got me doing."

"I'm so happy you went with our suggestion. Sonnet
one-sixteen is one of my favorites. It's all about what love is
and what it isn't," she answered.

"And don't forget, Simon," Jordan added, slipping into
trainer mode. "Your mind and body need to work together.
Bulking up and getting fit is good, but so is knowing the
difference between Jane Austen and Jane Eyre."

"They're not the same?" the boy deadpanned.

Georgie pressed her hand to her heart, feigning shock.

Simon laughed. "I'm kidding. I know Jane Austen was a

real person and an acclaimed author, while Jane Eyre is a fictional character created by Charlotte Brontë."

Georgie reached up and ruffled the teen's hair. "I should hope so!" she said as her fictional trifecta nodded approvingly at the boy's knowledge.

They'd met Simon after his grandmother had dragged the shy teen into Jordan's gym for the after-school fitness and nutrition program he ran during the week for high school kids. A skinny boy with his grades in the gutter, thanks to being bullied for his slight frame, Jordan took an immediate shine to the teen. And soon, the closed-up kid had morphed into a kind and confident, literature-loving student.

"Congratulations, Jordan and Georgie!" came a warm greeting from another friendly face.

"Maureen, it's great to see you," Georgie said, embracing the woman who had been like a second mother to Jordan and now, a godsend to them both.

The ex-wife of Jordan's former CrossFit mentor turned philandering douche canoe, Deacon Perry, Jordan had known Maureen for more than a decade. And she wasn't only a kind woman. She was also a gifted bookkeeper. With Jordan opening his own CrossFit gym, her bookstore revenue quadrupling, and the rapid expansion of the Own the Eights and More Than Just a Number brands, they'd hired Maureen to keep their finances in order.

"We saw you on TV!" Maureen's twin eleven-year-old daughters Mia and Mya chimed in unison.

"What did you think?" Jordan asked.

Mia's expression grew pensive. "It made me want a waffle."

"Me too!" her sister agreed.

The girls turned to Simon, who had started babysitting

them when Maureen was busy with the books, then pointed over to a grand waffle station near the white chocolate fountain.

"Simon, let's go get a mountain of waffles!" Mia cried, pulling on the boy's hand.

"Is that okay with you, Mrs. Perry?" he asked with a chuckle.

"It sure is, but don't eat too much. You don't want to get a stomachache," their mother cautioned.

The kids left, and Maureen turned to Dennis, who'd grown quiet. She extended her hand. "I don't think we've met. I'm Maureen Perry." She glanced between Jordan and his father. "And from the very strong resemblance, I'm going to guess that you're Jordan's dad."

The burly man's cheeks grew pink. "That's right. I'm Dennis, no, Denny Marks. It's nice to meet you, Maureen. Jordan's spoken of you, but he never mentioned how pretty you were."

Georgie glanced at her fiancé, who had turned to stone, seemingly in shock at the scene playing out before them.

"Aren't you sweet," Maureen answered, her cheeks growing pink as well. "Isn't it crazy that all the years that I've known Jordan, we've never met. But I'm sure we'll see each other more now since I'm helping Georgie and Jordan with their books."

"Jordan tells me you're quite the accountant." Denny shifted his weight from foot to foot nervously.

Was this Jordan's dad attempting to flirt?

"I recently took over ownership of an auto repair shop in the Tennyson neighborhood. I'd love to ask you a few accounting questions if you've got the time?" Denny asked with a bashful grin.

Maureen beamed. "I'd be happy to help."

Jordan's father plucked two glasses of champagne off a passing waiter's tray with the Rico Suave-ness of James Bond. "How about now?" he asked as his bashful expression made way for a confident swagger.

"I'd like that very much," she answered, taking the offered glass as Denny gestured toward a table.

"What the hell happened there?" Jordan asked, looking positively flabbergasted.

"Hold on. They're still in my line of sight," Georgie replied, watching as Jordan's father said something, and Maureen laughed, then leaned in and patted the man's hand.

"Was my dad flirting?" he questioned.

She stroked Jordan's arm. "It sure seemed like it."

"I don't know what to think about that," he said, looking like a kid who walked in on his parents doing the dirty deed.

"I think your dad has got a little Casanova mixed in with the car mechanic. It's sweet and a little surprising," she replied.

Jordan pressed his fingertips to his eyelids. "I just witnessed my dad making a move on Maureen."

"I'd venture to say, he's full-on making a move," Georgie added as Denny retrieved a pair of eclairs for the two of them. "Does it bother you?"

Jordan shook his head, and his bewildered grimace transformed into a more contemplative expression. "No, my mom's been gone for almost twenty years. I know how much he loved her, but I never thought of my dad as..."

"A smooth operator? A player? A real *Don Juan*?" she teased.

He pinned her with his gaze. "You're loving this, aren't you?"

"A little bit. You know me. The why date a ten when you

should marry an eight, Georgie Jensen, loves a good romance. And, thanks to a healthy appreciation for eighties love ballads, I can say with one hundred percent accuracy that your dad is a solid eight."

"I thought we agreed that relationships hinged on more than just a number," he countered.

"True. And it's probably only a little bit of harmless flirting. But they are two single adults. And who knows? Your dad's a great guy. Maureen is a lovely woman. They could totally hit it off and have a booty call or two."

"Jesus, Georgie!" Jordan said on a weary sigh as he glanced around the opulent room. "Is this wedding thing getting crazier by the second? When I got up this morning, I didn't anticipate a possible middle-aged booty call, a Belgian Waffle Princess, an engagement ring that doesn't fit, and now, CityBeat capturing our every move. Should I have whisked you away to elope instead?"

Georgie shook her head. "No way! If you think Botox wedding Barbie Lorraine Vanderdinkle is bad now, imagine what she'd be like if we told her we'd run off to Vegas to get hitched."

But she couldn't deny, especially after the last hour they'd endured, that running off to marry Jordan did sound heavenly.

Her mother meant well. She knew this. But she also knew Lorraine Vanderdinkle could go overboard. A little voice in her head reminded her of the years being shuttled from beauty pageant to beauty pageant, and her mom's desire for her to be the best—a perfect ten.

A foreboding prickle traveled down her spine and flip-flopped in her belly. "What if the wedding isn't perfect? What will people think? What impact could it have on the blog or our brand? What if we stopped being CityBeat's sweethearts?"

She'd wanted to make it big. She'd dreamed about becoming a CityBeat contributor and sharing her vision and advice with others. But had she and Jordan been wearing rose-colored glasses when they'd envisioned their future as quasi-celebrities?

"Georgie, it will be perfect because it's us," Jordan answered, but she could see the worry in his gaze.

The wedding crazy train had left the station, and he was just as unsure as she was as to what could lie ahead.

"Hold on," Jordan said.

Nonchalantly, he sauntered over to the pastry table, bypassed the god-awful pineapple, piled a plate with gourmet doughnuts, then returned like a triumphant explorer.

"Here, eat one of these. We don't do diets in More Than Just a Number. We'll stay true to ourselves. We're mindful and deliberate. No matter what, we're us."

She nodded. "Us, okay," she answered, taking the chocolate sprinkled treat when her mother materialized like the undercover pastry police.

"Pumpkin, no! Think of the wedding photos!" the woman said, knocking the sweet treat from her hand, then froze as the doughnut fell to the polished parquet floor with a sugary thud.

"Is that who I think it is?" Hector said, swooping in alongside Lorraine.

"I'd put out feelers, but the woman is like a ghost," her mother answered, staring at the entrance to the ballroom.

Hector pressed his hand to his chest. "I'd called a few people, too. She's an enigma. I've heard she has people scrape all her photos from the internet."

Lorraine shook her head. "I think it's her! She's a bona fide legend! She doesn't even advertise, and word on the street is she's booked out seven years."

"Lorraine Vanderdinkle, it appears the *bling* is here, at your party," Hector said like the Queen of England had wandered into the room.

The bling? Did her mother hire a rapper to perform? It didn't seem her speed.

Georgie waved her hands in front of Hector and her mother's faces. "Hey, what are you two talking about?"

"Me, Cornelia Lieblingsschatz," answered a husky voice with a thick German accent.

With a shock of white hair cut in an asymmetrical bob and dressed in all black with skin-tight leather pants and stiletto boots, Cornelia Lieblingsschatz was a cross between a dominatrix and a hot grandma.

"And you are?" Jordan asked.

"The wedding frau," her mother exclaimed in a frantic whisper, then curtsied—actually curtsied.

"We'd heard the rumors. We know of your power," Hector added with a deep bow.

"Is this a joke?" Jordan asked under his breath.

Georgie chewed her lip. Somewhere, in the back of her mind, she knew she'd heard of this woman. But she couldn't put her finger on *how* she knew of her.

"I am no joke," the frau answered, then held out her hand.

A young woman materialized out of the crowd and reverently placed a leather-bound notebook on the woman's waiting palm. She opened the thick book and stared at the hidden contents.

Georgie glanced at her mother and Hector, clutching

each other like two tweens at a Justin Bieber concert while Bobby chuckled.

"You are Georgiana Jensen, and you are Jordan Marks," the woman said without looking up.

Georgie shared a look with Jordan. "Yes, we are."

"Why is your engagement ring on the wrong finger?" the woman questioned sharply.

Georgie held up her hand. "It's a little too big. We're going to have it resized."

"Leave that to me," she answered as the young woman materialized again and slipped the ring off her finger like a pickpocket wedding nymph.

"Wait!" Georgie began when the wedding frau cleared her throat.

"You are a size five and a half, Miss Jensen. That ring is six and a quarter," she said, gaze still trained on her notebook.

"How would you know that without measuring the ring or even looking at Georgie's hand?" Jordan asked.

"Like your friend Hector Garcia said. I am Cornelia *Lieblings-schatz*, known to many as the wedding frau," she replied, blinging up the *bling* in her last name. "When it comes to nuptials in Denver, I know everything."

"Everything?" Jordan echoed.

"Everything," the woman replied as Howard appeared and nodded to the woman.

Georgie glanced between the two, but her stepfather quickly melted into the crowd.

"That's quite a claim, ma'am! Do you have any data to back that up?" Jordan replied.

Georgie shook her head. There was no time to worry about Howard.

The corners of the frau's mouth curled. "Miss Jensen

would prefer a simple, romantic wedding outdoors at the Botanic Gardens. But not a summer wedding! No, you love Colorado in the fall. You picture lights twinkling in the trees as you promise to love and honor each other."

Georgie's literary trifecta gasped.

"How do you know that?" she asked.

She'd never told anyone about her wedding day fantasy —not even Jordan.

He turned to her, mouth hanging open. "Is she right?"

"Yeah," Georgie answered, feeling like she was in a dream.

The wedding frau pinned Jordan with her crystal blue gaze. "And you, Mr. Marks, you never expected to find the kind of love you have found with Georgiana. You would follow her to the ends of the earth."

"Jesus!" Jordan gasped.

"No, not Jesus, only Mrs. Lieblingsschatz," the woman replied with the ghost of a self-assured grin.

"Frau Lieblingsschatz," her mother said with another curtsey. "What happens now?"

The woman closed her leather notebook. "I am offering the couple my services. The offer is on the table for two minutes."

"We have to decide in two minutes?" Jordan sputtered.

The wedding frau nodded.

"But know this, once you commit, you must follow all my instructions. I will be in the lobby awaiting your answer," she replied, then turned on her stiletto heel and left the ballroom.

Holy wedding ultimatum!

Georgie turned to Jordan. "What do you think?"

He took her hand and led her over to the milk chocolate fountain. "This lady seems to know what we want, and I don't think your mom will ever disagree with her."

Georgie glanced at her mother, who was still suspended in wedding frau shock, clutching Hector's arm.

"True. If it were up to Lorraine Vanderdinkle, we'd be getting married in some ballroom, probably even pinker and frillier than this."

He nodded. "With everything on our plate, this wedding planner guru may be just what we need."

"You're not worried about having to follow her instructions explicitly?" she pressed.

Jordan shrugged. "It's a wedding. How many instructions could she have for us? Pick your favorite flower. Fish or chicken. I think we can handle this, Georgie. Plus, her people already took your ring."

Georgie glanced at her ringless hand and then back to her mother and Hector, standing quietly like good little schoolchildren.

"It would be nice not to have to battle my mother or have CityBeat trying to call the shots," she agreed.

He held her gaze. "So, we're a unified yes."

Georgie nodded. "Yes."

They left the Pepto-pink ballroom and found the wedding frau standing in the lobby, jotting in her notebook.

"Frau Lieblingsschatz, we'd like to accept your offer," Jordan announced.

Georgie squeezed his hand. This was a good thing, right? This wedding woman, no matter how intimidating she looked or how bizarrely her mother behaved in her presence, seemed to know what she was talking about.

And she loved the Botanic Gardens in the fall. She'd dreamed of an intimate, romantic wedding there.

The woman had been spot-on.

Jordan met her gaze, and she knew whatever life threw their way, they'd be okay. She loved this man—her Emperor of Asshattery. Her reformed ten, who all along was a solid, loving eight.

Her partner.

Her best friend.

"Very good," Mrs. Lieblingsschatz said with the slap of the notebook closing.

The wedding nymph popped up and held out a pen and a clipboard. "We need your signatures on this contract and the confidentiality agreement."

Georgie signed her name, and Jordan followed suit.

"Where does she come from?" Jordan whispered, glancing at the wedding assistant.

"I don't know. It's a little disconcerting," she answered.

It was actually *very* disconcerting. But, with as nutty as this day had been so far, it was par for the course.

The young woman nodded to the frau, then flitted away.

"Your wedding will be in two weeks," the wedding planner announced.

"Two weeks?" she and Jordan exclaimed.

"Yes, and it will be the wedding you both have always wanted."

"Um...okay, thank you," Georgie sputtered.

This seemed too good to be true.

The wedding frau's lips twisted into a cunning grin. "And I almost forgot. Here's the first rule. No sex until after you're married."

4

JORDAN

Jordan froze and looked around the lobby for that lady with the contract they'd just signed.

He needed to tear that fucker up right now.

Maybe he'd gotten it wrong.

"I don't think I heard you correctly, Frau Lieblingsschatz. Did you say Georgie and I can't sleep together until after we're married?" he asked gently.

The woman narrowed her gaze. "It's only a couple of weeks, Mr. Marks. Are you unable to abstain for even a short period of time?"

"No, we could do it, but..." he began.

"You are a fitness trainer, yes?" the wedding frau asked, cutting him off as she opened her leather-bound notebook.

"I am."

"Do you believe people need to have strong bodies and strong minds?" she continued.

"I do."

She raised an eyebrow. "And what about hard work? Are you afraid of it?"

Dammit! This wedding woman had ninja skills when it came to marrying mind control.

"Jordan and I are up for any task. It's just that abstaining from sex seems a little strange in this modern day and age," Georgie offered with her plastered-on beauty queen grin.

This was not good. She only switched into full pageant mode these days when she got a whiff of Aqua Net hairspray, usually off some old lady who meandered into her bookshop.

"Modern day and age," the frau said under her breath with a coy smirk. She closed the notebook. "After you met, how long was it before you had your first kiss?"

"Well," Georgie began, sharing a nervous look with him. "We met in the park, and then an hour or so later, we learned we would have to work together in the Battle of the Blogs competition."

The wedding frau clucked her tongue. "That isn't an answer to my question. How long, in days or months, was it before you kissed?"

"Um...two?" Georgie supplied.

Cornelia Lieblingsschatz frowned. "Days?"

Georgie cringed but miraculously was able to hold the pageant expression. "Hours."

"You two became a couple two hours after meeting?" the frau asked, scribbling in her notebook.

Anyone else would have cracked under the questioning eye of this fearsome frau, but not his Georgie.

"No, I still pretty much hated his guts at that point," she answered as if she were addressing a line of judges.

"But you kissed him?" the woman pressed, smirk in place.

"Yes."

"Hmm," the wedding frau hummed. "Let's move on."

He shared a relieved look with his fiancée as his hammering pulse slowed.

Yes, they'd had a unique start to their relationship. They were the eight and the ten who, together, became more than just a number. It was all over the internet.

He wrapped his arm around Georgie, ready to take on the world. "Go ahead, Frau Lieblingsschatz."

"Sex," the woman said, dropping the s-bomb and sending his heart rate back into overdrive.

"What about it?" he sputtered.

"How long after meeting did you sleep together?"

Dammit.

"That happened about an hour after we kissed," Georgie answered.

The wedding frau pursed her lips. "And you stopped hating each other in that short amount of time?"

Georgie shook her head. "No, I thought he was an asshat at that point."

"*Asshat*?" Mrs. Lieblingsschatz repeated with a crinkled brow.

"Well, more like the Emperor of Asshattery," Georgie corrected.

This was not going as he'd expected. First time hate sex or not, they needed to keep up a united front. He'd hardly had a moment to think before the wedding nymph returned and whispered something into the frau's ear.

The frau nodded. "Ah, *eni blödhammel*."

"*Blöd* what?" he asked.

Mrs. Lieblingsschatz gestured toward the slight woman, standing next to a giant vase, and he did a double take.

Had she been there the whole time?

"My assistant did a rough translation of the English

word *asshat* into German. Georgie thought you were a stupid mutton when she met you, yes?"

His mouth fell open, ready to set the record straight when his fiancée nodded.

"Yes, exactly," Georgie answered.

The frau turned to him with an appraising eye. "And what did you think of Miss Jensen after you first met?"

"Well…" he trailed off, growing hot around the collar.

Georgie had made him crazy from the first moment he saw her. Granted, at the time, he was still completely committed to the hyper-masculine version of his Marks Perfect Ten Mindset protocol. And, in all honesty, it had made him act a lot like an—

"Asshat? Is that what you thought of Miss Jensen, too?" the frau questioned.

He felt his cheeks heat. "No, I didn't think she was an asshat."

"A stupid mutton?" the wedding planner pressed.

He pulled at the collar of his shirt. It had gotten damn hot in the lobby.

"Nope, not that either. I didn't like her shoes or her hair," he answered.

Christ! He sounded like an asshat or a *blöd*-whatever!

The frau emitted a disapproving humph as Georgie's worried gaze screamed for him to do something.

They needed damage control, and they needed it damn quick.

He cleared his throat. "I think both Georgie and I can agree, at that point in our relationship, we hadn't quite worked out our differences yet."

"But you kissed and slept together within a matter of hours," the woman supplied with another scribble in her notebook.

Jordan swallowed hard. When did this become a session with Dr. Ruth?

Georgie's pageant expression was back. "Have we qualified to advance to the next level of the wedding competition?"

The frau frowned. "What?"

Jordan patted Georgie's back. "What my lovely fiancée means is what happens next? Will you contact us? Should we exchange numbers?"

The wedding frau waved off his questions. "I have all your numbers. I already know everything."

"I bet you don't know our blood types," he tossed out, half-joking, but the wedding planner didn't laugh.

"O negative and A positive," she supplied.

He turned to Georgie. "Are you A positive?"

"Yeah," she answered wide-eyed. "Are you O negative?"

He nodded.

The frau watched them closely. "You did not know this about each other?"

He shook his head. "No."

Jesus! What kind of boyfriend, now fiancé, was he? What if something had happened to Georgie and God forbid, he needed to know these things?

The frau made another mark in her notebook, then glanced over at her wedding minion. The woman nodded and joined them with two swaths of fabric in her hands. No, not fabric—eye masks. She handed one to Georgie and the other to him.

"Come, now. We're leaving," the wedding frau said with a wave of her hand.

"What about our engagement party?" Georgie asked, glancing over her shoulder toward the doors to the ballroom.

"I'm sure your mother and the CityBeat founders will be able to entertain your guests and not mind your absence," Mrs. Lieblingsschatz answered as she slipped on a pair of Jackie O-esque sunglasses and headed for the exit.

"What the hell is going on?" he whispered to Georgie as they fell in step behind the Angel of Wedding Darkness.

She shrugged. "I'm not sure."

He threaded their fingers together. "What do you think about all this?"

Georgie lowered her voice. "I think I've heard of this wedding frau."

"You have?" he asked.

She nodded. "I'd heard whispers about an iron-fisted wedding planner from a few happy eights couples who wrote in to thank me for helping them find their way to the altar. But nobody actually talks about her. She was an urban legend to me until now."

He followed Georgie into the tight space as they navigated the spinning door.

"Urban legend or not, I was hoping our next stop would be our bed," he said, knowing exactly how Alice must have felt when she tumbled down the rabbit hole.

They exited the revolving door and found a black limousine with a man sporting a *do-not-mess-with-me* expression, holding the door open. Jordan glanced past the guy to see the wedding frau's black boots inside the sleek vehicle.

Georgie touched his arm and grinned up at him with her real smile, not the deranged beauty queen one, and he released the tight breath he hadn't realized he'd been holding.

"I think we go with it, Jordan. As crazy as this has been so far, this lady still may be better than, *you know who*."

"The Hydra of Denver," he answered in a theatrical tone.

Her not quite blue and not quite green eyes sparkled. "Something like that."

He lovingly tipped her chin up and brushed his thumb across her plump, kissable lips.

How he loved her!

The wedding frau was spot-on when she said he'd never expected to find this kind of love with anyone, let alone the most beautiful woman he'd ever set eyes on—even in a librarian cardigan and Birkenstock sandals. He leaned in, inhaling her sweet scent, so ready to kiss the woman he was going to marry when a loud guttural sound pierced the air.

"Miss Jensen, Mr. Marks, Frau Lieblingsschatz is on a schedule," the wedding nymph said, appearing from nowhere.

This lady was really starting to freak him out.

With a minute shake of his head, trying to get his bearings back, he helped Georgie into the car, and they took their seats across from the wedding planner.

"Please, put on the blindfolds," she directed without looking up from her notebook.

"You're serious about this?" he asked, holding up the silky fabric.

The frau set her notebook on the seat next to her and leaned forward. "I am taking you to a secret location. This place is only known to the very well-connected in the Denver wedding underground."

Holy hell! There was a Denver wedding underground?

This was the nuptial version of Neo being offered the red or blue pill in *The Matrix*. If he put on the blindfold, the truth would be revealed.

Could he handle the truth?

Well, the truth about what he could only guess were questions like, how many bridesmaids would they need, and how not to poke someone's eye out when throwing the bouquet. And then there was that saying, borrowed, blue, shiny, new...

Dammit! That didn't sound right!

Maybe there was more to planning a wedding.

"We have to do this?" Georgie asked.

Somehow, the frau's stony expression grew more stoic. "Your wedding is not only an important day for the two of you. As I understand it, several media outlets will have an interest in covering it. You two are popular like those girls on the internet, doing makeup tutorials for millions of people, yes? Like, teaching people how to get the perfect cat eye?"

He sat back and met the frau's gaze head-on. Did she think they were a couple of bogus social influencers?

"We help people live healthy and fulfilled lives," he corrected.

"But you write about it on a blog and then talk to a camera to share your thoughts?" she pressed.

"Yes," he answered, sensing the frau's trap.

"You are famous for not doing much more than discussing your beliefs."

He shared a look with Georgie.

"We do much more than that. In our blog and with our businesses, Georgie and I help people live better lives every day, Frau Lieblingsschatz," he answered, conviction lacing his words.

The wedding planner sat back. "Good! We understand each other. That's what I do to help couples plan their dream wedding. So, you're going to follow the Lieblingsschatz protocol, and that means you are to put the blindfolds on. Do not fret. We don't have far to go."

Georgie's gaze bounced from him to the silky fabric in her hands before she secured the blindfold over her eyes.

"Mr. Marks," the wedding frau prompted.

He put the damn thing on, then reached for his fiancée's hand. What he wouldn't do to rewind this day back to waking up with Georgie in his arms and his cock between her thighs. It was hands down the absolute best way to start the day.

An early riser for most of his life, he was always up before her. This allowed him the opportunity to brush an errant lock of hair from her cheek and pull her close while dropping kisses to her lips and chin and neck. He'd been anxious about the upcoming morning TV proposal he, Hector, and Bobby had planned. But in those moments when it was the two of them, curled together like sleeping cats, the sun barely a sliver in the sky, he'd forgotten his worries and had given in to his desire.

It wasn't hard to do with a goddess asleep in his arms.

He'd whispered her name, *Georgiana*, as he kissed the sensitive skin below her earlobe, and she'd hum a satisfied little sound, silencing any doubts in his mind. He'd massaged her breasts, working her sleep-warm body as his fingertips glided down her torso and always, morning after glorious morning, found her wet and ready for him.

Savoring her scent and her breathy sighs, he'd slide inside her slowly as their limbs tangled, their bodies growing desperate to thrust and rock and grind together beneath the blankets. Sweet lazy kisses intensified into heated gasps. His chest tightened remembering her nails, raking down his back as she met her release, crying out his name over and over until he couldn't hold back any longer, his hips pistoning as he teetered on the edge, ready to—

"Mr. Marks, are you coming?" came the wedding frau's sharp German accent.

"Am I what?" he shot back, shocked out of his predawn

fantasy fucking as if a bucket of ice had been poured down his trousers.

Georgie squeezed his hand. "We're here. You must have been meditating or something."

Or something, sweet Jesus! Was he so discombobulated that he'd rocked a complete sex rerun in his head during the car ride?

He slipped off the blindfold. "Sorry, I was..." He glanced from the stern wedding planner to his fiancée. "Meditating, like Georgie said. It's great for centering oneself to be at your most productive," he managed, throwing together one hell of a bullshit word salad.

The wedding frau produced another skeptical humph as he gestured for her to exit the car ahead of them.

Georgie leaned in. "Good save, Emperor. Did I happen to make an appearance in your *meditation*?"

"Silly, Empress of Asshattery, you should know by now that you're in every single one of my meditations."

"Are you ready for the Denver wedding underground?" she asked with a naughty glint in her eyes.

"No, but I've decided we've fallen down the Alice in Wonderland Bridal rabbit hole, and there's no turning back now."

Georgie slid out of the limo, and he followed, shielding his eyes from the bright sun. They'd parked outside a large building in an industrial area. Too bad he'd gone total recall sex replay or else he could have concentrated on where they were going. Luckily, a weather-beaten sign next to a rusty metal door revealed their location.

The Denver Porcelain Doll Factory.

"We're going to a doll factory?" he asked.

The frau tossed a snarky wink over her shoulder. "Mr. Marks, that's just the cover."

"Why a doll factory?" Georgie asked.

"You know how unnerving porcelain dolls are. Not even the most hardened criminal would try to break into a doll shop. I'm told people fear all the little eyes staring at them."

A chill went down his spine. "Are there any dolls inside?"

"Looks like you're about to find out," she said, keeping her features stone-cold.

"I'm starting to have a new appreciation for the underground bridal industry. They don't mess around," he said to Georgie, lowering his voice as the frau knocked on the door.

He glanced from side to side. "Is that a secret knock?"

The woman frowned. "Of course not! That would be ridiculous."

He bit back a grin and met Georgie's gaze. With her pink cheeks and lips pressed into a hard line, she was trying not to laugh either. And a sweet sense of contentment set in. This is how they'd get through the wedding madness. Together—the two of them.

Mrs. Lieblingsschatz ushered them inside. "Everything comes through here. This is where Denver wedding trends and cutting-edge front range bridal fashions are born."

He gasped, feeling like a CrossFit Dorothy right at the moment in the film where the little farm girl had left the black-and-white world of Kansas and emerged in the bright and glossy Oz.

Despite the building's dank exterior, the inside shimmered—actually fucking shimmered. Crates of flowers scented the air as rack after rack of lily-white dresses lined the far wall. A cluster of older women sat at sewing machines while young men carried boxes dripping with lace and puffy stuff that went under dresses. Shit! He didn't even know what it was called.

"Tulle," Cornelia Lieblingsschatz remarked.

He turned to Georgie. "Did she call me a tool?"

Georgie suppressed another grin. "No, the white fabric that went by us is called tulle, *T-U-L-L-E*. You made a funny face when you saw it."

"It's like a whole different world," he said as a guy swerved past them with a massive bin of rubber penises.

The frau waved off the dildo delivery dude. "Pay no attention. Those are very popular for bachelorette parties. Ours have super-charged batteries."

"I bet they do," Georgie answered wide-eyed.

The wedding frau pinned them with her gaze. "But that is not for you. You two are on the zero-fornication protocol."

He watched as the bins of cocks disappeared. With this no sex rule, it was a damn shame he couldn't detach his manhood and toss it into the bin to be locked away. After his dirty meditation in the limo, all he wanted to do was get Georgie naked.

The frau led them farther inside the cavernous space. "Today, we'll pick colors, flowers, the design for the dress, the cake, and find your perfect wedding rings."

"We can do all that here, in this place?" Georgie asked.

The wedding planner closed her eyes. "Do you feel it?"

"What?" Georgie asked.

"The magic," the woman replied.

"Yeah, sure," he and Georgie answered like two confused kids in calculus class.

Mrs. Lieblingsschatz walked them over to a large computer monitor and tapped the surface. A weather map donned the screen. "You're having a fall wedding. Lucky for you, on your wedding day, it will be sunny with a high temperature of eighty-one degrees Fahrenheit. Twenty-seven Celsius. Unseasonably warm."

"Wait a second. How do you know it's going to be eighty-one degrees on the third Saturday in October?" he questioned.

The frau met his gaze. "My contacts at NASA, and the National Oceanic and Atmospheric Administration, and years of my statisticians crunching Farmers' Almanac data to within an inch of its life," the woman answered, tapping the screen. "With everything I know, Mother Nature herself asks me for the weather forecast."

"That's certainly a lot of information! What else do you know?" Georgie pressed.

The wedding frau's smirk was back, and she walked past them. The click of her boots on the worn wooden floor echoed through the chamber as she began to speak.

"Your ceremony will take place outdoors in the Botanic Gardens at sunset, casting a golden glow and illuminating the vibrant reds, the deep shades of rose, and lush greens. You'll have your first dance under a pavilion, strung with thousands of tiny sparkling white lights." The woman walked up to Georgie and gently fingered a loose lock of his fiancée's hair. "You'll wear your hair up, Miss Jensen, with flowers from your bouquet threaded in."

"Like a Georgian wedding," Georgie whispered as if in a trance.

"Is this what you pictured?" the frau asked.

Georgie nodded, then turned to him. "What do you think?"

He pressed a kiss to her temple. "I'm good with anything that makes you smile like that."

"Hmm, no opinion," the wedding frau remarked, writing in her notebook.

Georgie's expression fell, and he shook his head.

"It's not *no* opinion. I just want Georgie to be happy."

"But are you happy?" Georgie pressed, her gaze brimming with worry.

He glanced around the wedding wonderland warehouse. "Yes, it's just that all this wedding hubbub isn't really..." he trailed off.

Agitation edged out the worry in Georgie's gaze. "It isn't really what, Jordan?"

"Georgie, I..." he stammered.

It wasn't like he didn't care about the wedding. But questions like should they have an indoor ceremony versus an outdoor ceremony weren't foremost on his mind. He didn't care if they got married at a truck stop in Timbuktu as long as she was the one walking up the aisle.

He steadied himself. He needed to come up with the right thing to say. Her gaze grew more pointed as his mind turned to mush.

"Georgie, I..." he tried again, but instead of looking angry, she closed her eyes and inhaled.

"What is that?" she asked on a dreamy breath.

"That would be the cakes," Frau Lieblingsschatz answered.

Georgie's face lit up. "We get to do a cake tasting?"

If he were a comic book character, this would be the scene with *phew* written above his head in huge block letters as the hero dodged a bullet.

"Jordan, they're baking cakes for us," she exclaimed.

He'd never been so grateful for empty calories in all his life.

For the next hour, he received a crash course in Weddings 101. A lot of it seemed like a load of bullshit and old wives' tales, but Georgie seemed to eat it up, and he quickly understood the old adage, happy wife, happy life.

"And now, Miss Jensen and I will part with you, Mr. Marks," the frau said as one of the wedding minions cleared away the flowers they'd settled on for the bouquet and centerpieces.

Georgie glanced at the row upon row of dresses lining the back wall. "Is it time to choose a dress?"

"Yes, the dress and the wedding rings," the wedding planner answered.

Georgie frowned. "I understand Jordan not being with me when I choose my dress. I want it to be a surprise for him. But why would we choose the rings separately?"

"In my many years of planning weddings, I've learned that the choice of wedding bands says quite a bit about a couple," the frau answered.

"Okay," Georgie replied, still with a slight crease in her brow.

Was this a test? There couldn't be a right or wrong wedding band, could there?

"Hans!" she called, glancing around the warehouse.

A small man with thick glasses emerged from behind one of the racks of dresses and joined them.

"Miss Jensen and I are going to attend to the dress, and Hans will take you to our ring room to select wedding bands," the wedding frau instructed.

He reached for his fiancée's hand. "I know you're going to look beautiful in whatever you choose."

"Good luck with the rings," she answered, giving his hand a squeeze.

The wedding rings. The rings they'd wear every day for the rest of their lives.

He hadn't thought much about their actual wedding bands. He'd been so relieved to find the antique engagement ring he hadn't considered the design of their bands.

"Come with me, sir," the man said in a gentle German accent, gesturing for him to follow.

Jordan watched as Mrs. Lieblingsschatz and Georgie disappeared into layer upon layer of billowy white dresses.

"The wedding frau is something else," he commented.

"You have no idea," Hans answered with the hint of a grin.

They snaked through the building until they reached the end of the hall, and the man unlocked a door. In gleaming lit cases, row upon row of rings sparkled under the lights.

"Wow, you guys must have over a million dollars' worth of jewelry in here!" he exclaimed with a low whistle.

"Try ten," Hans chuckled. "Now," he continued, pointing to the shimmering tables, "what do you have in mind for Miss Jensen?"

"I don't know," he answered truthfully.

"Take a moment to look. Think about what you love most about her, then choose," the old man instructed.

"No pressure, right?" he asked.

Why the hell was he so nervous?

Jordan gazed down at the multitude of rings when a sparkling number caught his eye.

"Could I see that one?" he asked.

Hans slid a black velvet display tray out from under the glass and gingerly removed a band.

"A very good choice, Mr. Marks. Pavé diamonds in platinum."

"Right, that's what I thought. Pavé makes a mean ring," he answered, trying not to sound like someone who'd never heard of a pavé diamond.

"Pavé is French for paved. It's a type of setting where the

diamonds are close together as if the ring is paved with the gems," Hans replied.

"That must have slipped my mind," he answered with the worst comeback in jewelry knowledge history.

Holy pavé fuck balls! Who was he trying to kid?

He stared down at the bank of rings, swearing they'd doubled or tripled in the short amount of time he'd been in the room. There were so damned many of them.

"I think Georgie would love this *pavé* ring," he said, staring at the sparkly circle.

The man nodded and slid the band onto a black velvet finger-looking object.

"And for yourself?" Hans asked.

"Something simple. I don't wear jewelry, no offense, man," he added, wanting to punch himself in the mouth for, again, sounding like his brain was pavéd with crap.

"None taken, Mr. Marks," Hans replied.

"And when I was a kid, I learned I had a nickel allergy," Jordan added, remembering the awful rash he'd gotten from a cheap gold chain he'd worn in a failed attempt to look cool in middle school.

"I see," Hans replied, selecting a tray. "I'd suggest choosing a platinum or titanium band. Those, unlike gold, do not contain any nickel."

Jordan watched as Hans placed the tray of nickel-free rings on top of the glass.

"You're a fitness trainer, correct?" Hans asked.

"Yes, and I operate my own gym."

"Then I'd suggest the titanium. It's hypoallergenic, and it resists corrosion from sweat or chlorinated water."

Jordan gazed at the sleek rings. "Really?"

"See what you think of this one with beveled edges," the kind man suggested, passing him the silver-colored titanium ring and teaching him what a beveled edge was. He would have called them ridges, but if he'd learned one thing today, it was that he may be able to knock out a thousand push-ups in one training session, but the mental stamina it took to choose something the size of a quarter damn near wiped him out.

"Beveled, huh," he said, sliding the band onto his ring finger, then stilled.

"It appears the ring is a perfect fit. I'll record your size, so we have it," Hans said, taking a small notepad from his breast pocket and jotting down the information.

Jordan couldn't pull his gaze from his hand.

"It hits home when you put it on, doesn't it, Mr. Marks," Hans observed, pocketing the notebook.

Jordan continued to stare at his hand. "Yeah, it sure does."

He'd wear this ring for the rest of his life.

"I think this is it," he said, unable to look away.

"Very good! May I have the ring back, or would you like to test drive it a bit longer," Hans asked.

"Here you go," he said, sliding the titanium off his finger.

He glanced around. Thanks to choosing the first two rings he'd laid his eyes on, he wasn't sure what to do with himself. He slid his hands into his pockets. "Should I wait here for Georgie?"

"No, no," Hans answered, returning the tray into the case. "Frau Lieblingsschatz likes to have the couples go through this process individually. You can wait in the room right through that door," he finished, then gestured with his chin toward the far side of the room.

Right. The wedding frau's ring test.

He thanked Hans for his help, then entered the waiting

room, and took a seat on the couch. He ran his hands down the scruff of his jaw.

Jesus, what a day they'd had, and it was barely lunch!

His stomach grumbled—a reminder that, except for a few bites of cake during the tasting, they hadn't had one thing to eat at their fancy champagne engagement breakfast. He thought of the carved meat station, and his stomach responded with an all-out rumble.

What he wouldn't give to have a tube of vegan cookie dough right about now! Despite teasing Georgie about her favorite treat, he couldn't deny the stuff was delicious. He was about to resign himself to flipping through a basket of magazines to kill some time when he caught a glimpse of a box of Twinkies on a bookshelf.

Not something he'd recommend in his More Than Just a Number fitness and nutrition blog posts, but desperate times called for desperate measures—and being trapped at a top-secret wedding warehouse surely fit the bill. He reached for the box and found three left.

"Hey!" someone called.

Jordan looked up to see the dildo delivery guy.

"Where'd you come from?" he asked.

"Back door," the man answered, glancing over his shoulder.

"Oh," Jordan replied. What the hell was he supposed to say?

The men stared at each other as if they were auditioning for a Wild West gunslinger role.

"Did you get those Twinkies off the shelf?" the dildo guy asked.

Jordan glanced at the box. "Yeah."

"Dude, those are my Twinkies."

"Can I have one?" he asked as his stomach doubled the plea by emitting a crazy growl.

The man's expression grew pinched. "I was going to eat them for lunch."

Jordan held up the box. "You were going to have three Twinkies for lunch?"

The guy shrugged.

Jordan squared his jaw and went into trainer mode. "I can't let you do that, man. With all that sugar, you'll be hungry in an hour. You need to be smart with what you eat."

"Dude, I'm trying," the man said, then stilled and gave him the once-over. "Wait, you're that guy. The CityBeat CrossFit guy!"

"That's right! My fiancée and I run the More Than Just a Number blog now."

"I know it," the dildo dude replied.

Jordan clucked his tongue. "Then, you should know you should not be eating Twinkies for lunch."

The man's gaze grew skeptical. "You looked ready to scarf down the box."

He had him there. But all was not lost.

"How about this," he proposed to the rightful owner of the Twinkies. "We do a quick strength workout, and then we each have one."

The guy scoffed. "Right here?"

"Hell yes, right here! There's never a bad time to get stronger," he answered, pumped at the prospect of slipping into trainer mode.

"Sure! Why not! I'm on a break," the dildo guy answered with an excited clap of his hands.

Jordan held the man's gaze going into beast mode. "Twenty burpees, twenty power squats, then twenty push-ups. Got it?"

"Got it!" the dildo man answered, hopping from foot to foot like a boxer ready to hit the ring.

Jordan rolled up the sleeves of his dress shirt. "In three, two, one! Let's go!"

He jumped, then hit the floor, knocking out his first burpee as his Twinkie owning trainee mirrored his moves. This felt good! He'd been a ball of nerves and anxiety, running on adrenaline for the past few hours. His limbs rejoiced with each push-up, each exertion. He could lose himself to the workout and harness the endorphin rush.

"What are you doing?" Georgie ask from behind.

"A micro workout with the dildo guy," he answered, lowering into push-up position when he remembered where he was and froze.

"I better get going," the man answered, hopping to his feet as he snagged the box of Twinkies and bolted through the back door.

Shit. He looked like a total nut job, and he wasn't even going to get a Twinkie.

He turned slowly to find Georgie, the wedding frau, and Hans staring at him.

"It's never a bad time to work in a little fitness," he offered, coming to his feet and clapping the dust from his hands.

"We need to have a discussion," the frau said as Hans spread a handkerchief-sized velvet strip onto the table in the room.

"Did everything go okay with the dress selection?" he asked as all those workout endorphins surging through his veins evaporated.

Georgie's expression softened. "I found exactly the style I want. I think you're going to love it, too."

"Then, what's the issue?" he asked.

The frau sat, and he and Georgie joined her as she unfolded the velvet fabric to reveal four rings.

"That's the ring I thought you'd like. It's made of pavé diamonds," he said, feeling like a damned ring expert, then shared a look with Hans, who replied with an approving nod.

Georgie chewed her lip. "It's just..."

"Just what? You don't like it?" he asked.

"It looks like something my mother would choose," she answered with a weak smile.

His heart sank. She was right.

He stared at the sparkling band. "I guess I can see that."

"I was thinking of going more simply with matching bands," she said and touched two silver bands—the choices she must have made with the wedding frau.

"I like the idea of matching bands. I didn't even realize it was an option." He reached for the rings Georgie chose, but Hans slid the bands away.

"No, no, those won't work," the old man said with a shake of his head.

"Why not?" Georgie asked.

"They're white gold, Miss Jensen, and Mr. Marks has a nickel allergy," Hans replied.

Jordan met the man's gaze. "You didn't tell her?"

"Hans wasn't with us for ring selection. It was only Miss Jensen and me," the frau answered.

Georgie frowned. "I had no idea there was nickel in gold. And when did you find out you had a nickel allergy?"

"I've known about it since I was a kid. I hadn't thought about in years. It's not like I wear jewelry."

Confusion and something akin to doubt flashed in her eyes.

First, it was their blood types, and now it was his allergy.

These weren't huge unknowns between them, but at this moment, with the look on Georgie's face, he wanted to get the hell out of there.

Hans handed Georgie the titanium band. "Your fiancé isn't allergic to this metal. It's titanium."

"It's lovely. Is titanium common?" she asked.

"It's a newer choice. But quite popular," the frau answered.

Georgie slid the large titanium band on her ring finger then gasped. "What about my engagement ring? I haven't seen it since this morning."

More like since the wedding frau's minion basically pickpocketed it off her finger.

"No need to worry. It's right here," Hans said, removing it from a velvet bag. "I'll be the one resizing it."

Hans handed her the antique engagement ring and slid it on with the titanium band.

"Old and new," Hans said with a chuckle.

"I love it, Jordan. What do you think?" she asked.

He took her hand into his. Despite the rings being too big, he loved it, too.

It worked.

Georgie removed the rings and handed them to Hans.

"There we are," the wedding frau said, flipping a page in her notebook. "And no need to worry. Your rings will be sized for you and ready by the time you return from bridal boot camp."

"What are you talking about?" Georgie asked.

"Boot camp. It's exactly what you need," she answered.

At the sound of boot camp, he was ready to do a damn cartwheel. He may not know about rings or flowers or fondant, but as a CrossFit trainer, he knew boot camp. He loved it. And how different could a bridal boot camp be from one of his training sessions? They probably added a wedding spin to it. Whatever it was, it didn't matter. Finally, this was something he understood!

The wedding frau tore out a sheet of paper from her notebook and handed it to Georgie.

"That's the address. My people will let them know you're coming," the frau instructed.

Georgie blinked with a puzzled expression. "When do we leave?"

What looked like one hell of a mischievous glint sparked in the wedding planner's eyes.

"Tonight."

5

"You leave for a bridal boot camp *tonight*? But you just got engaged this morning! And how do you have time for boot camp? Your wedding is in two weeks?" Becca exclaimed.

Georgie leaned over and rested her elbows on the bookshop's counter and cradled her head in her hands as Becca patted her back, and Irene smoothed the hair away from her face.

"Was that just this morning?" she said, staring at the wooden surface.

Between the *Wake-Up Denver* television proposal, followed by the Hydra of Denver's champagne breakfast engagement party, where, by the way, she received no champagne and no breakfast, and then, the whirlwind bridal speed date through the Denver wedding underground, she could barely see straight.

Oh, and thanks to whatever they signed for the wedding frau, the planner's assistant had informed them they weren't able to breathe a word about anything they'd experienced this morning.

She couldn't even tell her best friends she saw a giant container of sex toys with super-charged batteries.

"I'm so sorry I couldn't make it to your engagement party," Irene said, rubbing her belly. "This morning sickness is the real deal. And it's not limited to only the morning! What jerk named it morning sickness?"

Georgie straightened and smoothed her apron. "Don't feel bad. Jordan and I were only there long enough to see my mother in hyper-socialite mode before we had to leave."

"For the whole wedding planning thing, right?" Becca asked with a sly twist to her lips.

Georgie cringed. "Hold on. They gave me a glow in the dark card for what I can say about the wedding."

"Why would they give you a glow in the dark card?" Irene asked, sharing a perplexed look with her younger sister.

Georgie shook her head. "No, not glow-in-the-dark. It's called the Glomar response."

"What the hell is a Glomar response?" Irene asked, continuing to rub her hint of a belly.

Georgie grabbed the card from her purse, then cleared her throat. "I cannot confirm or deny that I have engaged in a contract with the entity known as the Denver Wedding Frau," she said, reading the laminated slip of paper the assistant had given her.

"So, you can't talk about anything related to your wedding? All we get is the date?" Irene asked.

Georgie sighed. "Think of my wedding like Voldemort, the event that shall not be named."

Hermione gave her an imaginary high five for her cleverness.

"But it's in two weeks! How will you get invitations out and have everything ready?" Becca pressed.

"She who cannot be named takes care of everything, and my mom has been generating and updating a wedding invitation guest list since I turned twenty-one," Georgie answered.

Irene stopped rubbing her belly and cocked her head to the side. "Your mom has a database of people to invite to your wedding?"

Georgie bit back a weary grin. "Please, don't tell me this surprises you?"

Irene sighed. "I guess not. Your mom is *very…*"

Georgie knew what her friend was thinking. "Lorraine Vanderdinkle is very, very. That truly sums it up," she answered.

Becca's brows knit together. "Could you at least tell us where you're having the ceremony? Are you doing it locally, or will a fleet of unmarked cars be picking up the guests and driving everyone to a top-secret location?"

Georgie tossed the glo-whatever card under the counter, glanced around the shop, making sure nobody was within earshot.

"It'll be at the Botanic Gardens at sunset," she whispered.

Becca pressed her hand to her chest. "That's so romantic."

"I love outdoor weddings," Irene added, then frowned. "But what about the weather? We are talking about Colorado in October. Snow, rain, blistering heat—anything can happen this time of year."

Georgie waved her off. "We've got that covered. It's going to be unseasonably warm that day."

"How do you know?" Becca asked, her voice brimming with disbelief.

"In addition to everything wedding related in this city,

our wedding planner, let's call her, the Matriarch of Matrimony, seems to control the weather, too," Georgie answered.

"Wow! The Matriarch of Matrimony sounds quite formidable," Irene remarked.

"She certainly seems to know her stuff when it comes to weddings. And she's not even scared of porcelain dolls," Georgie added.

"Wow, there's no way you could get me near a porcelain doll," Irene whispered with a sage nod.

"And what about bridesmaids?" Becca asked with her sly grin back in place.

Georgie pinned the woman with her gaze. "Is that your not-so-subtle way of asking if you'll be in the wedding?"

"Come on, Georgie! It's not every day your famous friend gets married." Becca huffed.

"I'm hardly famous, you guys," Georgie answered.

"Fine, infamous! Do you like that better?" Irene teased.

Georgie chuckled and shook her head. "Yes, I'd love for you both to be my bridesmaids."

The sisters squealed and hugged each other.

"I knew it!" Becca exclaimed. "Seriously, Georgie, where would you be without us?"

Becca was teasing, but her friend's words went straight to her heart.

While she'd only known the sisters a couple of years, they'd become an integral part of her life.

Georgie reached for Becca and Irene's hands. "I'd probably be working some job I hate to pay the bills. If it weren't for you two, I don't know where I'd be."

"And don't forget the giant douche canoe, Brice Casey. You do kind of owe him, too," Irene reminded her.

Georgie released her friends' hands and leaned against the counter. "Isn't it crazy. If I hadn't agreed to meet Brice for a date, and he hadn't told me he couldn't date me because I was an eight, I probably wouldn't have even started my blog —or met you, Irene. And then you wouldn't have introduced me to Becca."

"The universe works in mysterious ways," Becca said, nodding with an overdone contemplative expression.

"Any muffins in this universe?"

Becca gasped, dropping the theatrics. "Mr. Gilbert, I'm sorry! We got to talking, and I forgot about the muffins," she said, wiping her hands on her apron and placing the baked treats onto a large plate.

"Did Marjorie send you up here?" Georgie asked, eyeing the man.

"What?" he answered with a mischievous grin as he pressed a hand to his ear.

Georgie clucked her tongue playfully. "I see you're playing the *my-hearing-aid-is-on-the-fritz* game again."

She'd known Gene Gilbert and his wife Marjorie for her entire life. Friends of her deceased grandparents, she'd always thought of them as family. Gene, however, was quite a sly dog. His hearing aid batteries would often run out of juice at the exact moment when he and his wife were due to meet up in her bookshop with Marjorie's knitting club, who, on a side note, also enjoyed ogling Jordan.

She wasn't sure who was more excited when Jordan opened his gym next door. Her, or the horny blue-haired brigade as Gene now called the gaggle of octogenarians, currently settled in the cozy seating area near the shop's front window.

Becca hurried off to deliver the muffins to the ladies, and Mr. Gilbert settled himself on one of the stools she'd had installed in the new coffee shop area of the bookstore.

Gene glanced around the bustling space as shoppers perused the shelves. "You've come a long way, kiddo."

She followed his lead and took in the shop. Six months ago, she wasn't even sure she would be able to keep the lights on, but now, it seemed like all her dreams had come true. But a needling pang of anxiety festered in her chest.

"Don't do that, Georgie," Mr. Gilbert warned.

She tried to school her features. "Do what?"

"Get all worried."

"What makes you think I'm worried?" she asked, knowing that was probably the question every worried person threw back when they were attempting to seem unbothered.

Good God, though! After today's wedding bonanza, she was surprised she was still standing.

"Your grandmother Jensen used to do that, too. When things were going well, she'd get nervous and drive your grandfather bonkers," Mr. Gilbert offered.

Georgie swallowed past the lump in her throat. "I never expected so much so fast."

The man chuckled. "All I can tell you is that life moves fast, and I have to say, watching you get engaged on morning TV was quite an experience. But I guess all the kids your age are TV stars these days with the internet. Do you know, there's a fellow who films himself eating beans every morning?"

A peaceful warmth washed over her. A conversation with her favorite eighty-year-old was just what the doctor ordered to calm her frayed nerves.

She dusted a few muffin crumbs into her hand. "I did not know that."

"Beans, Georgiana!" Gene exclaimed as she caught Irene's eye, and the women stifled a laugh.

"That reminds me," Irene said, glancing at her watch. "I need to stop at the market for beans. We're making chili for dinner tonight."

"Are you going to film yourself eating it?" Gene asked.

"Probably not tonight, but I'll let you know," Irene answered with a teasing quirk of her lips as Gene shook his head.

Her friend picked up her purse. "And don't worry about Mr. Tuesday, Georgie. He can stay with us for as long as you're gone."

Georgie hugged her friend goodbye, then turned to Mr. Gilbert.

"Just because something is on the internet, it doesn't mean you have to watch it."

The man scoffed. "I was so damned proud I figured out how to get to your CityBeat site, I clicked on the first thing that popped up. Oh yeah, and congratulations on your engagement, by the way! I would have told you at your party, but you didn't seem to be there."

"This wedding is a little non-traditional, to say the least," she replied.

"And your mother is certainly happy," Mr. Gilbert continued.

Georgie eyed the man. "You know she lives for a good champagne fountain."

"And I know your dad's looking down on you from heaven and smiling, too," Gene added, his gaze softening.

Georgie felt her chest swell with emotion. "I wonder what he would have thought of all the hoopla?"

And then it hit her. She didn't have her father to walk her down the aisle. Sure, there was her stepfather, Howard. He'd always been kind to her and would probably do it if she asked. But he was always working or away on business.

She'd lived in the man's house for years but rarely saw him.

Her mother had fallen into the role of a Denver socialite and a pageant mom more than the life of a wife. Still, she and Howard seemed happy in their own doubles-tennis, drinks at the club way. But that wasn't the kind of marriage she wanted with Jordan.

"Your father would have seen that you were very much in love, Georgiana," Gene answered, pulling her from her thoughts.

Her father was a renaissance man. He'd loved fixing cars and reading literature. He'd awakened her love of reading and all things book related. Losing him as a girl had been dreadful, but she'd found comfort and companionship with the books her father had gifted her before he'd passed. She'd discovered her literary trifecta, the fictional helpers she knew in her heart her father had sent to guide her.

She wiped a runaway tear from her cheek as the excitement of the day got to her. "I think you're right."

After his death, Gene and Marjory Gilbert had been a godsend, taking her to the library between beauty pageants. A few months ago, when she was worried she wouldn't be able to keep the bookstore going, it was the Gilberts, bringing in their friends to buy books and purchase her baked goods, that had allowed her to get through the hard times.

She met her old friend's gaze and knew what she needed to do.

"Would you walk me down the aisle, Mr. Gilbert?" she asked.

Gene tapped his hearing aid. "This thing must be on the fritz. It sounded like you asked this old codger to walk you down the aisle," he teased, but his playful expression dissolved into a teary smile.

"Well?" she asked, her gaze growing glassy.

He steepled his hands and stared at his wedding ring. "Marjorie and I weren't able to have children. Did you know that?"

She shook her head. "I didn't know."

"We've always thought of your father as a son and you as a granddaughter, especially now that your grandparents have passed."

"You have?"

He patted her hand. "Why, sure! What do you think we're doing here in your shop all the time? Do you think we eat those muffins because they're good? We order them because we love you," he added, with a cheeky grin, but the shine in his eyes betrayed his snarky words.

She wiped another tear from her cheek. "Hey, codger, I've watched you eat three of my chocolate chip muffins in one sitting."

"Maybe they're not that bad," he countered.

"So, are you in on this crazy wedding? Will you walk me down the aisle?" she asked.

The man nodded. "I'd be honored to stand in for your dad, Georgie."

"What's all this?" Marjory asked, patting Gene's tear-streaked cheek as she joined them at the counter. "You're not reading *Chicken Soup for the Soul* again, are you? Sweetheart, you sobbed for days."

Gene kissed his wife's cheek. "No chicken soup books, dear. Georgie asked me to walk her down the aisle."

"Georgie, that's so lovely of you," the woman said, reaching out and squeezing her hand.

"I'm the lucky one. I'm so grateful to the both of you,"

Georgie replied with a wide, teary grin as the door to the shop opened, and Jordan entered the cozy space.

She waved him over. "Guess who's going to walk me down the aisle?"

"I am!" Gene answered before Jordan could even guess.

"That's terrific news," Jordan said, shaking the man's hand.

Her fiancé had grown especially fond of Mr. Gilbert.

"I see you don't have your cane with you, Gene," Jordan observed with a triumphant nod.

"Nope, I haven't needed it since I started training with you," the man replied, going into a bodybuilder pose that had them all laughing.

Jordan had talked Gene into a few training sessions that had bloomed into ongoing twice-weekly workouts.

"And there have been other benefits," Gene said, lowering his voice.

"Other benefits?" Georgie asked, stealing a glance at Jordan.

Mr. Gilbert slid off the barstool and straightened up. "Let's just say my wife doesn't mind having a more virile husband around the house."

Marjory blushed like a schoolgirl. "You're terrible, Gene! Now, come on. Let's let Jordan and Georgie have a moment together," the woman said, threading her arm with her husband's as they returned to the group of knitting ladies.

"It looks like Mrs. Gilbert is all over Mr. Gilbert," Jordan teased as Mr. Gilbert surreptitiously patted his wife's bottom before she took her seat.

"I'd say you've got a client for life. How was your workout with the high school kids this afternoon? Did you find a trainer to step in while we're at bridal boot camp?" Georgie asked, straightening a row of coffee mugs.

At the mention of boot camp, her fiancé beamed. "I did. Sara's going to fill in, and Simon said he'd be able to help out and run the after-school workouts."

"How about everything with the bookshop? Did you get things all squared away?" he asked.

She nodded. "Becca's able to step up, and a couple of the part-timers said they could take on more hours. Oh, and Talya, remember her? She's the high school student who's volunteering in the children's area. She said she could handle the story times for me."

A wolfish twist graced Jordan's lips. "It looks like we're ready for boot camp, baby. But I do have a bookkeeping question. Can you come with me to your office?"

"Maureen's not here," she replied, trying to read this man.

"We don't need Maureen for this," he answered.

Georgie signaled to Becca that she was going into the back as Jordan followed behind.

"What was the question?" she asked as she heard the door to the snug space close and lock before Jordan pressed her back against the door.

"I've wanted to do this all damned day," he breathed, peppering her neck with kisses.

With all the engagement excitement, they hadn't even kissed since he'd proposed.

She wrapped her arms around his neck and threaded her fingers into the hair at the nape of his neck. He smelled good, freshly showered, his skin still warm from the heated spray of water. She closed her eyes and inhaled the clean, earthy scent of his soap and imagined all those rivulets of water trailing down his cut abs and his muscled forearms.

"We shouldn't do this. We're on the no fornication protocol," she whispered on a sigh, but it didn't stop her from tilting her head to give him more access.

"This isn't fornicating. I looked it up. Fornication is consensual sexual intercourse. This is simply a guy making his fiancée come hard."

Holy hell!

He captured her mouth in a scorching kiss and lifted her into his arms. With her back against the door, Jordan's hard length pressed between her thighs.

"Georgiana, you smell so good," he breathed, digging his fingertips into the flesh of her ass as he ran his tongue across the seam of her lips.

"It's the scented dryer sheets," she said on a dreamy sigh.

Not the sexiest of replies, but it had been a long day.

A *very* long day.

She wrapped her legs around him and tightened her grip. Everything about this man's touch set her on fire.

"Have you been a naughty librarian this afternoon?" he whispered against the shell of her ear, and a delicious shiver cartwheeled down her spine.

Sweet Lord! The man could dirty talk.

"I organized a few shelves, then snuck a copy of the *Kama Sutra* in with the self-improvement books."

"You are one bad, bad girl. But I'll say this. That book did wonders for us," he answered.

"The best kind of stress relief," she purred, remembering how they'd used that excuse the first time they'd slept together.

"All the stress relief," he repeated on a sexy chuckle.

Jordan released her, setting her feet onto the floor before turning her away from him. Her back pressed to his hard torso as she craned her head to meet his kiss. His hand eased past the band of her skirt, and his fingers dipped into her panties. She lifted her arms and arched her back, giving him complete access to her body. He found her tight bundle of nerves and worked her in perfect little circles that had her gasping for breath within seconds.

"Do you like that?" he growled.

"You know I do," she panted.

He continued his magic between her legs as his other hand slid beneath her shirt and found her left breast. She pressed her hands to the door, steadying herself as Jordan's hard length rubbed against her ass as she rocked against him. With each brush of his thumb over her tight nipple and every stroke of his fingertips across her most sensitive place, the coil inside her wound tighter and tighter until she teetered on the edge of ecstasy.

"I know you're close," he said on a low, sexy rumble.

She was. God, she was. She parted her lips to answer when a faint knock came from the other side of the door.

Jordan froze. "Did you do that?"

She shook her head.

"It's me, Miss Jensen. I had a question about the children's story time schedule and a few things to go over regarding the Shakespeare Shuffle high school volunteer program. Miss Becca said you and Mr. Marks were working back here."

"It's Talya," she mouthed to Jordan.

"And, I'm out here, too. It's me, Simon. I have a question for you before you leave, Mr. Marks," the teen chimed from the other side of the door.

"Simon and Talya are right out there, and I'm..." Georgie whispered.

Jordan's cocksure expression gave way to a panicky cringe. "Give us a second, guys. I'm helping Miss Jensen get in a burst of cardio," he called out.

"Cardio in the office?" she mouthed.

"Let's be honest. Your heart rate was through the roof," he said with a smirk until she gestured to the door with two fifteen-year-olds on the other side, and his eyes went wide.

"Say we're doing work stuff," she whisper-shouted, which wasn't an easy feat with someone's hand in your panties.

"I was wrong. Miss Jensen and I are *not* doing cardio. We're doing *work stuff*," he called, and now she was the one cringing.

This man was a terrible liar.

"Do you think they know what we're doing back here?" he asked.

She stifled a nervous laugh. "They will if you don't remove your hands from my body."

"Jesus, you're right," he said, raising his hands like a football ref reacting to a field goal.

She smoothed her outfit then turned to her fiancé. "How do I look?"

His gaze raked over her body. "A little flushed. We may have wanted to stick with the cardio story."

She took a step back and couldn't help but stare. "Well, you look like you've got a party in your pants."

"It doesn't turn off like a switch," he whisper-yelled as he shuffled behind her desk and picked up a folder to mask the evidence of their non-fornication.

She glanced over her shoulder. Jordan strategically positioned the folder, then nodded, and she opened the door.

"What's up, guys?" she asked, willing her cheeks to *deflush*. Was that even a word? Her trifecta scoffed and shook their literary heads.

But she quickly noticed neither of the teens standing in

front of her cared about her wrinkled blouse or her flushed, pre-orgasmic coloring.

Simon's gaze bounced between the floor and Talya as Talya hugged a notebook to her chest, her gaze bouncing between the floor and Simon. It was like watching pubescent ping-pong.

Talya had started volunteering in the bookstore after the children's addition was finished. A sweet, quiet girl, when she'd come asking if she could help in the children's area to earn volunteer hours for her high school's honor society, Georgie was more than happy to oblige.

"Do you two know each other? You're both sophomores, right?" Georgie asked.

Talya nodded while Simon shook his head.

She frowned while the puberty ping-pong continued. Deciphering teen was like trying to read Greek.

She glanced over her shoulder to find her fiancé grinning like an idiot and holding a folder as if it were a stick of dynamite.

"Let's try something else. What can Jordan and I help you with?" she asked.

"Um, ladies first," Simon said, shifting from foot to foot.

"Okay, thanks," Talya replied, brushing the hair from her eyes as her cheeks grew rosy.

Hello, Teen Awkwardness 101.

Talya glanced at her binder. "Everything is covered for story time for the rest of the week. I wanted to make sure you were all right with me reading Eric Carle's books to the kids."

This girl was worth her weight in gold.

"That's perfect, Talya! His books and illustrations are engaging, and the children love his stories. It's a great choice," she said as the teen's cheeks grew a touch pinker.

Talya chewed her lip. "Okay, and one more thing. I have the volunteer list for the kids at my school who can help out during the Shakespeare Shuffle competition," the girl continued, then handed her a sheet of paper.

"You're going to be at the race?" Simon asked, his side to side nervous shuffle coming to a halt.

Talya nodded, and the teens stared at each other, neither saying a word.

Georgie cleared her throat. "Talya was kind enough to sign up to volunteer during the race and to recruit kids from the high school to take part and earn service hours."

"I'm signed up, too," Simon said, holding Talya's gaze.

"To volunteer? I don't remember seeing your name on the list," the girl replied with a creased brow.

Simon shook his head. "No, I'm competing. I'll be running and reciting a sonnet."

"Wow! That's really epic," Talya replied, brushing back her bangs again. "I'll be handing out cups of water to all the runners."

"That's epic," Simon stuttered.

"It's epic that you're running. I've seen you over at the gym and jogging through the neighborhood," Talya replied.

Simon's eyes went cartoon wide. "You have?"

The girl nodded, and Georgie stole a look back at Jordan. With the folder still in place, the man had gone beet-red, trying not to laugh while watching the most awkward conversation ever.

"Did you need to ask Jordan a question, Simon?" Georgie asked, needing to get these kids the hell out of there before she lost it, too.

"Oh, yeah! Mr. Marks, is it okay if we incorporate more upper body workouts for the next couple of days since a bunch of us are putting in the miles training for the run?"

"That would be epic," Jordan replied.

Georgie threw daggers at her fiancé with her eyes while simultaneously swallowing a belly laugh.

Not an easy feat.

"You work at the gym?" Talya asked Simon through her lashes.

He puffed up his chest. "I help Mr. Marks."

"That's epic," the girl cooed.

"I've seen you around the bookshop, you know, doing book stuff," Simon said, taking the teen awkward level up another notch.

Talya fiddled with the edge of the binder. "Yeah, I help out in the children's area."

"That's totally epic," Simon answered.

Georgie's eyes watered as she tried not to laugh. If she heard Simon or Talya say *epic* one more time, she would totally lose it. She took a breath and willed herself not to giggle.

"Hey, guys, do you know what would be great?" she asked, making damn sure not to use the word epic.

"What?" the teens asked in unison.

Georgie glanced at her watch. "If Simon could walk you home, Talya. It's about time for you to go."

"Yeah, sure! I'd be happy to walk Talya home. That would be—" Simon said, but Georgie cut him off.

"Super terrific! You better hit the road," she supplied.

The teens headed toward the front of the store, and she closed the door and met Jordan's gaze.

"Can I say it?" he asked with a naughty glint in his eyes.

"Don't you dare!" she warned.

Jordan dropped the folder and came out from behind the desk. He gathered her into his arms. "Georgie Jensen, you are totally epic."

"OMG, you're like totally epic, too," she said as they dissolved into a bout of laughter.

She rested her head against his chest and listened to the beat of his heart.

"Hey, Miss Jensen?" he said, running his hand down her back.

She looked up, ready for another round of epic giggles, but found her fiancé with a serious expression.

"Yes, Mr. Marks?"

He stroked her cheek as his gaze grew tender. "I love you."

This man.

She stared into his eyes—the eyes of her Marks Perfect Ten asshat turned her More than Just a Number fiancé. She could barely believe this man was going to be her husband.

"I love you, too," she said, pushing up onto her tiptoes to press a kiss to his cheek when their phones chimed.

Jordan leaned in, and their lips hovered a breath apart.

"You know what's not going to be epic?" he asked.

"What?" she said on a dreamy sigh.

He pulled back and kissed her forehead. "Being late to boot camp."

"Do you think we'll be okay?" she asked.

A wide grin stretched across his face. "Georgiana, boot camp might as well be my middle name."

She nodded. She had to stop herself from putting the cart before the horse. But the needling in her chest was back —the little voice sounding the alarm that trouble was just beyond the horizon.

6

"It looks like we lost the internet," Georgie said, holding up her cell phone and waving it around to try to catch a signal like a Wi-Fi wrangler, but he wasn't holding his breath. They hadn't passed a gas station or much of anything for miles, and he needed to help his fiancée take it down a notch.

"We are in the middle of nowhere, babe, and I don't think there's anything left for you to check. You've been working for the entire drive."

Georgie continued to wave the phone around, and he let out a weary sigh.

This may have been one of the craziest and longest days of his life.

And it still wasn't over.

After squaring things away at the gym and the book-store, he and Georgie had rushed home, threw the essentials into a bag, and hit the road. He'd received an email from the wedding frau's assistant, letting them know what to bring. There were a few cryptic lines of text, such as don't forget to pack dryer lint and a sturdy trowel, which had to have been a typo, but he wasn't too worried.

He knew boot camp. He loved boot camp.

The runs. The obstacle courses. The workouts.

Push-ups, pull-ups, and squats! Oh my! He was more than up for the challenge, and he could help Georgie get there, too.

They'd started working out together. She'd shaved eight seconds off her mile run. Not a hell of a lot, but when they'd started, she'd run a twenty-minute mile. A nineteen-minute and fifty-two-second-mile at least got her into the teens.

And as far as it being a bridal boot camp, that probably meant the program would entail couples' stuff like outdoor hikes and practicing how not to trip while walking down the aisle. Plus, he was with Georgie. The love of his life. If any two people could get through a challenge, it was the two of them.

They'd crushed Battle of the Blogs.

They were becoming household names.

As much as he hated the term *CityBeat Sweethearts*, he loved that a platform with hundreds of millions of people read what they had to say each day.

They could do this.

He did have a feeling the wedding frau may be keeping tabs on them. Her people had set this all up. But, again, it was boot camp, and he was a certified CrossFit trainer.

This was going to be cake. But not the kind with empty calories. This would be healthy cake, like the gluten-free recipe they'd shared on the blog last week, which had been fucking delicious, especially since he ate his test slice off Georgie's naked body.

Georgie's naked body.

And, hello, no fornication erection.

He shifted in the driver's seat, then glanced over at his fiancée. Thanks to all her frantic wiggling around, shuffling papers, and reaching into the back seat to pull her laptop out of her bag to attend to a zillion different projects, her skirt had slid up her legs.

A sight to see.

Toned and lean, he loved drawing his fingers up her calves, past her thighs, then spreading her out on the kitchen table like the naughtiest dessert.

He'd take that over cake any day.

They hadn't gotten to finish their no-fornication session in the office thanks to Epic Teen One and Epic Teen Two knocking on the door. And speaking of epic, he needed to get himself under control if he didn't want to show up to bridal boot camp sporting one epic boner.

"Okay, Jordan, I finished as much as I could before we lost the internet connection. And I texted with Becca and Irene. They say Mr. Tuesday is doing fine."

"That's good," he replied, trying not to think of her thighs.

She fished her mile-long to-do list from a stack of papers and tapped each scribbled item.

"I double-checked the scheduled blog posts for the next couple of days and made sure my Own the Eights book club recommendations were up to date, and I texted the director of the rec center where the Shakespeare Shuffle Competition is taking place. He let me know we have plenty of retired schoolteachers signed up to judge the recitations, and he says everything is good to go with the city regarding road closures for the race portion. But I still think we should double-check with the sponsors and the people making the ribbons for the winners, and—"

"Georgie, we're good, and we'll only be gone for a few days," he said, cutting her off before her brain exploded and fire blasted from her ears, or smoke came billowing out of her nostrils.

She crossed and uncrossed her legs, cracked her knuckles, then plucked a pen from her bag.

He glanced her way. "Georgiana, are you okay?"

Jesus! Maybe she had blown a gasket.

"Pull the car over," she answered, clicking the pen as if she were going for a pen click world record.

He stared at the mass of dense evergreens in all directions, towering majestically along the desolate two-lane road.

"Here? There's nothing around us."

"Yes, right here," she said, speeding up the tempo of the click chorus.

"Why?" he asked.

"Because I need you to do something for me," she replied as the clicks accelerated into a full-on click-tastic calamity of sound.

"I can't do it while driving? We're not far from the bridal boot camp. We only have ten minutes to go," he answered, checking the GPS.

She shook her head. "No, you can't do it while driving. That would be too dangerous."

"Too dangerous? What do you need me to do?" he questioned.

The clicks stopped.

"I need your help, Jordan. It's a Kama Sutra emergency," she said, lowering her voice as if she were asking him to save the world.

It only took a fraction of a second for his cock to tell his brain to tell his foot to hit the brakes. The tires squealed as earth and pebbles and bits of broken asphalt rose in a dusty plume with particles dancing in the golden glow of the setting sun.

Georgie gasped. "Wow! Remind me to use the Kama Sutra emergency line the next time I need you to unclog the shower drain."

"Do not pull a false alarm on the Kama Sutra emergency bell," he fired back as thoughts of their last Kama Sutra reenactment—a little reverse cowgirl on the kitchen floor, following their test bake of the healthy cake—flashed through his mind.

Georgie and cake. After the day they'd had, Christ, that sounded good right about now.

She clicked the pen. "Remember how we once used sex as not really sex but as a vehicle for stress relief?"

Did he remember? How the hell could he ever forget?

He held her gaze. "Are you asking if I've forgotten what it was like making love to you for the first time?"

She twisted the hem of her skirt. "No, I'm sure you remember. I was thinking we could get around this no fornication rule if the sex wasn't for gratification but for stress relief," she replied, nodding as if she were working this out on the fly.

"That sounds very reasonable," he replied, ready to unzip his fly and get down to some Kama Sutra business.

She chewed her lip. "I'm not sure if you can tell, but I'm a little anxious."

A little? Sweet Jesus, that was an understatement!

Luckily, over the past few months, he'd sharpened his boyfriend skills and was smart enough not to point out she was not only a little anxious but more like two pen clicks away from being cuckoo for Cocoa Puffs crazy.

"You do seem a bit on edge," he answered, damn proud of himself.

She blew out a slow breath. "If we were at a spa, I could get a deep tissue massage or, you know, random spa stuff to help relax."

He looked around. "But I don't see a spa."

"We are out of options when it comes to spas," she agreed.

His gaze dropped to her plump lips. "We need to take matters into our own hands."

The tip of her tongue wet her top lip. "It does seem like the only reasonable solution."

"Come to think of it," he said as his gaze continued its descent to her thighs.

"Yes," she breathed.

"I could really use a spa treatment, too," he finished as his blood supply headed south.

"It has been quite a day," Georgie added, her breaths growing shallow.

He cut the ignition and took off his seatbelt. "I want to be clear. What we're proposing is not sex. It's a spa treatment."

"Exactly! It's not sex," she answered, pointing at him with the pen.

"Bear with me a sec. I want to make sure I'm clear on what you're proposing," he said, using the last of his brain cells not already focused on the *no sex spa treatment* with Georgie to put together one final coherent thought.

They needed to be on the same page if, somehow, the frau ever caught wind they'd broken the no fornication rule. And if she did learn of their naughty disobedience, they'd need a plausible defense. After witnessing the wedding planner's operation today, he wouldn't put it past her to have bugged his car.

Georgie clicked the pen, and he unfastened her seatbelt with a click of his own.

"This spa treatment will consist of my cock *treating* your —" he began as her pen clicking drowned out his words.

"Yes!" she interrupted with a supersonic click speed that would put a woodpecker to shame.

"It works for me. I'm in!" he said, pulling her over the console and onto his lap.

"For the treatment," she said, still clicking the pen.

He plucked the damn thing from her fingers and tossed it into the back seat.

"That's right! For the treatment," he echoed, weaving his hands into her hair as their mouths crashed in a wantonness kiss.

What was it about breaking the rules that made this *spa treatment* so enticing?

She gasped against his lips. "Jordan, I need to feel you. I need it now."

His heart rate kicked up as his body went into complete carnal *spa treatment* mode. Had he ever needed her as badly as he did at this moment? It sure didn't seem like it.

Georgie pushed up onto her knees as he unbuttoned his pants and slid them down along with his boxer briefs, freeing his hard length.

"You are really ready for this spa treatment," she said, staring down at his cock with hungry eyes.

"I think you should know by now I do not fuck around when it comes to Kama Sutra emergencies," he growled.

"And spa treatments," she said with a naughty-girl twist to her lips.

"Especially, spa treatments," he reaffirmed, then reached under her skirt and threaded his fingers into the lace band of her G-string. "What are we going to do about these? Panties are prohibited for this treatment."

She gave him a playful pout. "This treatment room is

quite snug, and I don't have much room to move around. You'll have to rip them off. That is, if you're up for some panty ripping?"

Was he up for ripping the panties off the sexiest woman on the planet?

That would be a hell yes!

He snapped the lace of her G-string like a panty-ripping Incredible Hulk.

Georgie inhaled a tight breath as he tossed the remnants of her undergarments into the back seat to rest next to the damn pen.

He cupped her face in his hand. "The spa is open, ma'am."

"I've never needed the spa more," she answered, her gaze darkening.

He positioned himself at her entrance, the tip of his cock rejoicing in the wet heat of her sweet center.

He gave her a wolfish grin. "I see you're ready for your treatment."

"I need all the treatments," she said, closing her eyes as he teased her, sliding his hard length across her delicate folds.

He pressed a kiss below her earlobe. "I'm positive I can accommodate your request."

She pulled back and met his gaze as desire flashed in her eyes. "Shut up and fuck me!"

His eyes nearly popped out of their sockets.

Spa treatment Georgie meant business!

"Yes, ma'am!" he growled.

Lust coursed through his veins as he thrust inside her. Georgie rocked against him, and her knee bumped the recline button, putting them at the perfect angle for him to drive in, deep and hard.

"Yes," she moaned, gripping the sides of the seat.

He dug his fingertips into her ass, guiding her body in a punishing motion that rivaled even that of her rapid-fire pen clicks. Thrusting wildly, he inhaled her scent, closed his eyes, and let the friction build between them.

Months ago, from the first moment he laid eyes on Georgiana Jensen, his reaction to her had been visceral and all-encompassing. Their first kiss had left him wired and wanting more. Georgie and that messy bun of hers had worked their way into his heart. Her smile owned him, mind, body, and soul.

"You're beautiful, and you're mine. *Our love alters not with brief hours and weeks, but bears it out even to the edge of doom*," he whispered against her skin, incorporating a little Shakespeare into their spa treatment before claiming her mouth in a ravenous kiss.

All the sonnet practice with Simon was starting to sink in. He couldn't hold back his words as the intensity of their connection, and the heated friction between their bodies ignited into a raging inferno of sensation and desire. Thrust after frenzied thrust, their minds and souls melded together with no end and no beginning, surrendering themselves to pleasure.

Her breaths grew short as she wrapped her arms around him. She was close to meeting her release. He recognized the swell of her chest and the delicious grip of her core around his weeping cock. But he slowed their ascent into ecstasy, rocking her body in long, lusty strokes against him, deepening their connection and squeezing out each drop of hot, wet pleasure from their gasping bodies when something beyond the need for carnal release churned inside him.

This wasn't a stress relief screw. It wasn't a spa treatment.

And it wasn't even the excitement of doing the deed when they'd been instructed to abstain. No, this was more. This frenzied meeting of their bodies was a desperate plea for reassurance.

Can we do this?

Can we make it?

Is what we have together enough to endure the test of time?

Hovering on the precipice between pleasure and pain, he met Georgie's gaze.

"I meant every word I said to you. You're my everything."

Gasping as if that was what she needed to hear to quiet the anxiety buzzing through her body, she met her release, writhing and tightening around him. He followed her over the edge, pulling her close, anchoring them together as if their bodies knew some far-off storm was heading their way.

She sighed, and he slid his hand into her hair, savoring the warmth of their bodies as they wound down from the rush.

"I really like the spa," she said on a dreamy exhale.

He pressed a kiss to her temple. "I never thought of myself as a spa guy, but you've converted me."

She leaned back and ran her fingertips down his jawline. "We should probably get going, huh?"

"Probably," he said, trying to read her and see if the spa treatment worked in easing her anxiety.

She smiled, and, in the inky darkness that now surrounded them, he saw his Georgie.

"Thank you. I needed that," she said with a sated sigh.

He twisted a lock of her hair between his fingers. "Well, we had to give that poor pen a break."

She chuckled. "All right. I'm going to climb into the back and clean up. Did you pack the tissues?"

She maneuvered off his lap and into the back seat as he adjusted the incline and attended to a little cleanup of his own.

"Yeah, there should be a travel pack of Kleenex in my toiletry bag," he answered, getting situated.

"Oh no!" she cried.

He turned. "What is it? I know the tissues are there. I just did a whole blog post before we left on the necessities every guy should pack before they hit the road."

"No, the tissues are here, but I'm not going to have enough underwear. I packed for three days exactly," Georgie said, zipping her bag closed.

Dammit! He shouldn't have gone all sex hulk and torn them off—but panty tearing seemed so hot in the moment.

"I'm sure they'll have someplace to do laundry," he answered, totally not sure, but really, really hoping they did.

Georgie was an indoor curled-up-with-a-good-book-in-a-comfy-chair kind of woman. While she loved her meandering walks and communing with nature while meditating, after living with her the last three months, he'd learned she also liked the conveniences of indoor plumbing and their eco-friendly washer and dryer.

As did he.

Not to mention, his heavy-duty industrial smoothie maker was damn amazing.

"Do you really think they'll have laundry service available?" she asked, twisting her way back into the passenger seat and fastening her seatbelt.

"I'd imagine," he answered, starting the car.

They'd lost the last of the sunlight beneath the canopy of evergreens, and he turned on the headlights. After driving for a few minutes, what looked like a large structure up on a hill emerged between a break in the trees.

"That might be where we're headed," he said.

Georgie pressed her hand to the window. "It looks like a lodge. How fun!"

Thank Christ!

They could handle a lodge.

Lodges had clean linens and room service, and there may be an actual spa at this place.

A wave of relief washed over him as they came to a fork in the road.

"What do the directions say?" she asked.

"We're supposed to veer left," he answered.

They stared ahead at two signs. One read, Knotty Pines Lodge and Resort in fancy lettering while the other, more of a glorified piece of cardboard, read Alpaca Boarding and Wilderness Boot Camp.

The Knotty Pines Lodge sign had a huge arrow pointing to the right.

The fucking right.

"So, we're not supposed to turn right?" Georgie asked, staring up at the twinkling lights on the hill.

"No, the GPS says to veer left," he answered, swallowing hard.

"Could it be wrong? We're here for Bridal Boot Camp. The sign says wilderness boot camp," she offered up.

It also said fucking alpacas, but he didn't have time to worry about that.

"No, I'm pretty sure our destination is down that way," he said, glancing to the left down a dirt road.

Georgie was back to twisting the hem of her skirt. "Maybe it's another resort, and they're having a new sign made. It does get quite windy in the foothills. This might be a temporary thing. A quick fix," she said, her voice going up a nervous octave.

This was not good!

"That's got to be it," he agreed, doing his best to sound upbeat and not terrified at the prospect of running into an angry alpaca in the wilderness.

He took his foot off the brake, and the car inched forward as the headlights revealed a slice of duct tape on the cardboard sign with *bridal* written in angry block letters.

"I guess this is the bridal boot camp," Georgie said, staring at the sign.

He couldn't look away either. "Yep, it seems to be the case."

She glanced up at the twinkling lodge. "No Knotty Pines for us."

"I'm sure whatever is down this way is just as nice," he said, but the chill working its way down his spine disagreed.

Georgie nodded as he turned the steering wheel to the left and maneuvered the BMW SUV down a dirt road.

"Mrs. Gilbert says she loves knitting with alpaca yarn," Georgie threw out, her voice still hovering in that uneasy octave.

"I'm sure the animals are kept far away from the boot camp," he replied.

She nodded. "You're probably right, but it might be nice to pet one."

"Oh yeah?" he answered, working to keep his voice out of the *holy-shitballs-what-the-hell-were-they-walking-into* range.

But before he could dwell on the not so pleasant attributes of alpacas for another second longer, they pulled up to a giant gate.

He cut the ignition. "What do you think we do now? I don't see anything around here?"

"Let's see if we can open it," Georgie offered.

They got out of the car and walked toward the metal structure when the click of a shotgun being cocked stopped them in their tracks.

"Hello?" Georgie called, coming to his side.

"Are you here to try to steal an alpaca?" came a man's gruff, raggedy voice.

"No, sir," Jordan called back.

"You don't like alpacas?" replied the stern voice from the depths of the forest.

"They're lovely animals, but we're here for the bridal boot camp. I'm Georgiana Jensen, and this is my fiancé, Jordan Marks. Is this the right place?" Georgie asked, sharing a wide-eyed glance with him.

Jordan held his breath, praying this was not the right place when a woman's husky laugh peppered the air. Georgie gasped and grabbed onto his arm as a woman carrying a lantern emerged from the trees with a man close behind. Decked in camouflage, the couple looked like the grandparents' version of GI Joe figures.

"Buck, don't you tease these young folks. They're our last arrivals, the City *Feet* people who signed up last minute."

"Beat. It's CityBeat," Georgie corrected as the wilderness couple stared at them in the hazy darkness.

"And don't worry. We aren't expecting any special treatment," she added in what sounded a hell of a lot like her beauty pageant voice.

This was really not good.

"That won't be a problem here, miss. When it comes to braving the elements, nature decides what lives and what dies," the man answered somberly.

Holy apocalyptic boot camp!

Jordan glanced at his fiancée, now sporting a frozen grin.

"Ignore him!" the woman said, gesturing to the armed

older gentleman, who appeared ready to join a militia. "I'm Syd Slaughter, and this is my husband, Buck. We'll be leading the boot camp."

The Slaughters? This was right out of a horror movie.

This could not be right. The wedding people must have booked the wrong boot camp.

"We must have made a wrong turn. We're expected at a bridal boot camp," he said.

Syd gestured to the plethora of trees. "You're here. This is it."

"We are?" Georgie asked.

"Yes, this is the advanced wilderness bridal boot camp," Syd replied as Buck stared them down.

Advanced?

Georgie glanced around. "Where's the lodge?"

Syd turned to Buck, and the two broke out into laughter.

"Grab your gear and give Buck your car keys. He'll park your vehicle behind the brush," Syd instructed through a throaty chuckle.

"Why behind the brush?" he asked as he and Georgie grabbed their bags, then handed the old man his keys.

Buck's features hardened. "Because we are off the grid, young man. There will be no *Googly* maps or enemy drones taking pictures of my land or my animals."

"You mean Google maps," Jordan corrected.

Syd and Buck stared blankly at him. They had that scary look down pat.

"Is there Wi-Fi?" Georgie asked, cutting through the silence.

"No, ma'am! This boot camp is about living off the land and going toe to toe with Mother Nature. You can also hand me your phones. I'll lock them in your car along with any other electronics," Buck answered.

They didn't even get to keep their phones?

"Okay," Georgie replied wearily.

Syd cleared her throat and gestured with her chin toward Buck's backpack. "We do have one modern convenience for you."

"Great," Georgie answered, relief coating the word, as Buck reached around and pulled two items from the bag.

"As mandated by the judge, we have to give you these," the man said, handing them each a lanyard attached to a small plastic circle.

"What are they for?" Georgie asked.

"Death," Buck shot back.

"Death?" Georgie echoed in a panicked whisper.

Wilderness or not, what kind of boot camp was this?

Syd let out another husky laugh. "Buck, don't be so dramatic. It's only a tracking device. You can press the little button, and we'll come get you."

"Why would you need to come and get us? Aren't we here?" he questioned.

"We had a slight mishap a few years ago. We lost a couple of boot campers," Syd replied, a little too calmly for admitting they'd lost actual people in the wilderness.

Sweet Jesus!

"You lost them?" Georgie whispered in that same panicked tone.

"Only for four days," the woman replied with a nonchalant wave of her hand.

"We told them not to wander off," Buck mumbled, opening the gate.

"If you do find yourself in danger, press the button. Thanks to a court order, we'll get you in a jiffy. Now, let's get to camp," Syd said, gesturing for them to follow her as the lantern lit her leathery features.

Jordan fell into step next to Georgie, allowing Syd to stay a few paces ahead of them while Buck disappeared with the car keys.

"What have we gotten ourselves into?" Georgie asked under her breath.

"It's probably for show. You know, to make hipsters and city people feel like they're roughing it," he replied, hoping that was the case.

"I don't know the first thing about camping, Jordan. I spent most of my childhood parading around on stage in full makeup and five-inch heels. Do you know anything about wilderness survival? Were you a boy scout?"

He shook his head. "No, I spent my childhood hiding from bullies and reading comics in the library."

Georgie lifted her chin. "We're two capable adults. We advise people on all kinds of things. We should be able to figure it out. And, last week, we watched that nature documentary," she added with a hopeful lilt.

"Georgie, that nature show was on dolphins, and after five minutes, you fell asleep."

"Shoot! That's right," she whispered as his stomach growled.

He'd figured they were going to some fancy boot camp with a Paleo menu and organic produce that would make Georgie swoon.

"Syd, what's on the menu for dinner?" he called to the bobbing lantern light in the distance.

"Perfect timing! We're at the snack shack," she answered as they came upon a small shed.

The wilderness woman unlocked the door. With a clank and thud, she grabbed some items and threw them into a sack.

"A pound of deer jerky, six cans of beef stew, a gallon of

water, and, for a real treat, some canned pineapple," she replied.

Georgie made a sound between a yelp and a gag.

"That's dinner?" he sputtered.

She handed him the burlap sack. "Yep, these are your rations, and you can always get more water from the well."

Beef stew, deer jerky, and canned pineapple? This wasn't dinner. It was a recipe for constipation.

"That's it?" Georgie asked.

"If you trap a rabbit, we can cook it up, too. And don't forget to lock up your food in the bear canister. You'll find it next to where we've got you making camp. We haven't seen bears in these parts for years, but it's always better to be safe than sorry in the backcountry."

A bear canister!

Syd locked the shed, and they continued walking.

"Don't worry. I've got us covered. Just keep that pineapple away from me," Georgie whispered.

"What do you mean?" he asked.

"I've got a tube of vegan cookie dough in my bag. I wrapped it in an ice pack."

He shifted the sack of constipation rations and wrapped his arm around her. "God, I love you. Have I told you you're the most amazing woman on the planet?" he whispered back.

"We'll see how you feel when we run out of the dough," she teased, but that was a real possibility.

"Come on, you two. It's not far now," Syd called, trekking further into the middle of nowhere, Colorado.

They continued through the evergreens, dodging splintered trees and stepping carefully when the glow of a campfire crackled in the distance.

"We've got a full house. Ten engaged couples," Syd explained as two small canvas structures came into view.

"Yurts!" Georgie exclaimed excitedly. "I recently interviewed an interior designer and wrote a blog post about how people are turning yurts into luxury mini-villas with all the comforts of home. They're becoming quite the rage among millennials."

"Mini-villas and millennials?" came a voice in the dark.

Georgie shrieked, and he nearly dropped their bag of provisions.

"Who is that?" he asked.

"That's Buck! He's been tracking us since we left. You didn't notice him?" Syd asked.

"No!" Georgie said, back to clutching his arm as they came into a partial clearing.

"Buck and I live in that yurt for part of the year with all the creature comforts. The other yurt over there is the honeymoon yurt," Syd replied, pointing to the structures.

"We get to stay in a honeymoon yurt?" Georgie asked.

"No, this is advanced wilderness boot camp. You two will be pitching a tent with the rest of the engaged couples."

"A tent in October?" Georgie replied.

"It's our last bridal wilderness boot camp, and we've been assured the weather will remain unseasonably warm," Syd answered.

Damn that wedding frau and her weather magic! He should have waited and proposed at Christmas.

"And the alpacas?" he queried.

He had to ask about them, or else he wouldn't sleep a wink.

"We let them wander, but they usually stay near their enclosure just over that rock formation," Syd answered, holding up the lantern.

Okay, at least there was a wall of rock separating them from the beasts.

Syd passed him the lantern. "Take this. Your tent and camping gear are on that side of the clearing. Sleeping bags are next to the tent. It looks like all of the couples have turned in already. You'll get to meet them in the morning. We rise and fall with the sun."

"I don't see a tent," Georgie said, squinting past the campfire.

"Of course, you don't. You have to put it up," Syd replied.

"We have to put up a tent?" Georgie asked.

"We'll be fine," he said, taking her hand and growing hungrier by the second.

"See you bright and early," Syd called with a wave.

"And where are the restrooms?" Georgie asked.

"You brought your trowel, right?" came Buck's raspy reply.

They jumped, and Syd laughed.

"Don't let Buck get to you. He loves sneaking up on people," Syd said, giving her husband a playful smack on the arm.

"That's not creepy," Georgie muttered.

"What's that?" Buck asked.

"We brought a *towel*," Georgie supplied.

Buck cocked his head to the side. "*A towel?*"

"Yes," she answered.

"How are you going to dig a hole to take a shit in with a towel?" Buck asked.

Georgie's mouth fell open. "We have to go to the bathroom in a hole we dig ourselves?"

"Here, we've got an extra," Syd said, retrieving a small shovel propped against the yurt.

She held it out for him, and he took the shit shovel,

doing his best to touch as little of the handle as possible and praying his fiancée had packed hand sanitizer.

He glanced at Georgie and found her frozen in place, staring in horror at the gardening implement.

"Sweet dreams," Syd called in a singsong voice as the couple disappeared into the darkness.

7

GEORGIE

Georgie rubbed her eyes and attempted to bend her neck, listening as the vertebrae popped. The muscles in her back screamed for her memory foam mattress while her literary trifecta gasped in horror.

Lizzy and Jane were all for the great outdoors, but the Regency-era variety, where lovely servants, carrying wicker baskets and fresh linens, laid out a picnic of dainty watercress sandwiches and hard cheeses. And Hermione? That girl shrugged. How could she relate? She had a magical tiny tent that turned into a palace.

Georgie rolled her head from side to side then groaned. Damn magic. She could use some right now.

Despite Syd wishing them sweet dreams, last night had been an unmitigated nightmare. Neither she nor Jordan knew the first thing about putting up a tent. No tent knowledge, along with having to assemble the damn thing by lantern light, turned out to be an even bigger disaster. After hours spent poking tent poles every which way and a litany of swearing, they'd finally got it to stand.

Then, there were the sleeping bags that rivaled the scent of Jordan's father's ancient mothball encrusted tux.

She often cited the benefits of spending time in nature on their More Than Just a Number blog.

It was time to rethink that.

Jordan shifted in his sleep, and his mouth fell open as a rip-roaring snore tore through the tent.

Yep, her fiancé was a tent snorer.

The Marks snoring sound system activated when the man was without his goose down pillow. Last night, she'd tossed and turned, poking and prodding him, but he was out like a light and sawing logs like a lumberjack on steroids.

She brushed a lock of hair from his forehead. How many nights had she slept wrapped in his arms, peacefully dreaming? How many mornings had she woken with his muscled body pressed to hers and his hard length, ready to take her over the edge of ecstasy?

Never in her wildest dreams would she have imagined this is how they'd spend their first night as an engaged couple.

The only saving grace? At least, she hadn't needed to use the shit shovel...yet.

"Georgie? Is this a dream?" her fiancé, Mr. Tent Snorer, asked on a groggy exhale.

She blinked her burning, sleep-deprived eyes. "No, this is real, Jordan."

He shifted in the sleeping bag and gathered her into his arms. They'd opted to lay one flat to have some sort of cushioning and share the other.

"How'd you sleep?" he asked, his voice thick from actual sleep.

"Not great. You snore," she replied.

"I do?" he asked with a gruff, gravelly morning voice she usually loved. But this morning, all she wanted to do was stuff a pair of socks into his mouth.

"Yeah, pretty much all night long," she replied, lamenting her decision to pack light and not add an extra pair to her bag.

His sleepy gaze grew concerned. "Do I do that at home?"

"No." She sighed, feeling like an asshat. It wasn't his fault he was a tent snorer.

"I'm sorry, babe," he said against her neck, dropping kisses.

"Jordan, I don't think boot camp is for me," she murmured, melting into his touch.

He continued kissing a trail to her earlobe. "We could call the concierge desk and ask for housekeeping to bring up some earplugs."

She chuckled. "Yeah, along with a working toilet and a minibar."

He ran his hand down the side of her body then tugged at her fleece. "What are you wearing?"

"A T-shirt, a sweatshirt, and a fleece. I bundled up in the middle of the night," she answered.

He released the layers of fabric. "Are you warm enough now?"

She cuddled into him. "I've never slept outside. I didn't want to die of hypothermia."

"Georgie, we checked the weather before we left. It's not going to get even remotely close to freezing temperatures."

She sighed. "Your definition of *remotely close* may differ from mine."

"Let's warm you up," he purred in that sexy voice.

He slid his hand under her multiple layers of clothing

and stroked her back, drawing lazy circles with his warm fingertips.

She hummed her pleasure. "This, I like."

He slipped his hand into her yoga pants . "What about this?" he asked, caressing her tight bundle of nerves.

"That, I like even more." She wove her fingers into his dark, uncharacteristically messy hair. "Looks like you're going to be rocking some sex hair this morning, Mr. Marks."

"Two can play at that," he replied on a heated breath.

"It is the great outdoors. We can go a little caveman, can't we?" she answered as her sex brain kicked in and overruled her rational mind that yearned to return to civilization.

He captured her mouth in a kiss, then stilled.

She held her breath. "What is it?"

Oh no! She hadn't brushed her teeth, and, after all the tent hell and her fiancé passing out from exhaustion, she'd indulged in the one thing that never let her down.

Jordan frowned. "Have you been eating cookie dough?"

Her cheeks grew hot, and it wasn't from the sleeping bag hanky-panky.

"I was up most of the night, and I got bored," she confessed.

Tired, uncomfortable, and unable to escape her fiancé's snore-fest, she'd turned to her only salvation.

Vegan chocolate chip cookie dough.

"How much did you eat?" he asked as his frown deepened.

She buried her face in the crook of his neck. "Enough that we'll probably be eating deer jerky for breakfast."

"Georgie! You ate the whole thing?" he exclaimed.

"No!" she shot back.

"How much is left for us?" he asked.

She cringed. "An inch."

"An inch!" he cried.

Her cheeks burned with embarrassment. "I know. I'm sorry. I couldn't help myself. The few times I did fall asleep, I dreamed of my mother knocking that doughnut out of my hand. I needed something sweet."

He caressed her cheek as his features softened. "I guess if I want to enjoy any cookie dough, I'll have to keep kissing you."

She met his gaze. "That's sweet of you to take one for the team. I'm sure it's a real hardship."

"I'll show you a *hardship*," he whispered against her lips as his hand resumed stroking her most sensitive place.

Okay, this wasn't so bad. Maybe she could get into camping. Tent kissing was really nice and, when the love of her life wasn't snoring to beat the band, it was pretty hot being zipped up next to him in a snuggly sleeping bag.

She reached between them and palmed his hard length. "We've never done it in a tent."

"No, we haven't," he answered against her neck as he cupped her sex, rocking his palm against her in slow, delicious strokes.

She gasped. "And it wouldn't really be sex."

"It wouldn't?" he asked with a mischievous lilt.

"No, it's wilderness survival heat production," she offered as a near-inferno smoldered between her thighs, thanks to Jordan's touch.

"You are good at coming up with ways for us not to have sex," he answered in a tight breath.

"It's a gift," she said, then moaned as Jordan freed his cock from his pants.

It was time to get down to *not-sex* wilderness heat production.

She did a little shimmy-shake to get her yoga capris

down past her ass as he did a scoot-scoot twist to work his track pants to his ankles. Disrobing in a sleeping bag was not for the faint of heart, but her guy was clearly up for the task.

"Try lifting your leg and turning your hips," he offered, positioning himself at her entrance.

She shifted her body. "Hold on. I can hook my leg like this, and I think it'll work."

"Yeah, that's good," he said, gripping her hip and rolling on top of her until a sharp pain made her wince.

She sucked in a tight breath. "Ouch! Something hard is poking me."

A dirty grin stretched across Jordan's face.

She arched her back. "Not that, you, asshat! I think it's the sleeping bag's zipper."

Jordan's cocksure expression disappeared. "Let me roll us over so I can be on bottom."

"Okay," she answered, then caught a glimpse of the top of the tent, bowing and billowing inward. Thanks to their shit tent assembly skills, the unsteady quasi-shelter looked ready to topple over at any moment.

"Here we go. Get ready for the best wilderness survival heat production you've ever had," Jordan said with a sexy smirk as the tent began to heave.

"Jordan, wait," she said, a second too late.

Her CrossFit giant of a fiancé rolled to the side, catching the corner of the drooping tent and taking it with them as they maneuvered with the grace of a bull in a china shop.

With the tent resting on her head, she met Jordan's gaze and tried to hold back a chuckle.

"That was smooth," he teased as she shook her head, but before she could answer, a voice cut through the crisp morning air.

"What the heck is going on in there?"

Georgie gasped. "It's Syd. We can't let her know what we're doing," she whispered, knowing there was a good chance the wedding frau was in contact with the boot camp leaders.

Jordan's gaze registered her concern. He knew it, too.

"You're right," he whispered back. He turned his head toward the side of the tent. "Whatever you think we're doing, it's not sex," he called, then gave her a little wink.

"Not sex?" Syd parroted back.

"Why did you say that?" Georgie whisper-shouted.

Jordan grimaced. "I don't know. It was the first thing I thought of."

"If you're not having sex, then, what *is* going on in there," Syd pressed.

Georgie's eyes went wide, pleading for her fiancé to come up with a better explanation.

"Georgie got stuck in the sleeping bag," he offered.

"Try unzipping it," came Buck's voice.

Perfect. They had an audience. Who else was out there?

"Here, let me unzip the tent, and I can give you a hand," Syd offered.

"No!" she and Jordan cried in unison.

"We've got it under control. Give us a sec," Georgie called, squirming and jostling to pull up her yoga pants as Jordan did a weird inchworm jiggle to slide his track pants into place.

The tent scraped along the ground, scratching and grating against the tiny rocks and fallen pine needles. She turned to try to wiggle her way out when her elbow connected with Jordan's eye.

"Ow!" he yelped.

"I'm sorry," she replied, attempting to touch his face but only succeeding in poking his other eye.

"Jesus, Georgie!" he bit out.

"Do you two need the first aid kit?" Buck asked, with an amused bend to his words.

Jordan pressed his hand to his eye. "No, we're good."

"We're coming out," Georgie called, unzipping the sleeping bag and then unzipping the tent.

The bright morning sun blinded her, and she waved her arm, attempting to shield her eyes only to knock Jordan in the face for the third time.

"Babe, watch your hands," Jordan exclaimed.

"I can't see anything," she answered, blinking hard and turning away from the light as if she were a campground vampire—if those even existed.

Her trifecta shook their heads in disagreement. Of course, no respectable vampire would ever go camping. Georgie pushed her literary companions out of her mind as she crawled out of the tent. She blinked again as her eyes adjusted, only to look up to find a sea of hiking boots.

"Wakey, wakey, eggs and bakey," Buck sang out.

A wave of relief washed over her. "We get eggs?" she asked, staring up at the mountain man.

He frowned. "No, it's an expression. You get deer jerky and pineapple chunks unless you've got a rabbit or a squirrel hidden in that heap of a tent you want to cook up."

At the thought of that wretched can of tropical fruit, she pressed her hand to her mouth.

"Eat up and join us at the center of camp, sleepy heads. We're about to get started," Syd added over her shoulder.

Get started? She was ready for this nightmare to end.

Jordan helped her to her feet as she listened to the crunch of hiking boots heading away from them.

She scanned her fiancé's face. "Are you all right, Jordan? I didn't mean to hit you three times."

He rubbed below his eye, which had already taken on a yellow-green tinge. "It's okay, babe. I'll survive."

She cupped his face in her hands. "Want me to kiss it to make it better?"

His gaze darkened, but the man froze when a woman's voice caught them off guard.

"Jordy *Straws* Marks? Is that you?"

Georgie turned to see a young woman wagging her finger at them as Jordan's jaw dropped.

"Do you know her?" she asked her flummoxed fiancé.

"Of course, *Straws* knows me. We went to the same high school," the woman replied.

"Camille Pruitt?" Jordan sputtered.

"The one and only," the woman replied in a voice way too chipper for spending the night in a tent.

"Why are you here?" he asked, looking as if he'd seen a ghost.

"I'd guess the same reason as you, Mr. Straws. For the bridal wilderness boot camp," she answered, flashing her left hand adorned with a giant diamond ring.

Georgie turned to her fiancé. Straws was the cruel nickname the kids from Jordan's past had given him because of his gangly, pre-CrossFit body. He hated it. That nickname, accompanied by the thoughtless act of kids stuffing his locker with the damn things, had haunted him for years.

"He goes by Jordan now. That's his name," she corrected.

"That's right! Silly me! I should know that by now. My fiancé and I love your More Than Just a Number blog," the woman cooed.

"You do?" Georgie asked, crossing her arms and trying

not to allow the avalanche of skepticism to seep into her voice.

"Yeah, and you even know my fiancé, and Straws, I mean Jordan, does, too," Camille said, grinning like an idiot.

"I know your fiancé?" Georgie asked, completely stumped.

Camille gestured toward a man standing in the shade of an aspen tree. "Pooh Bear, come say hello! That CityBeat couple is here!"

Stepping out of the veil of darkness and wearing a ball cap with a Casey Pest Control logo, Georgie did a double take.

No, it couldn't be!

"This is my Pooh Bear, Brice Casey," Camille clucked.

"Hey, Virginia!" the supreme asshat and catalyst for her Own the Eights blog said with an idiotic grin.

She stared at the man. Of all the boot camps in all of Colorado, what were the chances of meeting this jackass here? Her usually loquacious trifecta could barely believe their fictional eyes.

"Her name is Georgiana or Georgie. Not Virginia," Jordan said, finding his voice and joining the conversation.

Brice put up his hands in mock surrender. "Dude, sorry! Lucky for me, you don't have a beer to dump on my head."

Then, Camille and Brice giggled. They actually giggled.

The last time she and Jordan had seen Brice Casey, it was the night she'd inhaled a boatload of Jell-O shots and entered a wet T-shirt contest at a rowdy Denver bar. Jordan had dumped a beer on Brice's head for making a Brice Casey-level douche canoe comment about her.

"But you have to admit, your name is confusing," Brice said, sharing a nod with Camille.

"It's so confusing because Georgia and Virginia are

states," Camille agreed with the logic of an empty paper bag.

"I think I've told you this before, but you should consider changing your name," Brice said as his expression grew serious.

"You want me to change my name because you can't remember it?" she repeated, incredulity lacing her words as heat bloomed on her cheeks.

Jordan must have sensed she was about to lose her shit and pressed his hand to her back.

"Well, Brice, Camille, how did you guys meet?" Jordan asked.

God bless this man for shifting the conversation.

Camille emitted an exaggerated sigh. "It's a beautiful story."

"It sure is," Brice agreed.

Camille's face lit up. "And we're famous, too. Brice is Colorado Rodent Royalty, and I'm the Plunger Princess."

Georgie shook her head to knock away the fatigue cobwebs. She had to be hallucinating from lack of sleep.

"Did you just say you were the Plunger Princess?" she asked.

"Camille's family owns a plumbing business," Jordan supplied.

"That's right! We're the largest family owned operation in the state. We've unclogged over a million toilets," the woman remarked proudly.

"And my family has been in rodent removal for five generations. Mice, rats, squirrels, if it's a rodent, we'll remove it," Brice added proudly, wrapping his arm around Camille.

Georgie's gaze bounced between the couple. Was this ridiculous conversation really happening? Could this be the result of ingesting the equivalent of twenty-two vegan chocolate chip cookies on zero rest?

"Our families have been friends for years, and Brice and I reconnected at a wet T-shirt contest," Camille continued.

At the mention of a wet T-shirt contest, Georgie snapped back.

"Was it the one I was in back in June?" she asked, addressing Brice.

"No, the next weekend," Brice replied with absolutely no shame in frequenting weekly wet T-shirt contests.

"It was meant to be," Camille gushed, pushing up onto her tiptoes to kiss Brice's cheek.

"Yep, Camille is the perfect ten I always knew I'd end up with. Plus, a couple of months before we reconnected, Cammie traded in her C's for D's," Brice added, gesturing to his fiancée's ample bosom like they were a rack of ribs.

"Pooh Bear, you are the sweetest man," Camille cooed.

Georgie caught Jordan's gaze. Had they somehow wandered into the twilight zone? When they turned left instead of right, had they entered some bizarro bridal dimension? She looked around, hoping a camera crew would jump out and say surprise. After the last night and even this morning, she'd be up for a day at the Ritz spa with her mother.

And that was really saying something!

"Are you guys ready for the competition?" Brice asked.

Jordan crossed his arms. "What competition?"

Georgie swallowed hard. There was no mention of a competition in the email they'd received from the frau's assistant, but, then again, there was no mention they'd be attending a wilderness torture event, either.

"A friendly wilderness survival skills competition

between the couples. Cammie and I love this stuff," Brice replied.

"You do?" Georgie asked.

These two barely had two brain cells between them. But at that thought, a kernel of hope bloomed. If these airheads could survive wilderness boot camp, surely, she and Jordan could, too.

"I was a highly decorated Girl Scout, and Brice was an Eagle Scout," Camille replied.

The kernel of hope faded.

"I was a beauty queen," she said, then clapped her hand over her mouth.

Brice and Camille stared at her, and she plastered on a high-wattage smile.

What the hell was wrong with her?

Was she intimidated by these morons?

No!

No, no, no, no!

She parted her lips to say she'd misspoken as the irksome clang of a cowbell rang out.

"We better head up. It looks like the race is about to begin," Brice said to his fiancée.

"Are you guys coming?" Camille asked.

"We'll see you up there," Jordan answered as Brice and Camille headed toward the center of camp.

Jordan turned to their floppy tent and pulled out their shoes and backpacks. "We need to get ready fast. Grab the deer jerky. We can eat after the race."

Georgie laced up, then opened the bear canister and placed the clump of meat into her backpack, while also keeping a watchful eye on her fiancé.

"What are the chances of two people from our pasts

showing up here? It's crazy!" she said as Jordan's features remained neutral.

He grabbed their water bottles. "I don't care what we have to do, Georgie. We're not letting those two beat us at anything," he said, his voice low as he glared at the stainless-steel containers.

"I don't think it's a real competition—" she began, but Jordan didn't let her finish.

"Did you not hear what the crown prince of rodent royalty said?" he shot back.

"I did, but I'm assuming it's all in good fun," she answered.

"Yeah, good fun, like pelting me with straws anytime I walked past the school cafeteria," he bit out.

She rested her hand on his back, feeling his muscles tense beneath her touch. "It's going to be fine. We'll ignore them. There are a bunch more couples here. I'm sure we'll barely have time to interact with Brice and Camille."

"Yeah, okay," Jordan answered with a pinched expression.

She pulled a strip of deer jerky from her bag and handed it to him. "Eat this. The Supreme Emperor of Asshattery requires sustenance."

He sighed, taking the hunk of meat as his shoulders slumped. "Sorry, Georgie. Seeing Camille brought back all the shit I thought I'd left behind. Are you okay? I'm sure you didn't expect to run into Brice Casey."

"Oh yeah! I'm totally good with bumping into the guy who was such a jerk it compelled me to start a revolution."

Jordan raised an eyebrow playfully.

"Okay, to start a blog. It's almost the same thing," she replied, holding his gaze, which, thankfully, had softened.

The clang of the cowbell cut through the air, calling

them to camp, and Jordan offered her his hand. She took it and savored the warmth of his touch. He brushed his thumb across the center of her palm, and she relaxed a fraction as they wove their way through the foliage to the center of camp to find the group already assembled.

Syd clapped her hands. "All right, wilderness couples! It's time for a scat race."

Georgie met Jordan's gaze, and his eyes lit up.

"Is scat a type of training like HIIT training?" he asked, radiating excitement.

Syd stared back blankly. "I'm not familiar with *hit* training."

Jordan lifted his chin, going into trainer mode. "HIIT, *H, I, I, T* stands for high-intensity interval training. It's a form of cardiovascular exercise where you alternate between bouts of high-intensity training and recovery periods. It's great for conditioning and improving metabolism."

"Is there any *shit* involved with your *hit*?" Buck asked with a quirk to his lips.

"Shit?" Jordan echoed.

Buck nodded. "Yeah, *S, C, A, T*, scat, is just a fancy way of saying shit."

Jordan took a step back, and his mouth fell open. "We're doing a race to see who can shit first?"

The entire group broke out into laughter, and Jordan's expression hardened.

"No, this is not a competition to see which boot camper can produce a bowel movement first, and of course, if you need to have one, don't forget your trowel," Syd advised as the couples nodded.

Buck took a step forward. "Teamwork is a cornerstone of any marriage. Part of being a committed couple is working together and understanding the lay of the land. Life isn't always a stroll through the park. The task at hand will have you trekking through the backcountry and identifying the different *animal scat* or feces. You know what feces are, right, Jordan?"

Another round of snickering percolated through the wilderness campers.

Georgie touched Jordan's arm and glanced up as a muscle ticked in his jaw.

"It's okay. I didn't know what it was either," she said under her breath. But her fiancé didn't meet her gaze.

"Not now, Georgiana," he mumbled, his posture going rigid.

"Jordan, it's not a big deal," she tried, keeping her voice low.

"Georgiana, can we listen to the directions so we can win this bullshit *shit* race," he bit back.

She dropped her hand from his arm. What the hell was up with this gruff *Georgiana pay attention* perfection attitude?

Then it hit her.

Perfection.

Shit!

She stole another look at her triggered fiancé, who, thanks to this wilderness poop race and the arrival of his high school blast from his unpleasant past, Camille Pruitt, had morphed into ten-mode. It had been ages since she'd seen this asshat and the true reigning Emperor of Asshattery. Sure, they joked about it now, but there was no denying the Class-A douche he'd been when they'd first met.

Syd gestured for their attention. "Every couple gets a clipboard. On it, you'll find a list of animals and a picture of their scat. Your job is to find scat from four of the ten animals listed. The first couple to complete this task gets to spend the night in the honeymoon yurt," Syd added.

"The honeymoon yurt," Georgie repeated as the thought of a real bed and a working toilet made her weak in the knees—or perhaps that was all the cookie dough and deer jerky. But still, the idea of not sleeping in a tent sounded like heaven on earth.

"And don't think you can cheat. Not all the scat on the list is found on our land. If you mark off each piece of shit, you are officially shit out of luck and lose any claim to the honeymoon yurt," Buck cautioned.

Georgie swallowed hard as Syd handed each couple a clipboard.

"Form a circle. We don't want you on top of one another. There's plenty of land and plenty of scat. We'll send you off in different directions, but make sure you've got your compass so you can track where you are on the map."

Georgie waved Jordan down. "Should we tell them we've never done anything like this before?"

With a stiff shake of his head, her fiancé nixed the idea. "No, we'll be fine."

"Are you sure?" she pressed, because, well, they were in the middle of freaking nowhere backcountry, and it seemed like a good idea to let someone know the only compass they ever used was the one located in Jordan's BMW's dashboard.

"Relax, Georgie," Jordan muttered. "They're sending us out in one direction. We'll turn around after we identify the shit and come back. How hard can that be?"

"Team high-intensity scat training, are you ready?" Buck called.

She and Jordan looked up to find all eyes on them.

Jordan puffed up like a peacock. "Yeah, we're ready."

"Turn around and on my count, head south, southwest," Syd said, checking her map.

"Are we running?" Georgie whispered.

"Yes, this is no meandering walk," Jordan replied as that muscle ticked in his jaw again. It might as well be his asshattery indicator.

"Three, two, one, go!" Syd cried.

Jordan shot into the forest like...whatever the hell sprints in the woods. A cougar? A mountain lion? Were those the same animal? Gah! Her trifecta shrugged as she glanced past a cluster of aspens, already starting their fall transition from green to gold. It was quite lovely, and she would have remarked on it if her fiancé hadn't bolted into the evergreens like a bat out of hell. She sucked in a breath and caught a glimpse of his gray hoodie as he scaled a large rock.

"Wait!" she cried.

Her backpack clunked from side to side as she held the clipboard and struggled to keep Jordan in sight.

"How are you going to find scat at that speed? And by the way, I've got the damn clipboard!" she yelled.

"I want to break from the group and get away from camp. I'm guessing the animals steer clear of it, so, keeping that in mind, the best scat is probably farther away," he called from over his shoulder.

Dammit! That actually made sense.

Ignoring the sour churn of her belly and her burning sleep-deprived eyes, she mustered all the strength she had because she had more than an inkling she was going to need it.

"Hurry, Georgiana! Run!" Jordan called.

Georgie clutched the clipboard and willed her legs to move faster.

"I am running!" she answered.

For the better part of the last three hours, they'd scoured the backcountry with their eyes locked on the ground in search of animal poop.

She caught her breath and slowed down.

Okay, calling it a run might be pushing it.

"Georgie, come on! I think I see something over by that tree," Jordan shouted.

Her fiancé's fecal matter focus had been unrelenting.

They'd found what they'd hoped was squirrel scat, jackrabbit scat, and marmot scat. She didn't even know what an actual marmot looked like, but she identified its damn poop. They had to find one more specimen of animal scat, and then they could return to camp.

She drew in a sharp breath and kicked it up into high gear, which was pretty much old lady walker speed by this point.

"I'm coming! Slow down!"

"We cannot slow down! You need to speed up!" he answered.

Heat rushed to her cheeks. "This is me speeding up!"

She was tired and hungry. All those muscles that had remained tensed and twisted last night during the Jordan Marks snore-fest begged for a respite from this shit show.

This literal shit show.

What she needed was a hot bubble bath. She could picture it now. Warm water. Bubbles, tickling her skin as she propped her feet on the side of the tub and reread her well-loved copy of *Pride and Prejudice*. She could sink into the scented water and listen as Jordan cooked dinner or played with Mr. Tuesday.

How she missed those days.

Those days?

OMG! Those days were two days ago! Two days ago, life had been perfect.

"Georgie, look out!" Jordan called.

"What?" she yelled back, but the smell answered.

She stared down at her shoe, smack-dab in the center of a giant pile of poop.

Jordan rushed over and took the clipboard from her. "Before you smashed the scat, did you get a look at it?"

She pressed her hand to her mouth, trying not to gag. She didn't know which was worse. Pineapple or poop?

"If I saw it, I wouldn't have stepped in it!" she snapped.

"Don't move! Let me try and get a better look," he directed with a stern expression.

"You want me to keep my foot in this pile of crap?" she shot back.

He met her gaze. "Yes, it's a competition, Georgiana, and we're not going to lose."

She scoffed but quickly closed her mouth and pinched her nostrils. It was damn hard to maintain being pissed off while standing in a pile of random animal shit.

Jordan, unaware of her discontent, crouched down next to her crap-encrusted sneaker. "It could be mule deer or elk scat," Jordan mused, staring at the pictures of poop on the clipboard. "Mule deer scat looks a little lighter in color, so I'm going to go with elk."

"Great! I'm onboard with elk. Can I move?" she asked.

Jordan gestured for her to stay put. "Wait a second. It could be mule deer. The shape of the piece of scat you missed is a little bit smaller. Or this might just be scat from a small elk. What do you think?"

"I think I'm standing in a pile of shit, Jordan! Actual feces! And you don't want me to move," she yelled.

"Calm down and stop being a drama queen, Georgiana. This isn't a wilderness beauty pageant," he replied, studying the clipboard.

Oh, hell no!

"What did you say?" she asked, lowering her voice.

"You've been kind of a diva today, babe," he answered, still staring at the damn shit.

"Diva? I'm a diva because I don't want to stand in animal fecal matter?" she tossed back.

Jordan looked up and met her gaze as a boisterous bout of yips and yeehaws rang out. They glanced over to see Brice with Camille on his back, laughing and cheering as they charged toward camp, dodging rocks and tree stumps like Mr. and Mrs. Outdoor Adventure.

"Just fucking great," Jordan mumbled.

"Can I please get my foot out of this pile of shit! Let's go with elk scat. I don't care!" she said, crossing her arms.

Jordan shook his head. "If you could be a little less beauty queen and a little more girl scout, we could have beat the Plunger Princess and her pest control prince."

She stared at the Emperor of Asshattery, who had garnered another title.

"You know what, Mr. King of Crap? I think I've earned a little luxury. I barely slept last night. I've been busting my ass, trying to keep up with you and scan this godforsaken wilderness for animal droppings. If anyone on this planet could use a fresh tube of vegan cookie dough and a pedicure, it's me!"

"We could put that on a sash! Little Miss *I Could Use a Pedicure*! Wouldn't your mom be proud?" Jordan muttered.

"Get up!" she growled, like a marmot, if they growled.

Dammit, she had no idea what sound a marmot made.

He glanced away from the clipboard. "Why?"

"Because if you don't get out of my way, my crap-covered foot is going to land square in the middle of your smug, scat-obsessed face."

"Don't be such a—" Jordan started, but the demon that lived in every woman pushed past her limit took over.

Her trifecta gasped. They knew that shit, scat, crap, or whatever you want to call it, was about to get real.

Hovering on the brink of losing her scat-despising mind, she leaned over and positioned her lips a breath away from Jordan's ear. "If you say diva or beauty queen one more time, Jordan Marks, Emperor of Asshattery and Reigning Sovereign of Scat, I'm taking the shit shovel, digging a hole, then tossing your perfect ten asshat ass inside."

8

JORDAN

"Remember, folks, no peeking! Do not look at your other half's answers," Buck cautioned as he walked the perimeter of the gathering area, observing the seated couples.

Jordan stared at the questionnaire in front of him, erased his answer, then chanced a look at Georgie. She didn't even glance up as she scribbled on the form as if she'd made it her life's work to mistreat pencils.

To say the last two days had been an unmitigated disaster was unfair to unmitigated disasters. A total and complete catastrophic shit show was more like it.

Yesterday, they'd lost the scat race, coming in dead last.

Instead of spending the night in the honeymoon yurt with real pillows and running water, they'd suffered through another night in tent hell. Well, truth be told, except for a sore back and aching neck, he hadn't suffered as much as Georgie.

After waking this morning, he'd found her already up. Sitting cross-legged on the other side of the tent, he watched as his fiancée finished off the last of the cookie dough, then licked the casing like a vulture intent on devouring the carcass of its dead prey.

And that wasn't the only odd thing about her.

At some point during the night, she'd taken her hair out of its bun. It hung around her shoulders in a wild chestnut mane. He sure as hell wasn't going to mention anything about it because he had no room to criticize her.

Yes, he'd been an asshat.

Yes, he'd fallen back on his worst coping mechanisms and regained his title of Emperor of Asshattery. Georgie's new moniker, the Sovereign of Scat, wasn't far off the mark either.

He'd taken the scat competition too far. He'd gone full-on Marks Perfect Ten Mindset.

But it wasn't like he didn't have a reason.

A switch had flipped inside him when he saw Camille Pruitt and stood there helplessly as she called him Straws. All his defenses had gone up. In the blink of an eye, he was that scrawny kid again, hiding in the school bathroom, waiting for the jerks and jocks to clear out. His childhood companions of shame and humiliation hit him again like a one-two punch.

And the whole embarrassing HIIT training versus scat training debacle didn't help either.

When the Plunger Princess and her rodent royalty fiancé, along with the rest of the boot campers, laughed at him, every insecurity multiplied, every frayed nerve bristled, and each hurt feeling from his past bubbled to the surface. And who was there to bear the brunt of it?

Georgie.

Still, he'd expected her to acclimate better to the task at hand. During the Battle of the Blogs, she'd taken charge.

Even when she'd momentarily lost her mind by entering a wet T-shirt contest, she'd won the damn thing.

Why'd she go all beauty queen diva on him?

What was different now?

He stared down at the questionnaire with the words *Engaged Couples' Compatibility Assessment* splashed across the top and found his answer.

Was he wrong to have proposed so soon?

Georgie was it. She was the one for him. He knew this in his heart and in his soul, but had he jumped the gun?

"Are you almost done?" Georgie asked, observing him with dark circles under her eyes.

He jotted down one last answer. "Yeah, babe, I am."

She tossed her mass of tangled hair behind her shoulder with a deft flick of her hand, took his form, then strode over to deliver the papers to Syd and Buck.

Did she think she was in a pageant? Is this what Georgiana Jensen morphed into on zero sleep?

He looked around at the other couples in their moisture-wicking shirts and khaki all-weather hiking shorts. It was like being trapped in an L.L. Bean nightmare. He and Georgie, thinking they were headed to a fitness bridal boot camp, had opted to pack workout clothing. It wasn't a bad call. He could easily hike and trek around the backcountry in track pants and a hoodie, while Georgie rocked yoga capris and sweatshirts. But they stood out—and not in a good way.

They garnered attention in the same way he had when he stood out as a gangly kid in middle school and high school, and likely, the way Georgie had stood out when she was competing on the beauty pageant circuit.

Freaks.

He hadn't been this person in years, and neither had she.

They were adored on social media. People made damn Pinterest boards devoted to them. The online world watched them fall in love.

What would they think now?

He glanced around the group while Buck and Syd stood in the center of the gathering spot, shuffling the papers and speaking in hushed tones.

Georgie returned and tapped his arm. "It looks like the judges are going to address us," she whispered with her shoulders back and chin raised as if she were preparing for the pageant spotlight.

He tried to muster a placating expression. She did not look like she was firing on all cylinders, and neither was he, but at least he'd gotten some rest over the past couple of nights. He needed to make sure she slept tonight. It wasn't like he was trying to keep her up, but the minute his head hit the poorly padded tent floor, he was out like a light. It wasn't the physical exertion that zapped his energy. He could run a marathon in his sleep. It was his nerves—this hyper-anxious state of trying to be the best that drained him by sundown.

Luckily, they only had one more night of boot camp. Then, they could get back to normal—whatever the hell that was. But it had to be better than this.

They'd cooked their can of beef stew, ate the sodium infused brown lump of food and made it through a morning couples' hike, without another scat hide-and-seek competition, thank God. Then, they'd completed a hands-on activity where Buck and Syd taught them how to craft a bow drill to make a fire in the wilderness.

He'd completed the task on his own. He was pretty sure Georgie had been sleeping with her eyes open in some state of half-awake lucid dreaming while the boot camp leaders led the lesson. And it was pretty cool, in a caveman sort of way, to make fire without matches or flipping the switch on a gas fireplace like they did at home.

He'd followed along with the group, constructing a primitive bow using a piece of wood the length of his arm and securing a cord to each end. Next, they made a fireboard —just a flat piece of wood with a little shallow circular indentation at the end. When it was time to construct the drill piece they'd wrap around the bow's cord to move back and forth in the fireboard's little hole to make the actual fire, Buck had handed each couple a large knife to sharpen the end of the wood.

There was no way he was about to allow pageant zombie Georgie to handle sharp objects, so he'd whittled the end of the six-inch sturdy branch into a point. Buck then gave each pair a flat stone with a shallow circle carved into the top, similar to the fireboard's slight hole. This socket stone, as Syd called it, was used to hold the blunt end of the drill piece in place while the sharp end fit into the fireboard's hole. Set up and ready to go, he'd bowed away like a violinist who'd pounded fifty Red Bulls, creating friction by moving the sharpened tip of the drill rapidly in the fireboard's opening.

It took a hell of a lot of effort, but he'd done it and made fire.

Take that, Boy Scouts!

Georgie leaned in. "I have a feeling this is the question and answer portion of the competition."

He nodded. She was probably right. They had just filled out a pretty bizarre questionnaire, and they hadn't done any touchy-feely couples' activities yet. Maybe this was the *Dr. Phil connect with your partner* portion of the bridal boot camp.

A wave of confidence washed over him—a welcome feeling. They could do touchy-feely.

He and Georgie were open books—or open blogs. They laid it all out on the line every day. They could do a couples' compatibility exercise in their sleep. And with Georgie's state of mind, that was a good thing.

"All right, couples," Syd said, addressing the group. "Let's have the gentlemen sit on one side of the circle and the ladies on the other."

Jordan watched as the men migrated to the other side.

"Are you going to be okay here on your own?" he asked, getting up.

Georgie glanced around with a high-wattage smile. "Of course! I'll be with the other contestants."

"Georgie? Babe? Do you know where we are?" he asked, two-seconds away from snapping his fingers in front of her face to get her to come back from whatever alternate universe her insomnia-riddled mind had entered.

She shook her head, then let out a weary sigh, looking a little more like herself. "Yes, I know where we are. I meant to say boot camp participants," she corrected, her tone more annoyed than spaced out, which under the circumstances, he'd take.

He glanced over as Brice Casey kissed Camille Pruitt on the cheek.

"I'm going to miss my plunger princess," the man cooed.

"Not as much as I'm going to miss my Pooh Bear, Bricey," Camille gushed.

Jordan couldn't look away. How could these idiots be so happy?

He stroked Georgie's cheek. "See you in a bit, babe," he tried.

She frowned. "You're going to be sitting across from me, Jordan. You'll see me the entire time."

And bam! She'd returned from beauty pageant purgatory and was back to being pissed off at him, which he deserved.

He headed toward the other side when Mr. Rodent Royalty himself, waved him over.

"Dude, there's a spot here," Brice said, scooting over on the log bench.

For fuck's sake! Was he going to have to sit next to Brice Casey? The douche who couldn't even remember Georgie's name and had brought Camille Pruitt and all her Straws baggage to his bridal boot camp?

So far, they'd been able to steer clear of the couple.

But not today.

He glanced around and found no other place to sit, then planted himself on the end of the bench next to the smiling prince of pest control.

Holy hell! Thanks a lot, wilderness gods!

He looked across the circle to see Camille Pruitt perched next to Georgie.

With the love of his life glaring at him and seated next to a woman who'd teased him about his skinny frame a decade ago, he blinked, taking it all in.

Was this hell?

"Isn't this something?" Brice offered, then blew Camille a kiss—an actual air-kiss like children did from the school bus as they said goodbye to their parents or like some duck-lipped millennial social influencer.

"It is certainly *something*," he replied.

Buck stood in the center of the circle as Syd handed a dry erase board and a marker to each of the men.

"Wilderness couples, get ready for some fun. We're going to play How Well Do You Know Your Better Half."

"Another contest? Awesome!" Brice announced with a fist pump in the air.

"We'll be going off the questionnaires you filled out," Syd continued.

"The couple with the most correct answers will win a night in the honeymoon yurt, and the couple with the least correct answers will spend the night out in the wilderness," Buck finished.

Jordan frowned. "I thought we were already in the wilderness."

Buck's expression hardened. "The real wilderness, away from camp."

There was a *real* wilderness? This wasn't wilderness enough?

"First question, gentlemen. Name your special someone's favorite book," Syd began.

A spark of excitement ignited inside him. Now, he wanted to fist pump into the sky like a damn douche canoe. Instead, he wrote out the title of the book placed prominently on Georgie's bookshelf at home.

Buck went down the line of men, asking for their response. One by one, the guys held up their dry erase boards with their answer. About half got it right, while the others got it wrong. His knee bounced as anticipation built, waiting for Buck to call on him.

He caught Georgie's eye, and she smiled at him. Not a deranged pageant smile, but a genuine Georgie smile.

She could feel it, too.

Victory was within reach.

And even better than victory—that honeymoon yurt

was going to be all theirs tonight, and boy, did he have a plan.

First, he'd give Georgie a solid six hours of sleep. But after that, it was going to be yurt sex city.

"Brice, hold up your board," Buck directed.

The pest control VP grimaced and lifted his dry erase board with the words *Little House on the Prairie* written in all caps.

Jordan's gaze darted to Camille, who gave a little pout.

"Why would you think that, Pooh Bear?" Camille asked with a scowl.

"It's the last book I saw you reading," he answered, shifting nervously on the bench.

Camille scoffed. "That was when we were ten years old."

Brice took off his Casey Pest Control trucker cap and scratched his head. "Have you read a book since then?"

Camille sprang to her feet. "Brice! I read my horoscope every day! Every day!"

Brice looked from Camille to Buck and then back to Camille. Was Mr. Rodent Royalty going to have to tell his plunger princess that reading her horoscope didn't count as reading an actual book?

Jordan bit back a grin. He loved watching Bricey Pooh squirm under the Princess of Plumbing's angry gaze. Now, was it the height of asshattery to laugh at another guy when his girl was shoveling shit right in his face in public?

Yes, it was.

If he were writing a blog post about interacting with people who didn't share your thoughts or values, he'd most certainly advocate for taking the high road and being the bigger person. That's what they'd do in their More Than Just a Number blog.

But today, today, he was taking the low road and not looking back.

He met Georgie's gaze, and she winked at him. Winked!

For a second time, the urge to fist pump into the air surged through him.

He was so getting yurt sex tonight—which would not be considered real sex and breaking the wedding frau's rule. They could file this act of debauchery under the mental health emergency tab.

Yes, sir!

Mental health was no joke and maintaining it through whatever means necessary, otherwise known as doing the naughty until they forgot what deer jerky tasted like, was just what the doctor ordered.

"Brice and Camille, you do not get a point," Buck said, then made a slash on his clipboard as Camille crossed her arms, and Brice hung his head.

"No biggie, man. You'll get the next one," Jordan said under his breath to the crestfallen Brice.

What did he really want to say to the ruler of rodent retirement?

Brice Casey, you are a loser, loser, loser, loser! Today, the Rodent Royalty regimen lives in shame. Take your plunger princess and forget about yurt sex.

Brice gave him a defeated nod. "Thanks, dude."

"Jordan, hold up your board," Buck said, moving on.

Jordan tried to maintain a neutral expression but could not help the corners of his mouth from curling into a cocky grin. He probably looked like Cruella de Vil, but he didn't care.

"I wrote *Pride and Prejudice*," he proclaimed as if he were the conquering force, preparing to take no prisoners.

Georgie let out an excited yip from across the gathering area.

"That is correct," Buck replied, making a tick on the paper.

Okay, a slash was bad, and a tick was good.

He caught his fiancée's eye, and she mouthed good job. He gave her a thumbs-up, and baby, they were back!

"Next question, gentleman. What is your special someone's favorite food?"

With his cocky grin still in place, Jordan picked up the dry erase marker and scribbled out five words.

Again, Buck started at the other end, ticking and slashing as the men answered the question.

"Brice, you're up," Buck said, working his way down the line.

Bricey Pooh mopped his brow with the hem of his shirt. "Cheetos," he answered with a wince.

"That is not correct," Buck replied with a sharp slash.

"Brice Hannibal Casey! Why on earth would you think Cheetos were my favorite food?" Camille called for all of Colorado to hear.

Jordan pressed his lips together in a hard line, doing his best not to laugh his ass off at the mention of Brice's middle name. What kind of parent named their kid Hannibal?

Georgie bit her lip, clearly trying to do the same thing.

Brice raised his hands defensively. "I wasn't sure if you wrote down the fancy food you order when we're out in public or all the stuff you eat when we get home."

Camille gasped. "My favorite food is organic Pad Thai with extra carrots and tofu. I have no idea why my fiancé would ever think it was Cheetos," she said, addressing the group.

"You did wolf down a bag in the car before we got here,

Cammie. That's why I went with Cheetos," Brice offered apologetically.

Damn! The guy was striking out hardcore.

Camille's eyes went wide.

"I mean...you only downed half a bag," Brice amended, but to no avail.

Camille looked ready to knock her bean spilling, or in this case, Cheeto spilling fiancé into next week.

"Let's move on," Syd offered, patting Camille's shoulder and helping her back to her seat.

Buck tapped the clipboard. "Jordan, what's Georgie's favorite food?"

Hello, sweet success!

"Vegan chocolate chip cookie dough," he replied, showing off the dry erase board. He even drew a tube of it below the words to highlight his artistic flair.

Georgie patted her heart, and his heart went flippity-flippity-flop. Sweet Jesus, it was good to have his Georgie back!

"That's right," Buck replied with a delicate tick to the score sheet.

That's damn right!

Nothing tasted as good as victory—not even raw vegan cookie dough.

"Since I'm down here, let's start with you for the next round, Jordan," Buck said, glancing at the clipboard.

"Hit me with your best shot, Buck," he answered, inhaling a lungful of fresh wilderness air.

Damn, maybe he was a wilderness aficionado after all!

"What's Georgie's favorite color?"

Georgie's favorite color?

His cocksure expression faded.

Shit!

He had no idea.

Think!

She loved books, but books came in every color of the rainbow. What else did she love?

He snapped his fingers. "Two colors. Black and white because those are the colors of our dog's fur," he answered like the damn king of the mountain.

Buck slashed the paper. "No, that's incorrect."

He gasped. "What?"

"It's rose," Georgie called from across the gathering area.

His mouth fell open. "Rose? How could it be rose? Isn't rose the same as pink? I thought you hated pink because your mom was all about that color," he asked, needing some damn clarification.

Georgie's cheeks flushed pink...rose. Whatever color it was, it wasn't good for him.

"Rose is not pink," she shot back.

He turned to Brice Casey. "Rose is pink, right?"

Brice glanced across the space at a sullen Camille. "Dude, my advice is to agree with Virginia."

Jordan frowned. "Who?"

"Your fiancée, Virginia, she's right over there," Brice said, pointing toward Georgie.

This idiot!

And wait a second. Wasn't he the idiot for asking for the rodent reaper's advice?

"I'd like to respectfully disagree," Jordan said, turning to Buck.

The wilderness boot camp leader cocked his head to the side. "You want to respectfully disagree with your fiancée's favorite color?"

Jordan came to his feet and ran his hands through his hair. "I didn't realize we were doing fancy colors."

"Rose is not a fancy color," Georgie replied, rising up from the log bench.

"It's pink, Georgie! Rose is pink, and you hate pink!" he replied as Brice sucked in a tight breath and shook his head.

"Dude, just agree," Mr. Rodent Royalty whisper-shouted.

Jordan glanced down at Brice Hannibal Casey. There was no way he was taking advice from this guy.

He shook his head. "I can't lose a point for this. I didn't even know rose was a color," he said as Brice grimaced.

"Rose is the shade of color halfway between red and magenta," Georgie called, looking to the women, who were all nodding.

He paced the length of the circle. "Okay, I get it, babe. But rose is a fancy color. I thought we were choosing from the Crayola box of eight crayons."

Buck shook his head. "Sorry, Jordan, but when I asked you what Georgie's favorite color was, at no time, did I say it was limited to the Crayola eight," Buck added, totally not helping a fellow man out.

Dammit! This is what he got for savoring Brice and Camille's dust-up, and that was nothing compared to the show he and Georgie were putting on for the group.

"Ask me the next question," he said, reclaiming his spot next to Brice.

Buck and Syd shared a glance.

"All right," the man began with a twist to his lips. "If Georgie were given the choice of a peanut butter and jelly sandwich or a peanut butter and honey sandwich, which one would she choose?"

He stared up at the man. Was this for real? His form didn't have any of these bizarre questions.

"Well?" Buck pressed.

"Um...jelly," he blurted, then watched Georgie's cheeks go from pink or rose to scarlet.

Georgie's hand flew to her chest. "It's honey, Jordan. Of course, it's honey! We wrote a whole blog post about the medicinal qualities of honey. Why would you think I'd choose jelly? What are you thinking?"

Jesus, what was he thinking?

He did a quick scan of the group to find all eyes on him.

"I didn't think. I said the first thing that came to mind. I had a fifty-fifty chance, and jelly is good, too, minus all the sugar and preservatives."

"Then why would you think I would have chosen it?" she shot back.

He couldn't think straight. Between the couples staring and Georgie glaring, his brain had turned to...well, jelly.

"One more question, Buck! I'm sure I'll get this one right," he said as a bead of sweat trickled down his back.

Buck and Syd shared another look.

"Are you sure?" Buck asked with an uncharacteristically wary bend to his words.

Jordan took a few breaths. "Do it."

Buck sighed. "What's Georgie's favorite way to unwind?"

"That's an easy one," he exclaimed, waving his hand in the air. "Sex!"

Buck slashed the page. "Nope."

Jordan gazed wildly around the group. "No! How could it be no? Georgie and I did it in the car before we got here. It's her go-to stress reliever."

The color drained from his fiancée's face. "My go-to stress reliever is to take a meandering walk!"

No, he couldn't let this go! They had to win that damn honeymoon yurt.

"I call bullshit, Georgie," he said as the entire female contingent gasped and stared him down.

No one spoke for what seemed like an eternity. Every pair of eyes bore into him from all angles. And Georgie? She'd been rendered speechless and stood on the other side of the gathering area with her lips parted.

Buck cleared his throat, then checked his watch. "It looks like we're going to have to bring this bonding experience to a close. It's time to send the losing couple out into the wilderness."

"And which couple would that be?" Jordan asked, but he knew the answer.

Buck glanced at that godforsaken clipboard. "Why, that would be you and Georgie."

9

"I'm sorry! I don't know what the hell I was thinking," Jordan said for what seemed like the millionth time.

Georgie shook her head and glanced down at the map.

Of all the scenic wilderness on the planet, this swath of Colorado backcountry was the last place she wanted to set foot. She trudged forward, passing Weariness Way and headed straight for Exhaustion Junction.

God, help them! What a day it had been, and it wasn't even close to being over.

And next to having little to no rest for the past couple of days, she and Jordan had lost...again.

Jordan had another Marks Perfect Ten meltdown, and now twenty people thought she was a sex maniac.

How could things have unraveled so quickly?

And they weren't the only ones on the brink of losing it.

With disheveled hair and dark circles under their eyes, her literary trifecta slumped in a heap on the imaginary floor with no words of wisdom or pithy retorts at the ready.

Life with a shit shovel did not agree with them either.

Georgie rubbed her eyes. "We have to keep going. The

map says there will be a red flag. That's where we'll find the tarp and the supplies for setting up camp tonight."

"Georgie, yell at me! Call me the Secretary of Scat. Chuck the poop shovel at my head. Say something besides only giving me direction updates," Jordan pleaded as she continued walking.

Muted by the thick blanket of clouds rolling in, the sun hung low in the sky, a hazy glowing circle. She used to love this part of the day. At about this time back in their real life, Jordan would be finishing up training his high school students, and she'd be tidying up the children's area after the shop's last story time. The butterflies in her belly would ready themselves, waiting for the bookstore's door to open. She always knew when it was Jordan, and it wasn't because of Mr. Tuesday's excited yips or hearing one of her employees greet him.

She knew he was on his way over to see her even before he'd left his gym. She could feel him thinking about her. She could see the sweet hint of a smile on his lips the second before he opened the door and entered the bookshop. They'd had it all.

Perfectly in sync.

Magically in love.

And now, hopelessly lost—literally and figuratively.

Syd and Buck had given them a map to the private wilderness camping location, otherwise known as the loser lot, where they'd been relegated to make camp and spend the final night. She'd taken the map, grabbed her pack, and set off with Jordan a few steps behind her.

He'd been back there the whole time. It was not an easy feat for this man to walk at a tortoise's pace, but that's where he stayed, streaming apologies for the better half of the last ninety minutes.

He felt terrible. She knew this.

She shouldn't have gotten so angry with him during the couples' quiz. The man was used to ingesting green smoothies and fair-trade coffee. And to make matters worse, in a delirious fit during a sleepless night, she'd dug a hole and buried the can of pineapple, depriving him of even the most awful of canned fruits.

Would a hit of vitamin C have helped her fiancé *de-asshat* himself?

Thanks to her midnight trowel skills, she'd never know.

After days spent eating deer jerky and beef stew, anyone's mind would be addled. He was out of his element as much as she was, but it wasn't the bickering or the fights over jelly and cookie dough that had her worried. No, something darker scratched in the corners of her mind—a little voice planting seeds of doubt.

If you two can't survive a few days without Wi-Fi, are you ready to pledge eternity to one another?

She stopped walking. "We need to do something, Jordan," she said, still staring at the map despite not knowing where the hell they were on it.

"Are you talking to me? Like, really talking and not acting like a sleep-deprived navigation app?" he asked with the sweetest, hopeful lilt to his voice it nearly broke her heart.

She stuffed the map into her pack, then set it on the ground. "You need to kiss me," she said as matter-of-factly as possible.

He observed her with a skeptical eye. "Is this a trick?"

After the last couple of days, she couldn't fault him for asking.

"No, just kiss me," she replied, tucking a strand of hair behind her ear and doing her best to look kissable after going days without a shower, which was not an easy thing to do. Luckily, her pageant training kicked in, and, at least, she had decent posture.

"On the mouth?" he asked with a dubious look.

"No, in my ear!" she shot back.

His eyes went wide.

"Of course, my mouth!" she clarified.

"I do want to kiss you, Georgie," he said, his expression softening.

She swallowed past the emotion in her throat. "You do?"

He took a tentative step toward her. "I'm sorry, Georgie."

She stroked the scruff on his cheek. "I know you are. I'm sorry, too."

"I don't know why I said those things and got so worked up back at camp," he confessed.

She cocked her head to the side. "I haven't exactly been at my best either."

A playful glint gleamed in his eyes. "Don't worry. I still love you, Virginia," he teased.

She chuckled, thinking back on Camille and Brice. "I can't believe his middle name is Hannibal."

"Right? What kind of parent would do that?" he mused.

She shrugged. "I hardly know anything about babies, but I know enough not to name one Hannibal."

"Can I tell you something awful?" he asked with a wicked quirk to his lips.

"Always," she answered.

"I thought it was hilarious Brice outed Camille for downing a bag of Cheetos."

"Hey, I ate a tube of vegan chocolate chip cookie dough," she countered.

"And that is what sets you apart from the Plunger Princess. You, Georgiana Jensen, and your binge food choice of overpriced organic cookie dough shows you've got class."

She shook out her wild locks of hair. "Classy like this?" she asked, striking a pose that would surely elicit Kardashian approval.

"Classy like you traded out your double Ds for quadruple Ds," Jordan replied, mimicking Brice's surfer-dude-crossed-with-a-pretty-boy voice while gesturing to her chest.

"If they can handle this, we can handle this, right?" she asked, dropping the shenanigans.

He cupped her face in his hands. "I know we can," he whispered against her lips before capturing her mouth in a sensual kiss.

This is what she needed. This man. Her More-Than-Just-a-Number, Jordan. She wrapped her arms around his neck, and he slid his hands from her face, down her back and pulled her body flush with his.

"Georgiana, I've missed this so much," he breathed between kisses.

But she wanted more.

Like a Ferrari, her libido engine roared to life, going from zero to sixty in the space of a breath. She swayed her hips from side to side and brushed against his hard length.

"You are a naughty wilderness girl," Jordan said, his voice growing gravelly, just the way she liked it.

"What's more *wilderness* than doing it outdoors?" she purred as he kissed the corner of her mouth.

Jordan gripped her ass, and delicious tingles engulfed her body.

"What kind of *not-sex* sex could we call it?" he asked, working his way over to her earlobe.

"Communing with nature *not-sex*. It's natural. Birds do it. Bees do it," she said in a breathy singsong voice.

"Even deer jerky-eating fleas do it," he replied, changing the words and making her giggle.

But before she could compliment him on his wit, his other hand worked its way down her back to rest on her butt, then stilled.

With both hands, he investigated her ass and gave her a mischievous pat down. "You're not wearing underwear," he remarked.

No, sir! She wasn't.

A coy grin bloomed on her lips. "I'm fresh out of clean panties. I hope this isn't a problem?"

"Commando in the wild?" he commented with a kiss to her neck.

"Pretty hot, huh?" she replied.

As if she were a green smoothie, he raked his gaze down her body and devoured her with his eyes.

"You have no idea."

She took a step away, coming out of his embrace. He watched her curiously as she turned her back to him. With the skill of a pageant veteran, she sauntered over to a large rock and bent over, presenting her booty like a work of art.

She glanced over her shoulder. "Ready to commune with nature?"

"I love communing with nature," he answered, sprinting over to her.

He gathered her unruly mass of hair, detangled it from the tracking device's cord around her neck, brushed it over her shoulder, then pressed a kiss to the exposed skin. But he didn't linger there for long. Jordan worked his way down to her waist, then peeled her yoga pants down to her ankles. The twilight air sent goose bumps down her body, but she didn't mind. She'd been in a sleep-deprived wilderness-hating haze, and the cool breeze combined with the heat of Jordan's body proved to be the perfect stimulant.

"I'm going to take you from behind like a National Geographic animal documentary," Jordan growled into her ear.

Under normal circumstances, that comment would have made her laugh her ass off. But, after all they'd been through, she could totally get into this animal sex thing.

Jordan shrugged down his track pants and boxers, then pulled her close and pressed his rock-hard cock against her ass.

"I'm going to fuck you like an animal, Georgiana," he said with another kiss to her neck.

A lightning bolt of lust shot through her body—or it could have been a real flash of lightning. At this point, her animal sex brain had taken over, and all she wanted was dirty girl take-me-from-behind *not-fornication* fornication.

She gasped. "We are hitting every naughty wilderness sex song."

Jordan pressed his fingertips into the flesh of her hip while the tip of his cock teased her entrance.

Georgie closed her eyes as desire flowed through her.

"Touch me," she moaned, and her fiancé knew what to do.

His large, skillful hand cupped her sex. With a deft caress, he teased her most sensitive place, working her in a rhythmic motion when something cold and wet pitter-pattered against her half-naked body.

"What's that?" she gasped.

"A little rain. I'm sure it will pass," he bit out as he slid inside her.

Sex outdoors in the rain for anyone to see? A wild sense

of excitement popped and crackled through her body—or maybe it was more lightning.

But what did it matter?

They were fearless adventurers, led by their primal desire for carnal release.

It didn't get more National Geographic *graphic* than that.

"I hope it doesn't bother you I haven't shaved in three days," she moaned as he rocked his hips, filling her completely with long, luscious strokes of his hard length.

He wrapped her hair in his hand and gave a pull, sending another burst of fireworks through her body.

"I haven't shaved either, babe," he answered in a low rasp.

She reached back and ran her fingers down the scruff of his jawline. "True, but you get sexy while I get hairy like an—"

Jordan froze mid-thrust. "An alpaca," he said, his voice losing its sexy growl.

She glanced back at her slack-jawed fiancé. "A what?"

"An alpaca, Georgie," he repeated.

"Yeah, alpacas are hairy. I was going to say ape. But sure, we could go with alpaca."

"Georgie, there's an alpaca right there," he said, still motionless.

A rumble of thunder cut through the gentle rain, ushering in a downpour, as she looked up to see the animal.

Jordan stepped back and pulled up his pants. "It's looking at us. It's watching us."

Georgie blinked away the rain and pulled up her yoga capris. Yes, the alpaca probably didn't care that they were bumping the wilderness uglies, but something seemed way off about being half-dressed in front of the inquisitive animal.

"Syd and Buck said they allowed their alpacas to roam around their land. This is probably one of them," she offered.

Panic marred Jordan's perfect stubbled face. "Georgie, I hate to tell you this but—"

She pressed her hand to his lips, silencing him. "Are you about to tell me you're afraid of alpacas?"

With her hand covering his mouth, he nodded.

As if the animal could sense Jordan's apprehension, the creature emitted a high-pitched squeal.

Georgie screamed, jumping back and dropping her hand from her fiancé's mouth.

"Oh my, God! Is that what they sound like?" she exclaimed, starting to get a little freaked out herself.

"Only when they're mad," Jordan answered as if he were narrating a Stephen King horror novel.

Her gaze bounced between the incensed animal and her panicked fiancé. "How do you know all this?"

"Do you remember where my goat phobia came from?" he asked.

She nodded, cupping her hand over her face to shield her eyes from the downpour. "Yes, you were at a petting zoo when you were little, and an asshole baby goat tried to eat your shirt. We cured you of that fear during the Battle of the Blogs back in June."

"There's something I didn't tell you about the petting zoo, Georgie," he began, staring at the massive creature.

She blew out a tight breath. "Is it that there was an alpaca there, and it tried to eat your shirt, too?" she replied, filling in the blank.

How many animals frightened her big, strong man?

"No, it didn't try to eat my shirt," he answered, fear lacing each word.

"Okay, then what?" she asked as the alpaca moved toward them, releasing another round of squealing pig meets screaming toddler shrieks.

"We need to run!" he cried, taking her hand and pulling her away from the agitated animal.

A bolt of lightning sliced through the sky as they dodged aspens with the alpaca in hot pursuit.

"Jordan, I'd bet all the vegan chocolate chip cookie dough in North America it's only chasing us because we're running. I don't think alpacas are naturally aggressive," she said, gasping to keep up.

"They can be aggressive," he replied, pulling her along as he picked up speed.

Trying to keep up with Mr. CrossFit Super Runner, she searched her memory for any relevant alpaca knowledge. Were alpacas and llamas the same thing? Were llamas nice? Did it matter?

She released Jordan's hand. "This is crazy! Stop running! I'm pretty sure alpacas are docile. I think I read something about them guarding chickens and sheep, and all Mrs. Gilbert's friends knit with their wool."

With rain trailing down his face, he shook his head. "We have to keep going! These are not ordinary animals! They've got giraffe necks, horse bodies with weird little puffy tails, and deceptively cute faces that look all sweet and innocent until..."

She wiped the rain from her cheeks. "Until what? You sound like you've lost your mind!"

Jordan stared over her shoulder. "Oh, shit!" he whispered.

She turned to see the alpaca with its head reared back. But, pissed off alpaca or not, she had no choice but to defuse the situation and save the man she loved from yet another animal phobia.

More than that—these animal antics had to end.

When they got home, she was going to make him write down the name of every creature he feared, big or small.

She reached toward the animal. "Hey, little guy! What are you doing out in the rain?"

She had to show Jordan this was just another one of his irrational animal fears.

"Georgie, don't get any closer!" he cautioned.

"Mr. Alpaca is a sweetie," she continued, not knowing if it was a boy or girl alpaca. But she was getting a strong guy vibe.

Jordan waved his hands. "He's not sweet, babe. He's about to..."

Before Jordan could finish, the little sweetie of an alpaca flung its wet head forward and opened its elongated, toothy mouth, as green phlegm spewed like the exorcist out of the animal. She turned her head away from the spray, stumbling back a few steps as the alpaca's putrid spittle storm hit the side of her face.

"What the hell happened?" she screamed.

"They spit," Jordan whisper-shouted.

Well, duh!

She touched her hair to find it sticky with alpaca saliva. "Why didn't you tell me they spit?"

"I didn't get a chance, and I figured you knew?" he answered.

"I don't know anything about these animals. I'm not even sure if there's a difference between a llama and an alpaca! How would I know they spit?" she yelled, growing more exasperated by the second.

He watched the alpaca warily. "Llamas spit, too. That's what happened to me as a kid."

"A llama spit at you?" she questioned, mentally adding llamas to the list of Jordan's fears.

He cocked his head to the side as confusion marred his expression. "No, an alpaca spit at me. Why would you think it was a llama?"

This was insanity!

She backed away from the alpaca, who, after emptying the grossest contents of its stomach on her face, meandered away, seeming to have lost interest in her after sliming her with God knows what. Alpaca bile? Alpaca puke? Whatever the hell it was, it was absolutely disgusting.

"What are we doing?" she screamed up at the sky, stumbling forward.

"Georgie, let me try to wipe some of it off," Jordan offered.

She stared at him, then took a step forward, but her other foot didn't make it to the ground. Thanks to an exposed tree root, she was now lying on the forest floor, staring up at the pouring rain in a slick of mud.

Jordan bent over her. "Are you okay, babe?"

She blinked back the rain or tears or rainwater infused with her tears and animal bile. At this point, she couldn't even guess how many substances were covering her body.

She extended her arms and legs like a kid making a muddy, deranged snow angel. "Do I look okay, Jordan? Do I look even remotely close to being considered okay?"

"I feel like this is another trick question," he said gently.

She'd had it. This was it. She was done with this bullshit boot camp. Done with deer jerky. Done with Brice and Camille and Syd and Buck and shovels—so freaking done with shovels.

"I have fallen, and I can't get up!" she screamed, which triggered the alpaca to scream, which then triggered her fiancé to cry out.

In the history of wilderness survival, never had there been a more pathetic display of outdoor survival skills.

Jordan collected himself, then offered her his hand. "I can help you up, Georgie. Come on. Let's get to camp and make a fire. You'll feel better after you warm up."

Prostrate on the ground, she blinked back the rain.

"How are we going to make a fire? It's raining cats and dogs, or llamas and alpacas," she answered in a shrill scrape of a voice.

He watched her as one would observe a ticking time bomb. "We'll get the tarp set up. Then we'll use the bow drill and the dryer lint."

"Where the hell are you going to get dryer lint?" she shot back.

Where'd he think they were? The appliance department of Home Depot?

"It was on the list. You were supposed to pack it," he answered in a crisis negotiator tone.

The man wasn't wrong, but she'd thought it was a typo.

"I didn't pack any lint from the dryer," she replied as Jordan's features hardened.

"Then, what did you pack?"

She stared up at him. "Lemon verbena-scented dryer sheets."

"Dryer sheets?" he echoed with a scrunched brow.

She nodded. "Yes, I told you. I brought lemon verbena-scented dryer sheets."

He shook his head. "What's verbena?"

"I don't know, but they're good for the earth, and they

smell all lemony sweet," she answered, getting a little tired of his know-it-all vibe.

"We use earth-friendly dryer sheets?" he questioned.

If she weren't afraid of choking on rain infused with alpaca bile, she would have scoffed.

"Of course, we do! Do you think I'd purchase earth-unfriendly dryer sheets?"

"I'd never given it much thought," he answered.

How sexist! Just because he was a man, it didn't give him a license not to care about non-toxic laundry products.

Her trifecta perked up and nodded their support.

"Like it or not, this is what we've got. Two lemon verbena-scented dryer sheets," she answered.

Jordan stared up at the angry sky. "Dammit, Georgie! That's not going to work! Since we won't be able to collect any dry tinder, we'll need to use the dryer lint to get a flame going. Don't you remember Buck and Syd's bow drill lesson from today?"

She didn't remember much of anything. The last three days had been more of a beauty queen meets Blair Witch montage.

"I remember watching you make the bow drill thingy for starting a fire, but I never thought we'd have to use it. I figured it was more of a souvenir," she said, sitting up.

Jordan ran his hands through his sopping mass of hair. "A souvenir? Do you know how hard it was, whittling wood and scraping shallow holes into pine? And then, there's the bowing. I'm in better shape than a gladiator, and it was still a hell of a lot of work to get it to start smoking."

Moment of truth—she'd spaced out big time during the whole arts and crafts segment of the day.

"I'm sorry, Jordan. I didn't know!" she said, throwing up her hands.

He paced back and forth. "You could have at least told me we were out here unprepared."

This asshat!

She reared back. "Unprepared? I'm not the one losing my shit at the sight of an alpaca."

"At least, I have the sense not to pet one," he muttered.

Holy alpaca farm! The Secretary of Scat was on thin ice.

"I was trying to help you see it was a harmless creature," she answered, trying to keep her voice even.

"But it wasn't harmless, was it?" he answered, going all Mr. Gotcha.

She started to stand, and Jordan extended his hand to help her, but she swatted it away.

"I don't need your help," she said through chattering teeth.

"You look like you need something," he shot back.

With perfect posture and her chin held high, she pinned him with her rain-soaked gaze. "Oh, I need something, all right! I need a bed. I need a shower. I need at least two tubes of vegan cookie dough. I need the Belgian Waffle Princess to make me a boatload of carb-infused deliciousness. And more than that, I need a fiancé who isn't afraid of alpacas!"

Jordan looked away and shook his head as she took a step toward him.

"What else are you afraid of, Mr. Big Strong Man? Turtles? Do their creepy shells freak you out? Elephants with those big floppy ears? Or, what about bunnies and their hippity-hippity-hop way of getting around?" she rattled off.

"I am not afraid of turtles or elephants," he mumbled.

"So, add bunnies to the list?" she replied with sarcasm coating her words.

He met her gaze. "I'm not afraid of bunnies either. But I've got something to say about that."

"By all means, don't keep me in suspense," she threw back.

He held her gaze. "Hippity, hippity, hop, hooray! I'm not sure if you've noticed, but it looks like we're spending the night soaked and freezing."

She glared at his symmetrically perfect face and reached inside her sweatshirt and pulled out the tracking device, hanging from the lanyard, then gripped the panic button.

"I'm done with this wilderness bridal boot camp bull-shit! I'm done with it all!"

Jordan raised his hands defensively. "Don't push it, Georgie. It's one night. We can do this. We can tough it out."

"Tough it out? What do you think I've been doing while you've been snoring like a sleeping bear every night?"

"Eating cookie dough," he replied accusatorially.

"That was one night!" she exclaimed.

"You could have left a little bit for me?" he countered.

She wiped the rain from her cheeks. "Is this what's happening? Are we going to pretend this is about cookie dough or shit shovels or llamas?"

"It was an alpaca," he corrected.

"It doesn't matter! Look at us, Jordan! The only time we're not trying to rip each other's heads off is when we're screwing! Maybe I am a sex maniac?"

He stared up at the pouring rain. "What are you saying?"

She steadied herself. "I'm saying that this is over."

She pressed the button and watched as the indicator light changed from a solid green to a blinking red.

"What happens now?" he asked as rivulets of water trailed down his face as a clapping sound came from behind a wall of rock.

"Now, you leave without your wilderness bridal boot camp completion certificate," Buck said with a final clap.

She and Jordan whipped around to see the wilderness expert and his wife coming around the rocks.

"How did you get here so fast?" she asked.

"Where do you think you are?" Syd asked, sharing a look with Buck.

"Way the hell away from camp, near the red flag," Jordan answered, but he didn't sound so sure.

Buck chuckled. "You're no more than a two-minute walk from camp. It's up this trail, past the rocks. Don't you recognize where you are?" Buck pointed to the alpaca. "Didn't Frankie give it away that you'd circled back?"

Georgie glanced at her fiancé, whose posture had gone rigid.

"Are you sure you want to give up?" Syd asked.

Georgie took another look at the sullen man she thought she knew.

"We're done."

10

"I can't believe you won't walk the five feet it takes to get to Jordan's gym from the bookshop. This is getting insane, Georgie. Your wedding is in two days! Two days! You guys need to talk," Becca whisper-shouted across the shop.

Georgie slid a copy of *Pride and Prejudice* onto the bookshelf and sighed.

The wedding may be in two days, but the last two weeks had flown by in a hazy blur.

Three hundred and thirty-six hours—not that she was counting—had passed since she and Jordan turned in their shit shovel and their engagement had turned into a full-blown shit show.

And just to be clear, it wasn't that the weather was hazy. Nope, the wedding frau was right. The last two weeks had been unseasonably warm and sunny with high temperatures near eighty degrees every day since she and Jordan had flunked out of wilderness bridal boot camp.

They'd driven back to their Denver bungalow in silence, and then Jordan had packed a bag, collected the contents of their dryer's lint trap, and left.

She couldn't blame him. She was the one who said they were done.

But what was she talking about? The boot camp from hell or their engagement?

And why didn't she know the answer?

In this alternate universe, time passed in a nebulous tumble of routine.

Yes, she went through all the motions. She'd open the shop. She'd close the shop. However, out of spite or out of morbid curiosity, she'd spent a ludicrous amount of time over the last fourteen days researching lemon verbena.

For the past two weeks, she'd written a myriad of blog posts on the perennial shrub. Lemon verbena required full sun to flourish. Perfect for attracting butterflies and hummingbirds, the drought-resistant plant could also be used as an essential oil or its leaves employed in making herbal teas.

She'd interviewed gardeners and spent hours online gazing at the herb's delicate white flowers hidden in a sea of deep green leaves.

Some sources claimed it was associated with supernatural forces and could protect against dark spells.

Unfortunately, her lemon verbena dryer sheet wasn't able to protect her and Jordan from whatever dark place they'd entered.

They communicated through the blog by going tit-for-tat with their posts.

She'd blog about the lemon verbena. Then, he'd hit back with a post touting the importance of pushing past one's mental blocks. She'd write about treatments to stop snoring, and he'd come back with the pitfalls of binging on raw cookie dough.

One thing was for sure. Under extreme stress, they'd reverted to the worst version of themselves.

The fragile beauty queen turned into an inflexible eight, and the former weakling turned into a hyper-masculine, single-minded ten.

"Seriously, Georgie! You've got to snap out of it. Has anyone else figured out Jordan left the bungalow?"

Or that she possibly kicked him out?

It was a legit question. Thankfully, only the perceptive Becca seemed to pick up on the disconnect between the bookshop owner and the fitness trainer next door. Not even Cornelia Lieblingsschatz or any of her wedding minions seemed to know.

"It's coming down to the wire, Georgie. Is the wedding still on?"

Georgie blinked and met her friend's gaze. "I think so."

Becca's jaw nearly hit the floor. "You think so? Your mother has invited all of Denver to this shindig, and that scary wedding lady is sending out emails left and right on wedding party etiquette and panty lines. Panty lines, Georgie! She made me send her a picture of my ass in the bridesmaid dress with the underwear I planned on wearing that day so her people could inspect it for *visibility issues*. First of all, who has people for that? And second, that's nuts! I get that she's a wedding genius, but sheesh, panty lines procedures?"

Georgie swallowed past the lump in her throat. She hadn't called off the wedding, and, as far as she knew, Jordan hadn't either.

But was it on?

She steadied herself and attempted to make sense of the situation. "Think of it this way, Bec. From what I've heard, the champagne engagement breakfast was a real hit, and

Jordan and I were only there for ten minutes. I'm sure, between my mother and the wedding frau, the actual wedding will go off without a hitch."

Becca left the counter and joined her next to the Jane Austen section.

"Have you hit your head?" Becca asked.

"No."

"Did somebody give you a pot brownie, or did you eat some magic gummy bears?" Becca pressed.

Georgie shook her head. "Nope, I've been sticking to my cookie dough, but even that doesn't taste so good anymore."

"There's no chance you've been drugged, or hypnotized, or had your body highjacked by aliens?"

"No, Becca! Have *you* been highjacked by aliens?" she asked, about done with her friend's antics.

Becca's expression grew serious. "I'm asking this because you said a wedding that didn't include an actual wedding could go off without a hitch. I know you've been in your head a bunch the past two weeks. But say that slowly and let me know if you still think people wouldn't notice a wedding without a bride and a groom?"

Georgie leaned against the bookshelf. "We're ready for a wedding."

They were.

They'd made all the big decisions during their whirl-wind of a trip to the Denver wedding underground.

At this point, there was no way of squeezing the prover-bial wedding toothpaste back into the pre-wedding tube.

Perhaps, out of the need for structure or routine or not wanting to let go, she hadn't hit the brakes.

She'd followed all the frau's instructions and had gone to her dress fitting and met with the hair and makeup people. She'd smiled and nodded politely at their suggestions. And it wasn't like it was odd that Jordan wasn't there. Many brides want to keep their dress and wedding day beauty preparations a surprise. She and Jordan had opted out of a bachelor or bachelorette party—it wasn't their thing. And, in lieu of a rehearsal dinner, they'd already decided to donate to a food bank.

As far as her mother, Hector, and Bobby—aka the Hydra of Denver—the frau had assigned them a slew of what she called transcendent wedding duties. What did these duties entail? She had no idea. But it had kept the hydra occupied and out of her hair.

In fact, she'd barely heard a peep out of them.

She glanced down at her left hand—the hand without an engagement ring. The wedding frau hadn't mentioned if it was back from the jeweler, and she hadn't brought it up.

A sinking feeling set in. Would she ever wear that ring again?

Had her words in the pouring rain sealed their fate?

"You're not answering the question, Georgie. Are you going to be walking down the aisle? Are you going to marry Jordan?" Becca asked gently.

What was she supposed to say?

She hadn't said anything to anyone about the catastrophic wilderness boot camp. Jordan was most likely bunking at his dad's place, and, for all she knew, he told his dad they wanted to be apart before the wedding.

But the one thing she knew for sure was the stalemate between them was real.

Neither had budged. Neither had reached out. Neither had waved the white flag.

The obstinate eight. The inflexible ten.

So much for being more than just a number.

"I..." she began when hushed giggles came from the children's area.

"We don't have another story time today, do we?" Becca asked.

Georgie checked her watch. "No, Talya should have finished up the last one over an hour ago."

"Want me to check it out?" Becca asked, glancing past the shelves of books. "It could be some kids horsing around."

Georgie shook her head. "I'll go. You watch the register."

Georgie wove her way toward the children's area. A bright and cheery space, when they'd designed it, she'd made sure to have cozy reading nooks built. These were great. Customers loved them, but so did teens, often with raging hormones, who, from time to time, she caught, reenacting the naughty scenes from the books in the romance section. She passed the now empty children's story time area, then froze.

"Love alters not with his brief hours and weeks, but bears it out even to the edge of doom."

Shakespeare. She'd know the line from Sonnet 116 anywhere. The lines Jordan had recited to her when they'd made love in the car before they entered Dante's ninth ring of boot camp hell.

She came around a table, stacked with the English bard's hardbacks and plays, and found Simon and Talya with their heads bent over a book.

"Edge of doom sounds super epic," Simon said, playfully bumping Talya with his shoulder.

"Well, this is Shakespeare's sonnet on his definition of what love is and what it isn't—and he's not messing around. You're right. It is pretty epic," Talya replied.

"Very epic," the teen agreed.

Talya blushed. "And there really isn't anything as epic as listening to someone recite it."

"Really?" Simon asked, meeting the girl's gaze.

"Oh, yes," she replied.

Simon played with the corner of the book. "Do you think I'm going to do all right in the recitation part of the Shakespeare Shuffle? It's important to my grandmother."

"Why is it so important?" Talya asked.

"She used to be an English teacher, and she's big on poetry," Simon answered.

Now, Talya gave Simon a playful shoulder bump. "You've been practicing and practicing with Mr. Marks, and you just sounded totally epic."

"I like practicing with you more," Simon said, his cheeks growing pink.

Talya bit her lip and twisted the sleeve of her hoodie. "I like helping you practice."

Georgie watched the sweet pair as young love blossomed before her eyes.

She and Jordan had helped Simon choose that sonnet for the competition back when they were experts on love—or, so they thought. She sighed, and it must have been one hell of a sound because it had the teens on red alert.

"Miss Jensen!" Talya said, bolting to her feet. "I didn't see you there. I finished up with the story time cleanup and..."

Simon sprang up next to her. "And...I finished up early with Mr. Marks at the gym and came here because..."

"Because at school today, I offered to help Simon with his sonnet practice," Talya finished.

With their cheeks rivaling the color of a beet, they looked as if they'd gotten caught making out behind the bleachers instead of the very tame act of reciting Shakespeare in a bookstore.

Georgie chuckled. "Nobody ever needs to apologize for reciting Shakespeare here. I'm glad you're getting some extra practice in before the Shakespeare Shuffle."

Simon shared a relieved glance with Talya. "Yeah, Mr. Marks has been preoccupied lately. He says he's busy with the gym."

Busy with the gym, just like she was busy with the bookshop.

"It's totally epic that you're getting married on the same day as the Shakespeare Shuffle. I picked out a dress and everything," Talya said with a dreamy expression.

"Me too!" Simon blurted.

"You found a dress that works?" Talya teased, glancing up at the boy through her lashes.

"Um...no, like pants and a shirt and a real tie that doesn't clip-on."

Georgie forced a grin. "I'm sure you'll both look great."

No longer the skin and bone lightweight, Simon shifted his strong frame from foot to foot.

"I was thinking since we're both going to be at the Shakespeare Shuffle and then we're going to Mr. Marks and Miss Jensen's wedding, it would make sense for us to go together."

"That would be epic," Talya answered, back to twisting her sleeve.

"Epic!" the boy answered wide-eyed.

"Totally epic," Talya replied as Simon's phone pinged.

The teens stared at each other.

"Simon, your cell phone," Georgie said, pointing to the forgotten device in the teen's hand and praying they were done dropping the word epic.

"Right!" He glanced at the phone, then frowned. "It's my grandma. She says she needs me."

"Is she okay?" Talya asked.

The teen shook his head. "I don't know."

"You better go," Georgie said, patting his shoulder. "And if you or your grandma need anything, reach out to—"

"I know, I know," Simon said, cutting her off. "Reach out to you or Mr. Marks."

Georgie nodded as the kids grabbed their backpacks and headed toward the exit.

She suddenly felt quite alone.

She glanced at the bright wall, decorated with children's drawings.

The wall that separated her shop from Jordan's CrossFit gym.

He was, most likely, on the other side.

Physically, only a few feet away—but emotionally, miles apart.

She stared at the barrier between them, her vision becoming blurry from strain or possibly the threat of tears until a wet familiar little nose nuzzled into her hand.

She scratched between Mr. Tuesday's ears. "Do you feel like a meandering walk, sweet boy?"

The pup's ears perked up as he ran around her in an excited loop.

A walk would do them both good. They'd been spending sixteen hours a day at the bookshop. If her restless limbs needed to move, Mr. Tuesday's must as well.

She headed to the front of the store, where Becca met her with Mr. Tuesday's leash.

"I heard the commotion. You must have said the *W-word*."

Georgie took the leash and fastened it to Mr. Tuesday's collar. "We've been pretty cooped up and could use the exercise."

"You could always go next door and ask to see a trainer. I'm sure there's one there who would welcome your visit," Becca said with a sympathetic expression.

Georgie shook her head. "Just the park today. I won't be long."

Becca nodded as she walked them to the door. "Take your time. Mrs. Gilbert's knitting group is at their Michael Bolton Fan Club meeting tonight. So, we won't be slammed, running back and forth, supplying them with pastries and coffee. Man, those women can knock back a doughnut hole or ten."

Georgie chuckled and shook her head, grateful for her friend's humor, then stepped outside.

Layered in shades of blue and gray, the dusk sky was the perfect backdrop for the Tennyson neighborhood shops, now beginning to flick on their outdoor lighting. The upbeat, eclectic vibe usually lifted her spirits.

Usually.

She set off down the sidewalk in the opposite direction of Jordan's gym. It was the most direct route to get to the park. But it wasn't the only reason she'd gone that way. An intrusive, foreboding thought she'd managed to ignore for the past two weeks, thanks to filling her days with work, work, and more work, reared its ugly head.

What if Jordan didn't want to be with her?

What if he regretted proposing?

If she saw him, she'd know. She'd see it in his eyes.

This limbo they'd been living the last two weeks had provided a buffer, but the clock was running out. In a matter of time, she'd either be married or single.

She continued down the sidewalk but slowed her pace when a woman in a flowing white dress and bracelets stacked up her arms, whipped off a pair of Gucci tinted glasses.

"Pumpkin, what a surprise!"

Georgie froze, and even Mr. Tuesday seemed at a loss, cocking his doggy head to the side.

"It's me, pumpkin," purred the yoga-fabulous hippie, standing in the middle of the sidewalk.

"Mom?" Georgie asked with the same confused head cock as Mr. Tuesday.

Lorraine Vandedinkle was a Chanel woman. Her daily attire included tailored suits, expensive silks, and bras that cost as much as a down payment on a time-share. And diamonds. The woman usually dripped in the sparkling gems, that is, until now.

"What are you wearing?" Georgie asked, as the being that had taken over her mother's body leaned in for a set of air-kisses.

"What the psychic energist suggested," the woman replied.

"Where's your assistant, Nicolette?" Georgie asked, glancing around for a competent adult to explain the complete one-eighty change in her mother.

"Nicolette and I parted ways. She's a Sagittarius," her mother whispered back as if it were a criminal offense to be born between November twenty-second and December twenty-first.

Georgie took in the giant crystal hanging off a chain around her mother's neck and the pound of turquoise rings, clicking along with the bracelets.

"What the hell is a *psychic energist*?"

"Language, pumpkin!" her mother said, then stilled and raised her palms. "Did the universe, or did Buddha tell you to use coarse language?"

"Um...Buddha," she answered, silently apologizing to the deity for throwing him under the bus.

"Then, curse away!" she answered with a grandiose wave of her hands.

Georgie glanced down the street toward her shop. It looked like the same neighborhood, but this version of her mother must have fallen through the space-time continuum.

"Could you define *psychic energist*, Mom?" she asked, not knowing where else to start.

"Of course! Cornelia Lieblingsschatz set me up with her."

Georgie's brows knit together. "Why would the wedding frau set you up with a psychic energist?"

Her mother went all *Namaste* and pressed her hands together. "Cornelia, in all her vast wedding wisdom, saw that Bobby, Hector, and I have a gift."

"For?" Georgie asked, stretching out the word.

Her mother's features grew somber. "For perceiving and identifying psychic energy given off by wedding favors."

Georgie watched Mrs. Yoga-Fabulous-Psychic-Energy-Vanderdinkle for a beat, then two.

Maybe her mother had eaten a tray of pot brownies?

No! She hadn't touched carbs since 2003.

"Mom, what does that mean for those of us not psychically gifted?" she pressed, still totally at a loss.

Before her mother could reply, a voice coming from behind answered.

"It means your mother and I have been visiting every candle shop in the city."

Georgie turned to find Howard Vanderdinkle, striding toward them.

"Howard, dear, it's more than just the candles," her mother chided.

"Right! There have been the chocolate shops and the nurseries with the potted succulents," her stepfather answered with the hint of a wry grin pulling at the corners of his lips.

She watched him closely. Despite the man being her stepfather, she didn't know him that well. But she sure as hell never imagined the business-minded venture capitalist frequenting shops with scented candles and house plants.

"Potted succulents?" Georgie repeated, trying to get back to whatever crazy track she'd landed on. This conversation had passed twilight zone zany and had gone straight to *Willy Wonka* weird.

"Yes, I have a gift for communing with them...and cacti. But we didn't want anyone to get pricked, so I'm focusing my energy on those fuzzy succulents," her mom answered as if her response sounded even a fraction close to normal.

Georgie nodded, unsure if there was a proper response when learning your parent communicated psychically with plants, chocolate, and candles.

She decided to switch gears.

"Mr. Tuesday and I are out for a little stroll."

Lorraine took a step toward her and moved her hands around.

"Yes, I'm getting that energy off you. I sense you need to walk," she answered, nodding to Howard.

"How about you go tackle the candles, honey, and I'll join Georgie on her walk," the man offered.

Her mother did the weird hand thing again. "Yes, I can feel your energy pulling toward Georgiana. I'll meet you at the Prius in twenty minutes," she said, then flitted, actually flitted, into the candle shop.

"Mom's being driven around in a Prius?" she asked, still watching her mother flit and flow through the shop's window.

Howard suppressed a grin. "No, your mother is *driving* a Prius."

Georgie gasped. "You're kidding."

"Nope, she's got them in six colors to match whatever her aura is that day," he replied, unable to hold back a chuckle.

Georgie's eyes widened. "Wow, the Denver Wedding Frau—"

"Knows how to handle a motivated mother-of-the-bride?" Howard finished.

Georgie gave her stepfather a teasing grin. "I had a different adjective in mind, but we can go with motivated. But I thought everything with the favors was done?"

"Cornelia has your mother double-checking the energy. That's what we're doing today," Howard replied with that wry expression.

"That frau doesn't miss a beat," Georgie answered.

"She certainly doesn't," he agreed with a knowing twist to his lips.

It was odd he called the wedding frau by her first name, but she dismissed the thought as Howard gestured for them to start walking, and she fell into step with a man she'd never joined for a stroll before. Sure, when she was a kid, she'd gone places with Howard, but her mother was always there, too.

They walked a few blocks in silence before Howard spoke.

"I owe you an apology, Georgiana," the man said, stopping her in her tracks.

"An apology for what?"

"For not making more of an effort to get to know you when you were growing up," Howard said, clasping his hands behind his back as they continued down the sidewalk. "I worked a lot, especially when your mother and I first married. But you and I never got to spend much time together, did we?"

"You were always kind to me, Howard," she answered, working to keep the surprise from her voice.

"But we've never talked, really talked, have we?" he mused.

The man was right. They hadn't.

They'd each occupied different parts of her mother's world. She and her mom had done pageants, and her mother and Howard had traveled, spent time at the country club, and attended numerous charity engagements and galas. When they were all together, the activity had centered on her mom.

"No, come to think of it, I don't think we have," she replied.

"But I have gotten to learn quite a bit about you these past few years," he said as they rounded the corner.

She frowned. "How so?"

"Your CityBeat blogs," he answered.

"You've read them?" she exclaimed, now unable to keep the surprise from her voice.

She would not have put Howard in the Own the Eights or More Than Just a Number target audience.

He nodded. "I have. I like to keep an eye on what's going on there."

"Why?" she asked.

"This may come as a surprise to you, but many years ago, one of the subsidiaries of my venture capital company gave Hector and Bobby the seed money to start CityBeat. My company is no longer associated with them, but I like to keep my finger on the pulse of past ventures."

"I had no idea," she said on a stunned breath.

"I know a good investment when I see one," the man replied.

A good investment.

She could sure use advice when it came to that.

"How do you know what's worth investing in and what's not?" she asked, training her gaze on the sidewalk.

"In its simplest form, the equation is risk versus reward," Howard answered.

"So, you want to take on the least amount of risk?" she pressed.

"Not always. When I read Bobby and Hector's proposal years ago, I saw two college kids with a lot of potential but little business experience," he answered.

"Then, why did you choose to give them the money?" she asked.

"Because, no matter how many times you run the numbers or pore over the forecasts, you've got to trust your gut. If it says yes, it's worth listening to."

She sighed. Unfortunately, her gut was all over the place.

She glanced down at Mr. Tuesday, padding alongside her. "I could use some investment advice. Could I run it by you?"

Howard nodded.

"I thought I wanted to invest in a company—more like merge with another company. Everything seemed perfect. The potential for long-term growth looked promising," she began.

"I'm sensing there was a hiccup in this *potential investment merger*," Howard commented with a sly expression.

Hiccup? Try an alpaca-sized, shit-shoveling, lemon verbena-scented hiccup.

"Under extreme stress, vulnerabilities were exposed," she replied, doing her best to stick to business jargon.

"That can happen," her stepfather agreed.

"Should I walk away?" she asked, her throat growing tight.

Howard mulled over her question as they circled the block and headed back toward the candle store.

"Can I tell you a story, Georgiana?"

"Sure," she replied.

"Before I met your mother, I was an even greater workaholic than I am now. Even then, I had teams of people working for me and could have easily spent my days golfing but chose to stay active in the company. I thought to maintain my level of success, I had to spend all my waking moments focused on business. I used to worry any deviation from the plan would decrease my profits. But your mother changed that. She helped me discover other parts of myself, other interests, other strengths. It wasn't always easy. I never enjoyed all those charity functions, but she made me see the impact I could have on the community. Now, I know she sometimes comes off as a bit of a socialite."

"Sometimes?" Georgie teased.

Howard chuckled. "But she cares. She truly cares and wants to bring people together, and she's brought out the best in me."

"I don't know if Jordan and I bring out the best in each other," she said as the words she'd kept locked away for two weeks came tumbling out. She froze. "I mean..." she stuttered, trying to think of something to say to counter her admission.

"I know this merger you're considering is your marriage, Georgie," Howard replied gently.

Panic welled in her chest. "How did you know I was talking about me and Jordan?"

Howard glanced over and raised a skeptical eyebrow. "A long-term investment that also included a merger?"

"I guess I wasn't fooling you with that," she replied, then gasped. "Mom doesn't know anything, does she? I haven't said anything. We haven't decided anything."

"No, and I think you and I can agree that allowing her to continue in her role as a wedding psychic energist is for the best."

"I don't want to let her down. I don't want to let anyone down. And the money I know you and mom have spent. It must be a fortune," she replied as the weight of her situation sank in.

"Let's not worry about that, Georgiana. You know it's not an issue for us," he replied.

She released a tight breath. "But, still..."

She'd been so preoccupied she hadn't even considered the cost of...*of calling off a wedding.*

It was too hard even to allow her mind to go there.

Howard rested his hand on her shoulder, halting the anxiety tornado inside her, as they stopped a few shops down from the candle store.

"Listen, you're right to view your marriage as a merger. It's the greatest merger anyone can make, and love, Georgiana, is the ultimate investment because, with love, you're not investing money, you're investing time. And time is a finite commodity. No amount of cash can buy you more. That's why it's such an important decision on who you'll share it with."

She held the man's gaze—this man, who for years, she'd

thought of as kind but distant. She'd never taken into account he and her mother had something special she'd never noticed.

Lorraine Vanderdinkle emerged from the candle shop—all flowing outfit and jangling jewelry. She slid on her tinted glasses, then waved to them with what Georgie used to call her mother's drinks-at-the-club smile stretched across her face. But now, she realized her mother was truly happy and deeply in love with Howard. A relationship she'd thought had been built on brunch at the Ritz and summers in the Maldives was a partnership grounded in mutual affection.

"With the time decision," Georgie began.

"Yes," the man answered, his gaze fixed on her mother.

"Is your gut a good barometer on making that choice?" she continued.

Her stepfather hummed a gentle chuckle. "No, Georgie, it's not. When it comes to that decision, it all depends on your heart."

Jordan stared at his phone, recording his every move, as his jump rope sliced through the air in quick, punishing whooshes.

"Double-unders are not for the faint of heart," he bit out, keeping his body straight and his abs tight as the rope passed under his feet in two revolutions for each jump.

Whoosh, whoosh!

Whoosh, whoosh!

He dialed up his pace, demonstrating the CrossFit-style of jumping rope. But this video wasn't only a tutorial for the blog. It was all he could think to do to combat the irritable buzz of nervous energy coursing through his body.

He hadn't slept a wink all night—the night before the Shakespeare Shuffle also happened to be the night before what was supposed to be his wedding day.

A muscle twitched in his jaw. "Elbows in. Light grip. Maintain those small circles with your wrists," he bit out, going faster.

Whoosh, whoosh!

Whoosh, whoosh!

"There is no room for mistakes. This exercise demands precision and determination. CrossFit ropes are thinner than your average rope, so if you lose focus for even a second...Dammit!" he cried as the rope whipped his shins.

So much for precision and focus.

"Son, what are you doing?" his father asked with a groggy voice.

Jordan dropped the rope and rubbed his shins.

That was a great question. What the hell was he doing?

He'd been a wreck since he'd packed a bag and left the one person he didn't know how to live without.

A wreck, not knowing if Georgie meant their time at boot camp was over, or if *they* were over.

During the drive back, after they'd been booted from wilderness boot camp, anger and humiliation had consumed him. But that heated emotion wasn't what had compelled him to leave without a word between them.

Anger and humiliation felt terrible. And yes, he'd indulged himself by spending a decent amount of time countering every one of Georgie's lemon verbena blog posts zingers with a zinger post of his own. But they could have worked past the tit-for-tat blog clash. No, what he feared went far deeper. It might even be ingrained into his soul.

Was she right to say it was over? Did she sense something he hadn't realized until now?

His disappointment and his unchecked ambition had made him act like the one man he never wanted to emulate again.

Deacon Perry.

His former boss.

His mentor for more than a decade.

Deacon was the man who'd changed his life. The man

who trained him. Deacon showed him not only how to transform his body but his entire life.

He'd idolized the man.

But he'd been blind to his faults.

A philandering husband. And absent father. He'd almost lost Georgie in his desire to follow in his former mentor's footsteps.

But, at his core, was he any different from the man who'd let him down?

He'd left the bungalow for two reasons. First, he hadn't had the strength to stay and ask her if it was really over. And second, he needed to know who he was before he promised to love, honor, and keep Georgie forever—if she'd take him.

He loved her too much to allow her to marry a monster —even if he were the monster.

He didn't want Georgie to suffer the pain Maureen had endured being married to the thoughtless, arrogant, and entitled, Deacon Perry.

But time was running out.

Jordan stopped the recording and sank into a kitchen chair, making sure not to meet his father's gaze. "I was putting together a jump rope tutorial for the blog. The acoustics are better in here."

His dad sat down across from him. "Talk to me, son."

"I told you, Dad, I was making a—"

"No, tell me what's going on with Georgie?" the big man said, cutting him off.

Jordan ran his hands through his tangle of hair. "It's wedding jitters. I thought it would help if I stayed here before the big day."

That's the line he'd fed his father when he'd arrived at his door. Dennis Marks had nodded and hadn't asked him about it since he'd taken up residence in the guest room.

It had been a perfect place to lie low. His father left early in the morning and wouldn't get home until late at night.

But it was a double-edged sword.

All those nights alone when he was lying in bed, longing for the life where he'd only have to glance over to find Georgie with her hair twisted into that damn messy bun he loved and her nose buried in a book, gave him ample time to dwell upon all his faults.

"I hate to break it to you, son, but today is the big day," his father said.

"I know," he answered with a heavy sigh.

Denny narrowed his gaze. "You're not going to jilt that lovely woman at the altar, are you?"

"Jesus, Dad!" he shot back.

"Well?" the man returned, crossing his arms.

Jordan shook his head and traced an imaginary line down the table with his index finger. "It's not like that, Dad. I don't want to hurt her."

"Then what in God's name are you doing here at the ass crack of dawn jumping rope on TV?" his father exclaimed.

"I wasn't on TV. I was making a video for the blog," he threw back.

"Would this be a video people will play on their phones and other digital doohickeys?" the man countered.

"Maybe, if I edit the part out where I shin-whipped myself," Jordan replied with a frustrated shake of his head.

His father sat back. "Then, I'm right."

Were they really debating what constituted as being *on TV*?

"Yeah, I guess you are," he conceded.

The man raised an eyebrow. "Would you like to know what else I'm right about?"

Jordan glanced up and met his father's gaze.

His father's expression softened. "You love Georgie, and you would do anything for her."

Jordan continued tracing the invisible line. "You're right. I would."

"Then, why are you here, Jordy? And don't feed me the line about not wanting to see the bride before the big day."

Jordan stilled his hand. "I told you. I'm here because I don't want to hurt her."

And I'm not sure if she still wants to be my wife.

But he couldn't say those words.

Denny leaned in and lowered his voice. "Why would you hurt her?"

Jordan closed his eyes and pictured Georgie's expression when he'd left the house.

Gutted. Utterly and completely gutted.

After the boot camp, the sleepless nights, and going at each other nearly nonstop, all he could see in her eyes was disappointment and heartbreak.

He'd wanted to take her into his arms and go back in time. But there was no going back—no undoing what had been done.

He pulled his gaze from the table. "Because when we were at the wilderness boot camp, I was a colossal jerk to her. I turned into..."

"Into Deacon," came a gentle voice from the far side of the kitchen.

"Maureen?" Jordan gasped. "Is there an accounting issue?" he asked, not sure why she'd be here at this early hour.

He turned to his father, whose cheeks had gone pink, then glanced back at Maureen, wrapped in his father's oversized robe.

"No, your books are perfect," the woman answered.

"Good morning," his father purred—actually purred.

"Good morning to you," she replied with a girlish grin.

"You slept here?" Jordan asked as his mind turned to oatmeal, unable to make sense of what was right in front of him.

She nodded.

"Did you fall asleep helping Dad with his books?" he asked, grasping at straws.

Maureen shared a furtive glance with his father, then joined them at the kitchen table.

"No," she answered with the curl of a smile.

"What about the girls? Where are Mia and Mya?" he continued.

Maureen shared another coy look with his father. "They had a sleepover with my folks."

"So, you had a sleepover with my dad?" he concluded, not about to be named super sleuth of the year.

"Is that what the kids are calling it these days?" his father teased, then lifted Maureen's hand to his lips and pressed a tender kiss to her knuckles.

Jordan's gaze bounced between the pair. "Am I awake?"

Maureen chuckled. "Yes, honey. Of course, you're awake."

"But it looks like..." he stammered.

"Like your dad got some?" his father asked with a wide grin.

"Denny!" Maureen said with a playful swat to his arm.

"When? Why? How?" Jordan uttered, still oatmeal-brained, and finding it difficult to form a coherent sentence.

His dad and Maureen gazed at each other like teenagers in love.

His father cleared his throat. "When? Last night. Why? Because Maureen is one of the kindest, smartest, most beautiful women I've ever met. And how?" He scratched his chin, then shared a knowing glance with Maureen. "It started in the kitchen, or was it in the car?"

Maureen mimicked his father and scratched her chin dramatically. "I'd say the car was foreplay, and the kitchen was where things started to heat up—right here on the kitchen table for round one."

Round One!

Jordan skidded his chair back from the location of parental hanky-panky.

"I don't want to know how many rounds!" he blurted.

"Three," his father whispered.

Jordan's jaw hit the floor.

"Dad! Stop! And how did you two even get together?"

"At your beautiful champagne engagement breakfast," Maureen answered.

His father nodded. "We got to talking, and then Maureen started helping me with my bookkeeping."

The two lovebirds stared at each other. If this were some middle-aged love story cartoon, this would be the scene where their eyes would transform into hearts.

"And one thing led to another," Maureen added sweetly.

Christ on a Cracker!

"You're my dad's girlfriend?" he asked, slow as molasses on the uptake.

Maureen resurrected that theatrical chin scratch move. "Maybe I'm your dad's booty call. It's like the thing you kids do with the swipe right," Maureen joked.

Jordan knew his mouth was hanging open, but he could not get it to close. Maureen was like a mother to him, and she'd just correctly dropped app hookup lingo.

"I don't know what I'd call it, other than two of the best

weeks of my life," his father said, again with the Rico Suave kiss to Maureen's hand.

"Are you going to keep seeing each other?" Jordan asked, regaining brain function.

His dad and Maureen went back to puppy-dog-eyes mode.

"I sure hope so," his father said.

"Me too," Maureen answered, then slid her gaze from his father and zeroed in on him.

"I think that's enough talk about your dad and me. We need to have a chat with you," Maureen said, watching him closely.

"Me?" he asked.

She nodded, then glanced at the floor. "Hold on. What is that?"

Jordan looked at the spot where he'd been filming the jump rope tutorial.

"It's dryer lint. I'll toss it in the trash," his father offered.

Shit!

Jordan shot to his feet and swiped the laundry remnant. "It's mine."

Maureen eyed him skeptically. "That's your dryer lint?"

He stroked the scented lint ball with his thumb. "Georgie's and mine. I took it from our place."

Maureen narrowed her gaze. "You won't talk to Georgie, but you'll keep her dryer lint? And don't try to tell me I'm not right. Remember, I do the books for both of you. I know you two are avoiding each other," Maureen chided.

His father grimaced. "What are you doing with Georgie's dryer lint, son? Not to mention, that's a pretty creepy thing to be carrying around."

"It smells like her," he said, staring at the bluish-gray lemon verbena-scented mass.

He glanced up to find Maureen and his dad with their heads cocked to the side, watching him as if he belonged in a padded room.

He waved off their concern. "It's not meant to be creepy. It's just…"

Just what?

The one thing he'd kept with him since he'd left?

The reminder of her scent and everything he longed for?

A memento of when he'd lost his shit—one of many times he'd lost his shit—when he'd learned she'd packed the damn dryer sheets and not the dryer lint?

"It's lemon verbena-scented," he offered as if that would somehow reduce the creeper factor.

However, from his father and Maureen's continued wary appearance, it didn't.

"What happened, honey?" Maureen asked, concern etched on her face.

He slumped into the chair. "I was a real asshat, Maureen. I made twenty people think Georgie was a sex maniac whose favorite color was rose, which I then said was pink and argued with her when she told me I was wrong."

"You are wrong. Rose is the color rose. It's the shade halfway between red and magenta," Maureen replied.

Jordan shook his head in astonishment. "Do all women know that? Is that something they take you aside for and share with you when you turn a certain age?" he asked, wondering if he was sick on the day they taught the quintessential rose-is-not-pink lesson at school.

"But that's not what brought you here, son," his father said gently.

"No, I told you. I don't want to hurt her. I don't want her attached to a man who might…" he trailed off and met Maureen's gaze.

"Cheat on his wife and stop spending time with his children to flounce around town with women half his age," Maureen finished.

Hearing her say the words was like a punch to the gut.

"I hate that Deacon did that to you and the girls. It's selfish and unforgivable," he said, his voice cracking with emotion.

Maureen nodded. "I agree. But what I don't understand is why you would think you'd be a husband like Deacon?"

He stared at the ball of lint. "Because when Georgie and I were at our worst, I reverted to the man Deacon wanted me to be. Someone who put winning, ego, and glory above all else."

Maureen covered his hand with hers. "And that's exactly the reason why you won't turn out like him."

He shook his head. "I don't understand."

Maureen's features softened. "Deacon doesn't want to change. I doubt he even sees his behavior as wrong. He writes it off, thinking because he's found monetary success, he's earned a certain kind of life where he can neglect his responsibilities. Don't you see, Jordan? He doesn't want to be a better man, and that's the difference. None of us are perfect. We all have our faults. But you want to do better. You want to be better for Georgie."

His gaze grew glassy. "She deserves it."

"She deserves you, honey," Maureen replied gently.

"I don't know if she wants me," he admitted.

Maureen squeezed his hand. "She's as broken up about this as you are. Remember, I work for you both. I've watched her mope around her shop the same way you've moped around your gym."

He blinked back tears. "This separation is killing me. I want to be with Georgie. I want to be the man for her."

"You are, son," his father answered.

"How do you know that, Dad?"

And there it was. The question that had him up wrestling with his demons until the early morning hours. Even if she'd take him back, how would he know that he could be the man Georgie deserved?

His big, burly father gave him a teary grin. "I know because you helped me become a better man. You showed me I wasn't honoring your mother's memory by wallowing in the past. For years, I hated myself for not dealing with her death better and for not being the dad you needed. But when I stopped hiding behind the mask of anger and disappointment, I was able to see there was a way forward. A way to look into my heart and know I could choose to do better. You changed your life, son. You grew strong in body and mind. Thanks to your example, I learned I was the one who had to choose to be better each day." He leaned in and lowered his voice. "You're not going to hurt Georgie. You might not always agree, but, at the end of the day, you'll always put her first. It's who you are. You love with your whole heart, Jordan. I'm the same way. We Marks' men sometimes get so caught up in our head, we lose sight of what our heart knows is true."

Jordan gazed between his father and Maureen. How he wanted to believe them. How he wanted to know for certain he could be the man these two people—who were so important to him—thought he could be.

"Let Georgie know how you feel. You're the man for her, son. All you have to do is believe that with your whole heart and lay off on stealing her dryer lint. It's damn creepy," his father added.

Jordan shook his head, grateful for the humor, but froze

when his cell phone, still resting on the table, began to vibrate.

"Is it Georgie?" his father asked.

Jordan picked up the phone, then cleared the emotion from his throat.

"No, it's from Simon Bacon's grandmother, Esther. She's in the hospital and asked that I come there immediately."

Maureen pressed her hand to her heart. "Oh no! Did she say anything else?"

He hammered out a quick response, then pocketed the phone and the dryer lint—creepy or not, he wasn't about to part with it yet.

"No, but I told her I was on my way. I can visit her before I have to get to the Shakespeare Shuffle for the competition. I'm guessing Simon is with her."

"Let me know if there's anything I can do to help," Maureen offered.

"I will," he said and headed for the door.

"And the wedding?" his father asked.

Jordan stared at the doorknob and released a tight breath. "I don't know, Dad. I need to make sure Simon and Esther are all right first, and then..."

Then, it was time to face the music. Time to confront his fears. Time to make his case to the woman he loved.

He glanced at his watch, knowing one thing for certain.

Time was running out.

12

Jordan sprinted through the sliding doors of the bustling hospital lobby and frantically gazed from side to side then stopped dead in his tracks.

With her hair twisted into a messy bun and wearing her running clothes, he stared at Georgie's back as she spoke to a nurse at the information desk. Unable to move, he watched her start toward the elevators. But after a few steps, she stilled.

Could she feel his presence?

Did she miss him as much as he missed her?

She had his heart. Could she still trust him with hers?

Emotion clogged his throat, and he forced himself to swallow. Every cell in his body screamed for him to run to her and take her into his arms. But he didn't move—not one damn muscle.

Turn around.

Turn around.

His mind went to the fictional characters Lizzy Bennet, Jane Eyre, and Hermione Granger—Georgie's trifecta. The literary trio she'd held dear to her heart since she was a girl.

"Ladies, I could use your help," he whispered.

Was it insane to call upon his fiancée's fictional besties? Sure.

Was he up for trying anything?

Oh, hell yes!

He held his breath as the trifecta came through and watched as, slowly, Georgie turned to face him.

He raised his hand in a moronic hey-there-hi-there idiotic wave and felt his cheeks heat.

Get it together, Marks!

She tucked a lock of hair behind her ear and manufactured an uneasy smile.

Of course, she'd be apprehensive!

He was the Emperor of Asshattery, who decided to throw down over the color rose. He was the Sovereign of Scat who turned a wilderness boot camp laundry sheet flub into an alpaca-sized fiasco.

She glanced around nervously, then started toward him. He met her halfway as her gaze traveled to a spot somewhere beyond his shoulder.

"Esther texted and asked me to come. She wrote that she had a pretty bad asthma attack last night, and the doctors kept her overnight," she said with the hint of a shake to her voice.

He nodded, wanting so badly to take her hands into his, but tried to remain composed. "Yeah, she texted me, too, but she didn't tell me why she was here. Just that she needed me to come to the hospital."

Georgie nodded. "She's on the fifth floor in the pulmonary unit."

He took a step toward her. "Georgie, I—"

She raised her hands defensively. "Jordan, let's get through this for Esther and Simon, okay?"

Jesus! She was right. What was he going to do? Spill his guts right here while a sick old lady and her frazzled grandson waited for them?

"You're right," he agreed, forcing his hands to remain at his sides.

He gestured with his chin toward the bank of elevators and stayed half a step behind her as they joined a cluster of medical staff waiting to go up. He couldn't walk next to her and risk the familiar urge to take her hand into his.

How easy it used to be.

He'd think nothing of twining his fingers with hers or twisting a lock of her hair.

How many nights had they sat side by side, keyboards clicking away as they worked on the blog? She'd mumble under her breath. Lost in her writing and completely unaware, he could hear her debating with herself. How he'd loved listening to her—loved the confident curl to her lips when she'd come up with a catchy line or a memorable description.

And her smile. How he'd missed locking up his gym and walking the few feet to her bookshop. In those few seconds, his breath would catch in his throat, knowing the minute he opened the door to the shop, she'd gift him the sweet, loving, slightly naughty expression reserved only for him.

All those little instances, taken one by one, could be seen as fleeting or insignificant. But together, they were everything.

If she'd take him back, he'd never take those perfectly mundane moments for granted again.

"Jordan," she called.

He blinked, having zoned out, to find the group packed into the elevator.

He wove his way in to stand next to her—their bodies

millimeters apart. She wrapped her arms around her body as the elevator started its ascent, then stopped on the second floor. The occupants trailed out, leaving only the two of them when he looked down and saw the sliver of dryer lint on her hoodie.

Without thinking, he rested his hand on her shoulder and plucked the fibers.

"What are you doing?" she asked with a startle.

He held up the freeloading material. "Taking the dryer lint off your jacket."

She glanced at her shoulder and smoothed the now lint-free fabric. "I grabbed my hoodie out of the dryer before I came here."

Okay, they were talking—it was about dryer lint, of all things, but it was better than nothing.

He held the lint to his nose. "It smells different."

She watched him warily. "The store was out of lemon verbena dryer sheets, so I got lavender-scented instead."

He took another whiff. "Smells nice."

"I like the lemon verbena better," she replied.

"Me too," he agreed.

She gave him a placating smile.

God, help him! He had to stop sounding like such a douche canoe!

The elevator dinged their arrival, and the doors opened.

"After you," he said, way too enthusiastically.

Why did every word out of his mouth sound as if he were auditioning to become a game show host?

He needed a plan—a plan free of asshattery and douche canoery.

Was *douche canoery* even a word?

Dammit! Focus!

What were the objectives?

Ester and Simon.

They'd check on the pair and make sure they were okay, and then...shit!

A large clock on the wall above the nurses' station flashed the time. They had less than an hour before the Shakespeare Shuffle. Granted, he and Georgie had made sure the event would run like clockwork with or without them. But they needed to be there. CityBeat would be covering the event as well as the rest of the local media.

Thanks to the Denver Wedding Frau—a sentiment he never thought he'd feel—and her uncanny ability to take charge of every aspect of their wedding, besides going to his tux fitting, nobody had bothered him with anything wedding related while they were in their engagement purgatory.

But here's the thing.

Everyone knew today was their wedding day—or, at least, that it was supposed to be their wedding day. There was a damn countdown clock on CityBeat's homepage.

"Here's Esther's room, five-sixty-nine," Georgie said, pointing to the placard.

Sixty-nine?

Was it a sign?

Sixty-nine was totally their thing—and not even in a dirty way. Okay, it absolutely was in a dirty way, but, when they'd first met and learned they'd be competing together back in the Battle of the Blogs, Bobby and Hector had told them they had a sixty-nine percent audience overlap between their blogs. At the time, it seemed ludicrous any of his now-debunked Marks Perfect Ten Mindset blog followers could find anything useful in Georgie's Own the Eights posts.

She glanced over her shoulder at him, and he would

have sworn he'd detected the hint of a grin pulling at the corners of her lips.

Was he imagining things now?

"Are you ready?" she asked, lowering her voice.

He nodded.

Georgie knocked gently, then opened the door. "It's me. I mean, it's us, Georgie and Jordan."

He bristled. That didn't bode well!

"Come in, come in," came Esther's raspy voice.

They entered the room to find her in bed.

"Thank you both for coming," she said, then waved them over.

Georgie sat on the edge of the bed and hugged the woman. "How are you feeling?"

Esther adjusted the breathing tubes hooked around her ears. "Better. This unseasonably warm weather is playing havoc with my asthma, but I didn't call you two here to talk about me."

"Is Simon all right?" he asked, lowering himself to sit on the other side of the bed across from Georgie.

"Simon's fine, but he doesn't want to leave my side. I sent him out to get me some real coffee from the shop down the block. Even that was a struggle to persuade him to leave for fifteen minutes," she replied.

"I can understand that. I'm sure he's worried about you. We all are," he answered, sharing a glance with Georgie, who nodded her agreement.

Esther took Georgie's hand, then reached for his. "I'm going to be fine. I think Simon knows this, but he needs a nudge to feel okay about leaving me to compete in the Shakespeare Shuffle. As a retired high school English teacher, I'm sure you can understand this is very important to me. He's worked so hard, and you both have helped him so much."

Jordan squeezed the woman's hand gently. "He's a great kid, Esther."

"He is. He's stronger and more confident, and I have the two of you to thank for that. Since he started working out in your gym and hanging out in the bookshop, his real smile is back. You two have changed his life," she said.

"I don't know if you could say that. Simon was always a good kid," he replied.

Esther released a shaky breath. "But he was headed down a dark path. He'd retreated into himself. I could tell him a million times that he was smart and funny, but I'm his grandmother. He needed to hear it from someone else, someone he admired. That's where the two of you came in. You challenge him. You helped him see the person we all knew was inside of him." The woman glanced between them. "You've also taught him about love."

"Love?" Georgie repeated, surprise coating the word.

Esther nodded. "I'm not sure how much Simon's told you, but his parents aren't allowed to have contact with him."

"He's never mentioned them to me," he replied.

"Me neither," Georgie answered.

"It's not a happy story. His parents had gotten mixed up in drugs, and his early years were tumultuous, to say the least. He'd never been around a couple who loved each other. You see, I've been a widow for almost twenty years now, and Simon never knew his grandfather. I suspect he wasn't sure what real love between a committed couple looked like before meeting the two of you. He talks about you all the time. You've had a great impact on his life."

Georgie swiped a tear from her cheek. "That's very kind

of you to say. We're grateful he's a part of our life," she added, catching his eye, then turning back to Esther.

Our life?

That had to be something. She still thought of them as having a life together—or that they used to have a life together.

His gaze washed over Georgie, and the slight hint of a smile she gave him when she caught him looking at her was there, barely a breath beneath the surface of her schooled features.

"You know, he has a girlfriend now. He and Talya spend just about every waking moment together," Esther continued.

"I suspected there might be something going on between them," he replied.

"He says she's *epic*," the woman added with a glint in her eyes when the door to the room flew open.

"Mr. Marks, Miss Jensen, what are you doing here?" Simon asked, carrying in a large to-go cup of coffee.

"They're here to take you to the Shakespeare Shuffle," Esther said in a firm, don't-mess-with-grandma tone.

But the kid wasn't having it.

"I told you, Grandma. I'm not leaving you," he answered firmly.

"Sweetheart, you heard what the doctors said last night. They only kept me overnight for observation. And the nurse stopped by after you left to tell me I'll be released later today," Esther replied.

The teen set the coffee on the bedside table. "I should be here."

"No, you should be at the race. You've worked too hard to miss it," Esther replied.

Jordan glanced between grandmother and grandson and saw the pain in Esther's eyes.

"How about we do it together, Simon?" he offered.

Simon frowned. "You want to run the race with me?"

"Why not?" Jordan asked, switching from concerned mentor to motivational trainer.

Simon shrugged.

"You don't think you can keep up with me?" Jordan pressed, knowing how to challenge the teen.

The kid scoffed. "I can keep up. But what if I mess up the sonnet," he said, deflating as he glanced at his grandmother.

Jordan pinned the teen with his gaze. "We've been training for this from the moment you entered the gym. And you've got the sonnet down. I've listened to you recite while running, jumping rope, and doing deadlifts. I'd venture to say you could recite it while being chased by an alligator."

Simon's expression softened. "Maybe."

"Jordan's right, Simon. I overheard you practicing with Talya. You're ready," Georgie added.

"Talya," Simon repeated, as a grin spread across his face at the mention of the girl.

Jordan shared a look with Esther, and she gave him a conspiratorial wink.

"Look at the time! You need to get going!" the woman said, pointing at the clock on the wall.

Simon's gaze bounced between them, then landed on his grandmother. "Are you sure?"

She waved him off. "Yes, and it's not like I won't be able to watch. You set up my laptop so I can ride the web."

"It's surf the web, Gram. And yes, I've got the CityBeat site bookmarked for you," Simon answered, retrieving the laptop from a bag on the floor and setting it on the bedside table.

"There you go! Now, give me a hug," she replied, folding her grandson into her embrace.

Jordan followed Georgie to the door to give Simon and Esther some privacy to say their goodbyes.

"Does Simon know?" Georgie asked under her breath.

"Know what?" he murmured back.

"That we..." she began but stopped when Simon joined them.

He held her gaze, but he couldn't read her. What was she saying? Did Simon suspect they were living apart or that their wedding may or may not take place in the next handful of hours?

With one last wave to Esther, the three of them left the room and rode the elevator down to the first floor.

"Where'd you guys park?" Simon asked as they walked out the sliding doors into the fresh morning air.

He and Georgie spoke at once, with her pointing in one direction and him in another.

The boy frowned. "You guys didn't come together?"

Jordan threw Georgie a worried glance. "No, we didn't, but that's because—"

"I had a few errands to run this morning," she finished.

"Okay," Simon answered, not sounding convinced.

Jordan gave the kid his best fake grin. "Let's take my car."

"Is everything okay?" the boy asked.

"Yes," he and Georgie answered in the same rah-rah, go-team-go voice.

"Are you guys feeling okay?" Simon pressed.

"Yes," they answered again, channeling a deranged cheer squad.

"I bet you're excited for today," Simon continued as they walked to the car.

"Sure! We couldn't have gotten better weather for the race," Georgie answered with an expression as fake as his.

"No, I mean for *your* wedding?" Simon said, getting into the back seat as they buckled their belts in the front.

"We sure—" he began, not knowing what the hell to say when Georgie interrupted.

"Let's focus on one thing at a time, Simon. Do you need to stretch? Do you want to take another look at the sonnet? I can pull it up on my phone," she offered, still sporting that plastic grin.

Simon perked up. "No, I think I'm as ready as I'll ever be, and you guys should use the sonnet today, too."

"For what?" Jordan asked, merging into traffic for the short drive to the community center.

"The wedding! The sonnet is all about what love is and what it isn't. It would be perfect for you! But you probably already know that since you were the ones who recommended it," Simon replied.

Jordan glanced over to where Georgie was twisting the cuff of her hoodie.

"I don't have it memorized like you do, Simon," Georgie answered with a nervous laugh.

"Mr. Marks probably does. He's listened to me recite it a million times," the teen countered.

"Let's focus on you, champ," Jordan said, catching the boy's eye in the rearview mirror.

"You guys aren't in a fight, are you?" Simon asked as the worry returned to his face.

"No, it's nothing like that," Georgie answered.

Simon leaned forward and pressed his elbows to his knees. "You guys haven't been hanging out at the bookshop very much these last couple weeks."

Shit! The last thing he wanted to do was upset Simon.

"It's been a busy time with the Shakespeare Shuffle and..." Georgie began, her eyes begging him to help her out.

"And everything else going on with us," he finished.

Jesus! Could neither of them even say the word *wedding*?

The teen gave them an unconvinced half nod.

Simon looked up to him and Georgie just as he'd looked up to Maureen and Deacon all those years ago before Deacon lost his way. And there was no way in hell he was about to let Simon think he didn't love and respect Georgie. He swallowed hard, trying to come up with something encouraging to say when Georgie placed her hand over his.

"We're going to be okay," she said, giving it a gentle squeeze.

"We are?" he answered in a cracked voice, not meaning for it to come out as a question.

"I hope so," she said, blinking back tears.

He threaded his fingers with hers and rested their clasped hands on the console as they cruised down the boulevard.

"Back to mushy. That's more like I remember it," Simon said, feigning teen mortification at their display of affection.

But what the hell was going on? Was Georgie only doing this to make Simon feel better before the race? It felt genuine. But could the tears in her eyes be tears of sadness —the tears over something about to end?

He couldn't let that happen.

They approached the community center, and reluctantly, he released her hand. "I better let go so I can park."

"Right," she answered, clasping her hands nervously in her lap.

Instantly, he missed her touch, hating the loss of the connection he longed for over the last two weeks. He turned into the parking lot across from the community center and found a spot. He cut the ignition as his gaze traveled to the teen in the back seat, and he pushed aside the emotion welling in his chest.

Simon was their priority now.

Georgie opened the car door. "Jordan, why don't you stick with Simon. I'll go check in with the director and our volunteer coordinator. I'll catch up with you two during the race," she said, gifting the teen a grin before exiting the car.

He watched Georgie jog up to the volunteer stand. When would he see her again? He needed to carve out a moment to get her alone—to apologize, to make her see they were meant to be together.

It couldn't be over between them. It simply couldn't.

"Mr. Marks, are you ready?" Simon asked.

Ready?

Jordan swallowed past the lump in his throat. Was he ready to find out if the woman he loved would take him back? And what if it was over? How the hell would he go on?

"It looks like it's you and me, big guy," he said to the teen, doing his best not to sound defeated.

"Yeah," Simon replied, nodding to himself as if he were turning something over in his mind.

They got out of the car and surveyed the bustling rec center.

Jordan cleared his throat. "Let's pick up our race bibs and get warmed up."

He needed to get Simon moving. Hell, he needed to get out of his head and get himself moving.

Once they started running, he could figure out what he wanted to say to Georgie. And it wasn't like she'd catch up to them in the race. Yes, with a hell of a lot of training, they'd knocked a little time off her mile, but she still got passed by spry senior citizens out power walking.

He breathed a cautious sigh of relief. There was still time. The wedding wasn't until later this afternoon.

A shiver traveled down his spine.

What kind of guy doesn't know if his wedding is on or off hours before the big event?

He shook his head and willed the thought away. He couldn't go there. Not yet. Not while there was still a chance.

They checked in, grabbed their race bibs, and headed toward a crowd of runners gathered at the starting line. Along with participants of all ages, the place was packed with teens, amped up and horsing around, preparing to run the 5K, then complete their Shakespeare recitation.

"Do you think I'm going to look like a fool?" Simon asked, shifting his weight from foot to foot.

Jordan met the kid's gaze. "No, not at all."

Simon glanced over at a group of teenage boys. "They're from my school. They're athletes."

Jordan checked out the jock squad. "Did they ever bother you?"

"A few comments here and there. But not much anymore," the kid answered, but Jordan knew the damage had been done.

Simon might not be that skinny kid anymore, but it didn't erase the years of teasing.

He rested his hand on the boy's shoulder. "Listen, those guys don't matter. Not one bit. You're strong. You're fast. They'll be eating our dust."

The teen swallowed hard. "You believe that?"

"I do," he answered, conviction lacing the words.

Simon chuckled. "You're going to be saying that again soon, Mr. Marks."

Jordan frowned. "What are you talking about?"

"*I do,*" the teen tossed back with a twinkle in his eyes.

Jordan nodded, praying the uncertainty churning in his belly wasn't apparent on his face.

How he hoped Simon was right.

He glanced around, looking for Georgie, and instead found a crew of people in CityBeat T-shirts heading their way. Barry emerged from the pack and jogged up to them.

"Everything looks great! Hector and Bobby wanted us to make sure and get plenty of footage."

Jordan shook his head. Christ, the irony! Last time he'd run a race, he'd been in a world of shit with Georgie, and CityBeat had been there to record and livestream their reconciliation.

That had turned out for the best. He'd spilled his guts in front of the world, proclaimed his love, denounced his asshattery, and got the girl!

A wave of hope washed over him, tamping down his nerves until the cold, hard punch of reality knocked away any temporary relief.

This was different. This time, everything—their careers and their relationship—was on the line.

"Mr. Marks, it's almost go-time," Simon said, then gestured to a large digital clock as the crowd called out the countdown.

Five.

Four.

Three.

Two.

One.

The race horn cut through the air, and the pack took off.

"Let's go!" he said, as he and Simon wove through the pack of runners.

The pound and grind of hundreds of sneakers eating the pavement rumbled around them. Simon held his own, meeting him stride for stride as they pushed to the front of the pack.

"Are you ready to hit our personal best speed?" he asked the boy.

"Let's do it," Simon huffed between tight breaths.

They kicked up their pace, passing clusters of participants. His arms sliced through the air, driving him forward as the kid maintained top speed next to him.

1K down.

2K down.

3K.

4K.

As they passed the signs, marking their progress, Jordan watched from the corner of his eye as Simon lifted his chin, growing more confident with every stride until they approached the jocks.

"You've got this, Simon," he said under his breath as one of the kids glanced at them.

"Hey, check out Bacon Bits!" the guy blurted out like a true meathead.

Bacon Bits? Jesus! Jordan thought back to his stupid nickname, Straws. It looks like the jock squad hadn't gotten more creative since his days brushing off taunts. He glanced over at Simon, ready to give the kid a pep talk but found him smiling.

Without missing a beat, Simon dialed up his pace. "Looks like you're getting passed by Bacon Bits, asshat," Simon called as they sailed by the group of speechless athletes.

Jordan bit back a grin.

"Sorry about the language, Mr. Marks," the kid panted.

"I didn't hear anything," he answered, tossing Simon a

wink when the hum of what sounded like a weed whacker on steroids rang out from behind.

Was some asshat riding a motorbike in the race?

He glanced over his shoulder to find—not an asshat— but Georgie!

With her hair streaming around her shoulders and determination written all over her face, she snaked her way through the herd of runners, nearly taking out one of the jock brigade, while vrooming the peewee engine of a cotton candy electric pink scooter.

"Jordan, it's not over!" she called, waving, then almost wiping out before gaining control of the tiny motorized skateboard.

"What are you doing, Georgie?" he asked as she zoomed up alongside of them.

"I needed to tell you something, so I decided to run the race with you guys," she answered over the buzz of the sputtering engine.

"But you're on a scooter, Miss Jensen," Simon bit out.

"I know! Isn't it great? I borrowed it from a little girl. No meandering run pace for me today! Now, I can keep up," she answered, vrooming the grip and nearly eating it again.

Holy hell! He couldn't believe nobody had stopped her. Then again, Georgie Jensen on a mission was nothing to mess with.

"What do you mean, it's not over?" he asked.

"I mean—" she began, but Simon cut in.

"Miss Jensen is right! It's not over. It's time to take it up into high gear," the teen panted.

The finish line came into sight, and he glanced over at the kid. "Are you ready to take first place?"

"We're in the lead?" Simon breathed, glancing around wide-eyed.

Jordan dialed back his pace. "We are. Run past the tape. It's all you."

"No, Mr. Marks, let's finish together," Simon replied, red-cheeked and smiling ear to ear.

"You got it," he answered, so damn proud of this kid.

He glanced over at Georgie and found her blinking back tears.

Was she talking about the race or their relationship?

Of course, she wanted to be here for Simon. But the skip in his heart couldn't help hoping she was there for him, too.

He glanced at the still smiling Simon.

"Let's do this!" he called, adrenaline pumping through his veins as they cranked it up to a full-out sprint and broke the race tape.

"We did it!" Simon cried, gasping for breath as they slowed down.

Jordan shook his head. "One more hurdle, kid," he replied, catching his breath and gesturing toward the tables staffed by teachers.

"The sonnet," Simon breathed.

Georgie cut the scooter's motor and removed the pink unicorn helmet. "You're ready. You can do it, Simon."

"Do you think so?" he asked, his cheeks going from pink to white.

"I know you can," she replied, squeezing his hand.

"Simon!" came Talya's voice as she ran toward them with a sour-faced girl running behind.

"Can I get my scooter back, lady?" the girl, who couldn't be much more than ten, asked with a pinched expression.

"Sorry, Miss Jensen! This girl recognized me from volunteering in the bookshop and asked if I'd help her get her scooter back."

"Thanks for letting me use it," Georgie said, handing over the helmet.

"You didn't ask. You grabbed my helmet off the sidewalk, strapped it on your head, and then told me you'd give me a whole tube of cookie dough if I let you ride my scooter," the kid shot back, not amused.

"It was important for me to catch up with these guys, but I didn't give you much choice, did I?" Georgie replied with a nervous chuckle.

The girl grabbed her scooter. "I know you're the bookshop lady, and you better believe I'll be coming for your cookie dough."

"Don't you worry. It'll be there for you," Georgie answered.

The girl made one of those I'll-be-watching-you gestures then kick-started the little scooter like a member of the fifth-grade version of Hells Angels and sped off down the street.

Jordan stared in awe at his scooter-swiping fiancée—well, hopefully still his fiancée. But before he could say anything, Talya clapped her hands excitedly.

"It's sonnet time! Are you ready?" she asked Simon.

The kid nodded. "I've never been more ready in my life."

"You're going to be so epic," she cooed.

"It's totally epic that you're here," Simon replied.

Jordan cleared his throat, cutting through the epic amount of teen hormones. "It would be really epic if you won the race and aced the sonnet. You should get to it."

"Right!" Simon answered, snapping back.

Talya and Simon jogged over to the table staffed with retired teachers, and Jordan exhaled a shaky breath as Simon's voice carried over to them.

Let me not to the marriage of true minds admit impediments.

"He sounds good," Georgie said with a nod toward the teen.

Jordan watched as she wiped a tear from her cheek. Was she just emotional to see Simon win and complete the recitation, or was it more?

And what the hell was he supposed to say?

I'm sorry?

Please, don't say it's over?

I've been carrying around your dryer lint for weeks?

No, none of it was right. None of that got to the heart of what he wanted to convey.

Simon's voice grew louder.

Love is not love
Which alters when it alteration finds,
Or bends with the remover to remove...

Simon's recitation of Shakespeare's sonnet on the definition of love was the answer.

He took Georgie's hands into his, listening as the teen continued.

Oh, no! It is an ever-fixed mark.

Mark! It was a sign. This was what he needed to say to the woman he loved. He stared into Georgie's eyes as Simon continued.

That looks on tempests and is never shaken;
it is the star to every wandering bark,
whose worth's unknown, although his height be taken.
Love's not Time's fool, though rosy lips and cheeks
within his bending sickle's compass come...

"What are you doing?" Georgie whispered, her gaze bouncing between him and Simon.

"Can I join in, Simon?" he called to the teen.

Simon glanced over his shoulder. "Sure thing, Mr. Marks!"

Georgie frowned. "What's going on, Jordan?"

He swallowed hard, then joined the teen. "*Love alters not with his brief hours and weeks, but bears it out even to the edge of doom. If this be error and upon me proved, I never writ, nor no man ever loved*," he whispered softly, finishing the sonnet along with Simon.

"Jordan, I'm so—" she began, but he stopped her.

"Wait! Give me a chance to explain. Shakespeare is right about love. Real love is constant. It doesn't stop when things get tough. And we love each other, Georgie. We've known it from the beginning. We're supposed to be together. Our love is meant to last." He reached into his pocket and held out the lint. "I've kept this with me the whole time. Smell it. It's not the lint I just pulled off your hoodie. It's the lemon verbena-scented lint I took before I left."

"You've been carrying around the dryer lint?" she asked.

He nodded. "Yes, because it reminded me of you."

She stared at the bluish-gray fibers. "This reminded you of me?"

Dammit! This was not going the way he wanted!

"Yes, but it also reminded me I was a fool to freak out about it at wilderness boot camp. I reverted to asshattery, and you were right about me becoming the King of Crap. I turned into my worst self. I see that now. I see it so clearly, and it's not what you deserve."

Georgie pressed her fingertips to his lips, silencing his rant.

"What I deserve is an asshat who loves me enough to carry around my dryer lint and quote Shakespeare to me in front of the world."

"You do?" he breathed.

"What I was going to say was that I'm so sorry," she said gently.

He couldn't pull his gaze from her shining blue-green eyes. "Why should you be sorry?"

"I should have trusted that we could get through anything. I should have believed in our investment in each other. I shouldn't have decided to quit the boot camp without talking it over with you. I was mad, and I forgot how strong I was—how strong we are when we work together," she replied, holding his gaze—her beautiful eyes imploring him to believe her.

He shook his head. "But I argued with you over the color rose and told a group of people you were a sex maniac. I let an alpaca spew all over you. And don't forget, I lost my shit over a dryer sheet. I think you had the right to be upset," he replied, then wanted to duct tape his mouth closed.

She patted his cheek. "You are not making a great case for yourself, Mr. Marks."

She was right. This was it. This was his moment to set the record straight.

He steadied himself. "I love you, Georgiana. And if you'll let me, I want to spend the rest of my life proving to you that I will never be reckless with your heart. Please, say it's not over."

She nodded, mulling over his words.

"There are six things we need to discuss first," she answered carefully.

A spark of hope ignited in his chest. "We can talk about whatever you want."

She held his gaze as a tear slid down her cheek. "Number one, alpacas can be real asshats when they want to."

He cupped her face in his hands. "Agreed. Total asshats."

"Number two. You promise to always sleep with your

goose down pillow and will seek appropriate medical care if you ever start snoring again."

He nodded. "Goose down pillows for life. And I'll keep an ear, nose, and throat doc on speed dial."

"Three," she stated, her tone resolute. "The words *shit shovel* will never be spoken between us again."

A shiver spider-crawled down his spine at the thought of that godforsaken implement of horrors.

"Agreed. From this moment forward, we are firmly on team toilet," he answered, somewhat aware of the muffled laughter around them. But it didn't matter. Georgie was here —with conditions—and he was ready to agree to all of her terms.

"Four," she continued. "Lemon verbena will become the official scent of the More Than Just a Number blog."

He stroked her cheek with his thumb. "It was my favorite even before I knew what it was."

Georgie released a shaky breath. "Five, and this one is tough for me, but I'm a strong woman, and I can accept the truth, no matter how hard it may be."

Nothing moved. It was as if the universe itself were bracing for Georgie's stipulation. But, good God! What could she be talking about?

She lifted her chin. "Number five, the color rose is *kind of* pink—even though it is its own color and holds its own on the color spectrum."

He gasped. "Really? It is pink? It looks pink to someone not versed in nuanced color shades. Then again, it could be me. Should we have my vision tested? It could be that," he rambled, then shut his damn mouth, again, wishing for some duct tape, when she turned on the stink eye.

"Kind of pink," she said, lowering her voice.

Point taken.

He nodded, getting the message loud and clear.

"Okay, I agree. Rose is kind of pink but still a solid color all on its own. And six," he pressed—so ready to put these two weeks of hell behind him and move forward with the love of his life.

"Six is about time," she said as another tear trailed down her cheek.

"What about it?" he whispered.

"Time is precious. It's the most valuable thing we have, and I want to spend as much of it as humanly possible with you. We're not over. We'll never be over. The Emperor and Empress of Asshattery have a long reign ahead of them," she finished, gazing up at him.

A rush of gratitude coupled with an unwavering love for this beautiful, intelligent, driven woman washed over him.

He sank onto one knee, blinking back tears. "I did this all wrong the first time. I thought proposing on TV would be romantic. I had no idea everything would turn into a circus. All I want in this world is to walk through it with you. Georgiana Jensen, we don't need the cameras and the fame and the notoriety. Between you and me, right here, right now, I am asking you to marry me." He glanced at his watch. "In four hours and forty-seven minutes."

A heartfelt chorus of sighs erupted around them.

He held Georgie's gaze. "Are there a bunch of people watching us?"

She looked from side to side. "Yep."

"Are they recording us with their phones?" he continued.

She nodded. "Along with a couple of news crews and Barry."

"Hey, guys! This is some great stuff," the CityBeat producer chimed through a sob.

"So, what do you say? Are you ready to join the Empire

of Asshattery to rule the blogosphere together?" he asked, unbothered by the spectators because only one person mattered now.

The one person who always mattered.

Georgie parted her lips, but before she could answer, a horn rang out, playing the first four notes of "Here Comes the Bride."

They looked up to see a giant RV with Acme Pet Grooming Mobile painted along the side.

The tinted driver's side window cracked an inch.

"Jensen and Marks, get in," came a woman's commanding voice with a thick German accent.

13

"We have the assets. Let's move," the wedding frau said to the driver of the enormous vehicle.

"Mrs. Lieblingsschatz, what is all this?" Georgie asked, climbing the few steps into the mobile pet grooming RV.

Dressed in her signature black, the frau gestured to a sofa. Georgie and Jordan sat on plush cushions in what looked nothing like the interior of a mobile pet grooming vehicle.

"This is crazy," Jordan said under his breath, glancing around at the marble flooring and sleek cabinetry in what could only be described as the most luxurious recreational vehicle on the planet.

"Is that a fireplace and wine chiller?" Georgie asked, hardly able to believe her eyes.

The frau huffed. "Of course, there's a wine chiller! You can't drink champagne at room temperature."

"What is all this?" Jordan questioned, tapping a computer screen built into the wall only to have his hand smacked away by a miffed German wedding planner.

"This is the last resort," the frau answered.

The woman pressed an icon on the screen, and an actual table rose from the floor while the mobile mansion's engine purred as the RV merged into traffic.

The frau settled herself into a posh club chair across from them. "Do you know what my marriage success rate is?"

Georgie shared a look with Jordan. "Pretty high," she guessed.

"It's one hundred percent," the frau replied, crossing her arms.

"But that almost changed, didn't it, *liebchen*?"

They glanced over and found Hans from the Denver wedding underground, pushing past a curtain hiding the rest of the RV and sauntering toward them.

"What are you doing here, Hans?" Georgie stammered.

"Did you think I lived in that warehouse like a wedding ring elf with the dildo guy?" the man asked with a teasing expression.

Georgie shared another perplexed look with Jordan.

What the hell was going on here?

The man took the chair next to the frau, then patted her knee.

"We weren't sure about you two after that business with the alpaca," he said with a sly grin.

Jordan frowned. "How do you know about the alpaca?"

Hans glanced at the frau.

"Tell them," she said with an exasperated wave of her hand.

"What did you think you were wearing around your necks at the wilderness boot camp?" Hans asked.

"A tracking device," Georgie answered.

"Yes, it was a tracking device, but it was also a microphone," Hans replied. "Didn't you notice you were the only ones at the boot camp wearing them?"

Georgie gasped. The whole boot camp experience had been so jarring, so utterly discombobulating, she hadn't even noticed if the other participants were wearing the special lanyards.

"Syd and Buck said it was for our safety and that it was court-mandated?" she answered.

Mrs. Lieblingsschatz chuckled. "Aren't they creative! They're dear friends of ours."

"Ours?" Georgie repeated. "You two are together?"

"Married fifty years today," Hans said.

"You're kidding?" Georgie exclaimed.

She'd pegged the woman as a spinster matchmaker!

"Don't look so surprised. To orchestrate love, one needs to understand it completely," the frau replied.

"Happy anniversary," Georgie sputtered.

Jordan lowered his voice. "How do you know Syd and Buck? Were you guys all in the special forces together, or were you spies, once upon a time, thwarting global espionage?"

Georgie nodded. It was a reasonable assumption. After their experiences with both couples, she wouldn't be surprised to learn they'd overturned a corrupt government or rescued kidnapped political prisoners back in the day.

The wedding frau released a full-belly laugh. "No, our time-share in Florida is next door to theirs."

"Time-share?" Georgie echoed.

"Yes, near Cocoa Beach. Syd and Buck aren't always roughing it in the Colorado foothills," the woman replied.

"And Buck is quite an accomplished pickleball player," Hans added.

The frau nodded. "We do need to practice before meeting them on the court again."

Georgie stared at the wedding frau and Hans as the pieces of the puzzle came together.

"Hold on! Did you *orchestrate* the whole catastrophic wilderness boot camp experience?"

The wedding frau's expression grew serious. "As a couple, you needed to lose."

"Lose?" Georgie exclaimed.

"Why would you think that?" Jordan asked.

"We do our homework," Hans replied.

Georgie glanced between the pair. "What makes you think we needed to lose?"

"Let's see," the frau began. "You two are the top bloggers on the CityBeat website. You both won the Battle of the Blogs. You run successful businesses, and before you set foot in the boot camp, you lived together in a cotton candy, lemon verbena-scented, picture-perfect world surrounded by books and bodybuilding equipment where you had ample sex and fawned all over each other. Would you disagree with that assessment?"

Jordan leaned forward. "Cotton candy isn't in keeping with the healthy eating aspect of our blog. If you wanted to depict our lives pre-boot camp, I'd suggest vegan chocolate chip cookies accompanied by a protein shake, but I get what you're saying."

"You needed to have your relationship tested," the frau said, lowering her voice.

"Why?" Georgie asked.

"To know your marriage would last," Hans added gently.

Cornelia Lieblingsschatz relaxed into the chair. "You see, I can plan a wedding at the drop of a hat. I have the finest caterers and the most sought-after dressmakers and floral designers at my beck and call. But here's the thing people forget. A wedding lasts only a handful of hours, but a marriage is meant to last a lifetime."

"What would make you think Georgie and I wouldn't have a marriage that would last?" Jordan pressed.

"Because you weren't in possession of one vital piece of information," Hans replied.

Georgie frowned. She didn't like this one bit. Who were these people to decide what they needed as a couple?

"And what would that be?" she challenged.

"You needed to know that even at your worst, your love and commitment to each other would carry you through the hard times," the frau answered.

Georgie's trifecta nodded.

Holy wedding bells!

The woman was right.

"You, Georgiana, will always be a little bit of a beauty queen, and Jordan will always be a little bit of an over-achieving asshat. That's the word, right? Asshat?" the frau asked, turning to Jordan.

He shrugged. "Asshat or the Emperor of Asshattery. It's up to Georgie to make that call."

Hans pinned them with his gaze. "What you need to understand is when you agree to marry someone, you commit to marrying the whole person. That includes all the quirks and the peculiarities. There will be good times, and we pray they outweigh the bad. But life isn't always fair, and you need the knowledge of knowing your love will get you through whatever obstacles come your way."

Georgie sat there, completely stunned when Jordan reached for her hand and twined their fingers together.

"But we almost didn't make it," he said, the words coming out cracked and broken.

"Ah, but that's where you're wrong, Mr. Marks," Hans corrected.

The hint of a smile bloomed on the frau's lips. "In the days after you left the boot camp, neither one of you said a word about calling off the wedding. You're both stubborn as mules, but your hearts know what matters most."

Georgie drummed her fingers on her thigh. "But after hearing everything we said to each other during the bridal boot camp, how could you think that? Even I didn't know until today what was going to happen," she added.

Without a word, Hans pulled two small felt pouches from his pocket. He poured the contents of the first bag into his hand. There, sparkling under the lights and as beautiful as the day Jordan slipped it onto her finger, was her antique diamond engagement ring.

"I think you always knew you'd be wearing these," the man said, slipping a pair of matching titanium wedding bands from the other pouch.

"Our rings," she whispered, staring at the bands glinting in the light.

Hans passed her engagement ring to Jordan. "Here, Mr. Marks, let's have you do the honors. I sized the ring myself, so it should fit perfectly."

Jordan carefully took the ring from where it rested on Han's palm, then turned to her.

"Let's see if the second time is a charm," he said with a slight shake to his voice.

She held out her hand and watched as Jordan slid the engagement ring onto her finger.

And time stopped.

The breath caught in her throat, and everything stilled.

Life provides so many memorable moments. Snapshots in our minds as crystal clear today as they were when they occurred. The day she received her very own library card. The minute she set foot in the animal shelter and saw Mr. Tuesday. Her first encounter with Jordan, shirtless and glistening in all his hot-bod glory and brimming with a life-supply of asshattery.

"Hans, look! One of the prongs is bent," the frau said, but Georgie couldn't look away from her fiancé.

"It must have happened in my pocket. It's a quick repair. I can fix it now," Hans replied, reaching for her hand.

"No, it's just as it should be," she answered.

"But it needs to be perfect," the man countered, leaning in to examine his work.

Georgie shook her head. "No, it's better than that. It's us. It's who we're meant to be—all flaws and jagged edges. All asshats and pageant princesses. It's everything."

Jordan held her gaze. "We aren't big on perfect, but we know how to be us."

"I see," Hans said, sitting back in his chair.

"Now, all you have to do is stay inside the ring," the wedding frau remarked.

"What does that mean?" Georgie asked.

Hans shared a knowing look with his wife.

"It's the advice the rabbi gave us fifty years ago before we married," the man replied.

Cornelia tapped the titanium wedding rings reverently. "He told us to look at our marriage as if we were inhabiting the inside of the wedding band."

"Often, you're together in the center, loving and cherishing each other," Hans continued.

"But, if your husband enrages you by eating the rest of the *käsekuchen* while you're sleeping," the frau said, eyeing Hans.

"German cheesecake," Hans translated with a chuckle.

The frau continued. "Then, you are on opposite sides of the ring. But you never leave it. You never break the bond. Yes, of course, I am not naïve enough to believe every marriage can last. But I'll tell you this. Hans and I make it our priority to ensure the marriages we bless and facilitate are the kind that will." She turned to Hans. "You know, I'm still mad about that cake."

Hans took the frau's hand and kissed it. "It was a damn good cake."

Georgie observed the couple. "That's beautiful."

The frau's expression grew thoughtful. "It was. Not too sweet and just the right firmness."

Georgie shared a look with Jordan, expecting to find him amused. Instead, he looked guilt-ridden.

"What is it?" she asked him.

"We broke your rule, Mrs. Lieblingsschatz. The one about not..." he said, trailing off as his cheeks grew pink.

"Fornicating," the frau supplied.

Oh no!

"Are you still telling couples that?" Hans asked.

"It worked for us, didn't it?" the wedding frau answered.

Jordan cocked his head to the side. "That wasn't a real rule?"

"Some rules are meant to be broken," the frau replied.

"Good, because we broke this one. Like really, really broke it," he answered.

"It also sounded like you made your own rules to bypass my mandate," the frau added.

Georgie shook her head. "Then, why do you even use it?"

"A little reverse psychology. The forbidden is often the most desired," the woman answered.

"That's for sure," Jordan replied, blowing out a relieved breath.

Mrs. Lieblingsschatz folded her hands in her lap. "The truth is, I was always going to plan your wedding, Georgiana."

Georgie's jaw dropped. "You were?"

"Yes, it's in the contract Hans and I signed many years ago when we decided to expand our wedding planning business."

"I don't understand. How would you know that you were always going to plan our wedding?" Jordan asked.

A smirk pulled at the corners of Cornelia's lips. "Not your wedding, Mr. Marks. Georgiana's wedding. Her stepfather wrote it into our contract."

"What?" Georgie shot back. "I thought my mother contacted you."

"She did, but she doesn't know about this either. You were just a girl when your stepfather's company invested in the Denver Wedding Frau."

"Howard set this up?" Georgie asked, hardly able to believe it.

"Howard Vanderdinkle is discrete, but he wanted the best for you when you decided to get married. Hans and I are the best, so being a prudent investor, he stipulated that his financial support hinged on providing our services to his new stepdaughter when she was ready."

"Wow, I had no idea," she answered, thinking back to a few days ago when she and Howard had their first real heart-to-heart.

First, it was the realization he'd invested in CityBeat and now, to learn he'd cared enough about her to solicit the skills of the city's best wedding duo, made her see the man in an entirely different light.

"That's why Hans and I needed to make sure Mr. Marks was the right match for you," the frau finished.

"So, you sent us into the wilderness and made sure the Plumbing Princess and Mr. Rodent Royalty were there, too?" Georgie asked.

Was there anything these two couldn't coordinate?

The wedding frau narrowed her gaze. "What are you talking about with plumbing and rodents?"

"There was a couple at the boot camp. Jordan knew the woman from when he was in high school, and I knew the man. He was a real creep to me a few years ago and was the reason I started the blog that led me to Jordan."

"We had nothing to do with that, Miss Jensen," Hans replied.

"That was all the universe, adding its own test. And appears you passed with flying colors," the frau added.

Georgie sat there gobsmacked—completely and utterly gobsmacked.

She blinked. Hardly able to believe all that had gone into their wedding and into preparing them for married life. She glanced from the wedding duo to her fiancé—a man who'd proposed to her twice, opened his heart and proclaimed his love for her in front of the world, again, and had carried her dryer lint with him to keep her close.

And that wasn't all.

She'd learned of Howard's affection and the kindness of Mrs. and Mr. Lieblingsschatz—three people she'd never imagined had silently had her best interests at heart for many, many years.

"Can we make a change to the wedding ceremony?" she asked.

The frau frowned. "What kind of change?"

"Our family friend, Mr. Gilbert, is walking me down the aisle. Do you think I could have two people do that?"

"Howard?" Jordan asked.

She nodded and blinked away a fresh wave of tears. "Yes."

The wedding frau snapped her fingers, and a wedding minion emerged from behind the curtain and nodded.

"It's done," the woman replied.

"Where did she come from?" Jordan asked, glancing at the set of thick white curtains separating this section from the rest of the RV.

"What's back there?" Georgie asked.

"The salon," the frau answered.

Jordan craned his head to try to see past the thick drapes. "There's a salon back there?"

"I told you when we picked you up. This was our last resort. We're a fully mobile undercover wedding machine. We've got everything here to prepare for your nuptials."

Georgie tried to get a look. "There are people back there?"

"Yes, and they're all waiting to get you primped and polished," the woman replied.

Georgie pressed her hand to her abdomen as butterflies took flight in her belly.

"My dress is here?"

"Of course," the frau answered with a wave of her hand.

Jordan cringed. "And my tux?"

"Yes, but with a slight adjustment," the frau replied.

"I can't smell it from here. That's got to be a good sign," he said with a touch of relief.

The wedding frau snapped her fingers again, and another assistant emerged from behind the curtain, holding a sleek black tuxedo.

"That doesn't look like my dad's tux," Jordan said, inspecting the jacket.

"He gave us permission to alter the garment," the woman answered.

The assistant carefully opened the jacket to reveal an electric blue lining.

"I think this is a much better way to honor your family tradition, Mr. Marks," the frau added.

Jordan released a relieved sigh. "I couldn't agree more."

"And there was plenty to make a garter for Miss Jensen," Hans added as the assistant procured the wedding staple from the breast pocket of Jordan's jacket and placed it on the table.

Georgie glanced around, still blown away by how everything had come together when she remembered the old wedding adage.

Old, new, borrowed, blue.

"Wait! There's something we've forgotten. We've got old with my vintage ring. New, with the titanium bands. Blue, with Jordan's tux. But what about borrowed?"

"Hans," the frau said with a twinkle in her eyes.

The man retrieved another felt bag from his pocket and produced a hairpin adorned with an arrangement of tiny pearls.

"The borrowed item should come from a happily married couple. We have two borrowed gifts for you," Hans explained.

Cornelia Lieblingsschatz gazed at the hairpin. "I wore this when I married Hans. We'd be honored if you wore it today."

Georgie gently touched the delicate pearls. "It's lovely. I can't thank you enough."

"And the second is the date," Hans replied.

"The date?" she repeated.

"Fifty years ago, Hans and I were married the third weekend in October," the frau added.

"This date was good fortune for us, and we hope to pass it along to you," Hans said, taking the frau's hand.

"And don't forget the mother," Mrs. Lieblingsschatz said, rolling her eyes.

"My mother?" Georgie asked.

The frau leaned in. "Could you imagine what Lorraine Vanderdinkle would be like after a three month, six month, or even a yearlong engagement?"

Georgie shuddered. "There's not enough psychic energy in all the universe for her, Bobby, and Hector."

"Psychic energy?" Jordan questioned.

She cupped Jordan's cheek in her hand. "It's a long story, but we pretty much owe Mr. and Mrs. Lieblingsschatz for the rest of our lives."

Jordan held her gaze. "It looks like we're the real deal, messy bun girl."

"You're going to be *really late* if we don't get things moving," the wedding frau said, then clapped her hands.

The curtains parted, and a team of people stood at the ready.

"These are the best of the best. We've got stylists, seamstresses, aestheticians, manicurists, and makeup artists," Mrs. Lieblingsschatz supplied.

"It's showtime," Hans said with a glint in his eyes, coming to his feet.

The wedding frau gestured for them to follow her into the mobile salon, but Jordan shook his head.

"Hold on! Georgie never answered me," he said, taking her hands into his.

She frowned. "What are you talking about?"

"After the race—after I proposed, again. You never got to answer."

She stared up at him. "Isn't it obvious?"

"I want to hear you say it," he replied, his gaze growing dark.

This man. This handsome, part-time asshat and full-time love of her life.

"Georgiana," he chided, the four syllables sounding good enough to eat.

Her trifecta fanned themselves as she pressed up to her tiptoes.

"You know my answer. Yes! A thousand times, yes!" she whispered against his lips, again, stealing the line from Lizzy Bennet's sister.

He dropped her hands and pulled her into his embrace. Their lips met, and all she wanted to do was melt into his touch.

"Let's never go two weeks without kissing again," she gasped as he threaded his hand into her hair.

"Let's not go two hours," he growled as their connection grew more heated by the second.

"Two minutes," she countered, needing more of him, all of him until the "Here Comes the Bride" horn blasted through the RV's cab.

They pulled apart and found everyone smiling, except the wedding frau, who had her hand poised on the computer screen.

"Do I have to press this again? We have a wedding to prepare for! After thousands of nuptials, I've never had a wedding delayed. Not once! And it's not happening today!"

"I better let you go," Jordan said, twisting a strand of her hair between his fingers.

"You probably should," she answered.

He pressed a kiss to her temple. "Promise me one thing."

"Anything," she answered.

He held her face in his hands, a sweet gesture he'd done more times than he could count. But the next time he did it, he'd be her husband.

He caressed her cheek with his thumb. "Don't let them make your hair too perfect. You know how much I love a messy bun."

14

"You can't see me in my dress, Jordan."

"Not even a little peek?" her fiancé asked from the other side of the thick curtain separating them.

She bit back a grin. "No."

"A teensy-tiny look?" he pleaded.

Georgie wanted to shake her head at her persistent soon-to-be husband, but she didn't want to mess up the delicate flowers the hairdresser had painstakingly placed into her bridal-beautiful messy bun.

She glanced in the mirror and lifted her hand to touch one of the petals of a dainty white lemon-verbena blossom.

It was a nice touch—and confirmation Mr. and Mrs. Lieblingsschatz had heard everything during their wilderness boot camp blowup. Luckily, if they did think she was a sex maniac, they were polite enough not to mention it.

But, holy alpaca phlegm!

While she understood the motivation of the wedding frau to push their limits as a couple, she never wanted to attend another wilderness boot camp—not for all the vegan chocolate chip cookie dough in the world.

And she wasn't kidding about banning the word *shit shovel*. As much as she enjoyed gardening, she'd never look at a trowel the same way again.

"You smell good," Jordan said from the other side of the curtain.

"Like our laundry?" she teased, inhaling the sweet scent.

"I love the way our laundry smells," he replied.

"And I love you, but I hope you don't have my dryer lint in your pocket," she teased.

"About that..." he answered, trailing off as the muffled sounds of her fiancé shifting and, most likely, parting with the incriminating evidence made her press her lips together to stifle a chuckle.

If Jordan Marks was a superfreak dryer lint hoarder, then he was her superfreak dryer lint hoarder.

She glanced over at a full-length mirror and sighed, taking in her appearance. With Jordan under strict orders not to come over to her side of the RV, all they had to do was wait another thirty minutes until they'd made it to the Botanic Gardens.

In an ivory empire waist gown, harkening back to the age of Jane Austen, and her hair just as she and Jordan liked it, wound into a wedding-chic, messy bun with tendrils framing her face, she'd never felt more lovely or more ready to become Mrs. Jensen-Marks.

Of course, she was going with a hyphenated last name. But it wasn't only her sense of autonomy guiding her in the decision. Jensen wasn't only her last name. It was her father's last name, and she intended to keep it to honor the man she knew was looking down on her and smiling.

"Not too bad, huh?" she whispered to her trifecta, who wholeheartedly approved of her attire.

"Are you talking to them?" Jordan asked.

She could hear the smile in his voice.

"I hope you don't think it's strange that you're marrying someone who converses with her childhood imaginary friends."

He chuckled. "Not at all. I asked for their help today."

She gasped. "When?"

"When I saw you in the hospital lobby. I knew if you sensed I was there and if you turned around, it meant our connection hadn't been broken."

"You asked Lizzy, Jane, and Hermione to get me to look at you?" she shot back.

"Yep, and it worked," he replied, sounding quite proud of himself.

Georgie blinked back tears, wondering if her father hadn't played a little part in that, too, when the RV lunged forward, and she scrambled to stay upright.

"Are you okay?" Jordan called.

"Yeah, but why are we stopped?"

"It's the engine. It's completely seized," the driver called.

The wedding frau appeared from the back of the RV.

"No, no, no! This cannot be happening!"

After the beauty experts had finished getting them nuptial-ready, they'd dropped them off in the city. But with time to spare, the wedding frau had directed the driver to make another loop before she and Jordan were to meet a pair of Bentleys, waiting in Denver near the gardens, to make their grand entrance.

"We'll call for a car," Hans said, from over on Jordan's side.

"There's no time. We're in the foothills," his wife replied.

The foothills?

Georgie went over to a tinted window and nearly fell over when she saw a familiar sign.

Actually, two familiar signs.

A pair of signs she'd never forget for the rest of her life: the welcome sign for Knotty Pines Resort and a cardboard sign, directing poor souls to hell on earth, otherwise known as wilderness boot camp.

"What are we doing all the way out here?" she asked.

The frau ran her hand through her asymmetrical bob. "I told the driver to go this way. It's exactly thirty minutes from Buck and Syd's land to the Botanic Gardens. I had everything timed perfectly."

"What about calling up to Knotty Pines? Surely, they'd have a car to lend," Hans offered.

Mrs. Lieblingsschatz whispered something in German that sounded like a curse. "This is the week they're closed down for maintenance to prepare for the winter season. It's only tradesmen and cleaning staff."

"What about Buck and Syd? I bet they've got a stripped-down Hummer or a military Jeep hidden on the property in some bunker," Jordan tried.

"No, they're already in Florida," the frau lamented, holding out her phone to reveal a text message along with a picture of Buck and Syd, donning tennis whites and holding champagne flutes.

"Do you think they'd mobilize the National Guard or send a flight for life helicopter?" the wedding frau mused.

"*Liebchen*, you can work magic with weddings, but activating the armed forces in the name of a wedding may be beyond your reach," Hans replied.

But what were they to do?

Georgie glanced out the window as a white van rumbled down the road from Knotty Pines.

"I'll stop that van and see if we can get a ride!" she said, heading toward the front of the RV.

"I'll come with you," Jordan called.

Georgie froze. "You can't! I don't want you to see me."

"You're not going out there on your own," he answered, picking this moment to go all alpha CrossFit trainer.

"Fine, cover your eyes."

"With my hands?" he asked.

"Yes, with your hands!" she answered, sharing an eye roll with the frau.

"What if I have to protect you from some lunatic driving around the foothills in a creepy van and, accidentally, look at you?" he pressed.

This was getting crazy. If anyone was about to look like a lunatic, it was a woman in full wedding attire, flagging down cars in the middle of nowhere.

"Close your eyes. I'm coming over," she said as an idea popped into her head.

Georgie whipped open the curtain and feasted her eyes on her handsome fiancé.

"Wow, you look amazing!"

"Not too bad, right?" he answered, eyes closed.

"Here, I've got something that will prevent you from seeing me, even if you accidentally open your eyes."

"What is it?" he asked with a furrowed brow.

She slid her dress up, removed the garter, then pulled it over Jordan's eyes.

"There! I'm a MacGyver bride! That should keep you from seeing me."

"What if the driver of the van is some nut?" he asked.

"Then, I'll tell you, and you can slingshot my garter at him. Come on," she said, taking him by the hand.

The van rumbled toward them, and she positioned herself right in its path. Waving wildly, she squinted, trying to read the lettering on the vehicle's windshield, then froze.

It couldn't be!

She narrowed her gaze, double-checking what she'd read.

"You are never going to believe this, Jordan!"

"What is it?" he questioned, looking side to side—for what reason, she didn't know.

All the man could see was electric blue fabric and lace.

The van slowed, and the driver craned his head out of the window.

"Virginia?"

Georgie's jaw dropped.

"Is that who I think it is?" Jordan asked, disbelief coating his words.

Georgie blinked once, then twice, and lo and behold, sitting in the driver's seat of a Casey Pest Control van was the one and only, Brice Hannibal Casey.

"What are you doing out here?" Brice asked, getting out of the van.

She gestured to her dress. "We're trying to get to our wedding."

Brice sucked in a tight, cringeworthy breath. "Knotty Pines is closed. You can't get married there. Plus, I was taking care of a little pest problem, and that ballroom is Dead Mouse City at the moment. Wait," he said, glancing down the road that led to Buck and Syd's place. "Are you getting married at the wilderness boot camp? Depending on how many guests you have, you're going to be digging a lot of holes."

Georgie gave the guy a placating grin. "No, we need to get to the Denver Botanic Gardens."

Brice pushed up his cap and scratched his head. "What are you going to do there?"

God, bless him! This man was not the sharpest tool in the shed.

"We're supposed to get married there. That's why I'm in a wedding dress and Jordan's in a tux."

"Hey, man, looking good!" Brice said, unfazed, as if it were commonplace for him to run into people, sauntering around in bridal gear.

"Brice, can you drive us to Denver?" Jordan asked.

"Sure, but you've both got to ride in front. My equipment takes up the back," he answered, pulling the cap back onto his head.

"Thank you! We'll ride anywhere," Georgie answered.

Never in her life did she think she'd be so happy to see Brice Casey.

The Lieblingsschatz wedding duo exited the RV and joined them on the road.

"We've got a car coming, but the driver says he's fifteen minutes away," Hans said.

Georgie breathed a sigh of relief. "That's all right! We can all ride in Brice's van."

"Sorry, Virginia, no can do. Like I said, the back of the van is full. I can only fit two," Brice replied.

The wedding frau hurried to the van's passenger side door and gestured for them to get in. "You and Jordan need to go. My people are already at the venue. Everything will run like clockwork, and Hans and I will arrive as soon as we can."

Georgie took Jordan's hand and led him to the van.

"Thank you for everything, Mrs. Lieblingsschatz," she said, growing emotional.

The wedding frau's features softened. "You're wearing my hairpin, Georgiana. I'm Cornelia to you now."

Georgie reached out and squeezed the woman's hand. "Thank you, Cornelia."

The frau's gaze grew glassy, but before a tear could be shed, she cleared her throat.

"You, pest control guy!"

Brice straightened up like a soldier. "Yes, ma'am!"

"You need to drive quickly, but you also need to drive safely. Can I trust you with this task?"

"Aye-aye, captain," Brice answered, saluting the frau.

"I don't want to see one wrinkle on that dress! Do you understand?" she threatened.

He saluted again. "No wrinkles! Sir, yes, sir!"

Brice opened the passenger side door for them and guided the blindfolded groom onto the seat. "You're going to have to sit on Jordan's lap, Virginia."

She settled herself on her fiancé's lap, and Jordan's body vibrated with suppressed laughter. At this point, she didn't care if Brice called her Virginia, Georgia, Tennessee, or Madam Michigan. He just needed to get them to the gardens.

She adjusted herself on Jordan's lap and clumsily buckled them in

Jordan wrapped his arms around her. "This is it, isn't it?" he whispered into her ear.

"Is what?" she whispered back.

"Exactly how you pictured your wedding day," he said with a smirk.

"Isn't this what every girl dreams of?" she teased.

"Not Cammie," Brice said, popping the gearshift into drive.

"Did you guys break up?" she asked.

"It was the Cheetos that got us," Brice replied, shaking his head.

"I'm sorry to hear that," Jordan said.

"Me too. Camille seemed great," she added.

Brice sighed. "She is great, but now she's with Johnny Squat Johnson."

"Who is Johnny Squat Johnson?" she asked, unable to stop herself.

Brice's shoulders slumped. "A better fit for her. His dad owns a company that provides porta-potties for outdoor events. It makes sense that the Prince of Potties would end up with the Princess of Plumbing."

"That's a real bummer, Brice," Jordan said as his cheeks turned red from his clever little pun.

Georgie elbowed her fiancé in the ribs, then covered her face with her hands, not wanting to laugh at this poor man.

She glanced around the van, littered with invoices and takeout wrappers, needing badly to change the subject if she didn't want to break out into a giggle-fest.

"Brice, I didn't know you worked out in the field. I thought you were the Vice President of Operations at your company."

"I am," he answered with a resolute nod.

"I figured you'd be in an office."

"My dad's the president. He gets the office. I need to learn the business and get my hands dirty. That's what he tells me, so, here I am," he added with a thoughtful expression.

She stared at this man who'd been the catalyst for getting her to this moment. This person she'd pegged as an absolute jerk, who may be more than a jackass mouse killer with good hair.

Emotion welled in her chest. "Brice, I need to thank you."

"For what?" he replied.

She sighed as contentment washed over her. "For being a real douche canoe."

"Jesus, Georgie!" Jordan gasped.

"No, I'm serious, and I mean it in the best way. You might not be able to remember my name, but without you and that awful first date we had years ago, I don't know if I'd be marrying the man of my dreams today."

"Georgie's right! We both owe you," Jordan said earnestly.

"I should thank you guys, too. I've learned a lot from your More Than Just a Number blog. And you're right! I was a douche canoe. I think I got a lot of chicks over the years because I have great hair."

"Man to man, you do have good hair," Jordan said, holding out his fist to get a bump from Brice.

"And, Virginia," Brice said.

"Yes," she answered, because why the hell shouldn't she answer to it.

"You were never an eight," he answered solemnly.

She patted his shoulder. "Thanks, Brice. That's kind of you to admit."

"I read one of your posts on the importance of honesty, and I have to tell you something," he continued.

"Please, go ahead," she said, starting to like this More-Than-Just-a-Number-reading Brice Casey.

"You're more like a seven-point-five. But I rounded up," he replied with the expression of a blissfully clueless golden retriever.

Jordan's head dropped to her shoulder as he shuddered with another round of barely restrained laughter.

"I appreciate your honesty, Brice," she said, shaking her head as the van pulled up to the Denver Botanic Gardens.

Brice shifted the vehicle into park and glanced over at

them nervously. "I got you here in one piece, and your dress looks okay to me. Do you think that German grandma ninja lady is going to come after me?"

She couldn't hold back a chuckle this time. "No, I think it's safe to say you saved the day, Brice Casey."

"You sure did. Thank you," Jordan added as the passenger door flew open.

"Pumpkin! What are you doing in a pest control van?"

Georgie scanned the sidewalk in front of the gardens' main entrance to find her mother, looking sorceress elegant in a flowing rose-colored gown. Howard stood beside her with Mr. Gilbert and Jordan's dad close by. Maureen and the twins waved to her as the girls spun in circles in their matching flower girl dresses, while Irene, her husband, Becca, and Mr. Tuesday, adorned with a smart doggy bowtie, brought up the rear of the entourage with Barry, phone in hand, filming their unorthodox arrival.

"Is the whole crew here?" Jordan asked.

Georgie gazed at the group. "Yep, and Barry's here livestreaming, and FYI on the dresses—my mother and bridesmaids are all in—"

"Rose-colored gowns," Jordan replied. "Hans dropped that important piece of information while you were having your hair done, so I wouldn't make the mistake of calling them pink."

She smiled, taking it all in.

"Hans and Cornelia don't miss much, do they?"

"They sure don't," he answered.

"Well, come on, pumpkin! I still need to check the harpist's psychic energy before she begins to play," her mother exclaimed.

Georgie caught Howard's eye, and her stepfather tossed her a wink.

Jordan's father offered her his hand and helped her from the van.

"You look beautiful, Georgie," the man offered with tears in his eyes.

"You sure do," Mr. Gilbert added, pressing a kiss to her cheek as the *ding-ding* of a bike bell rang out.

"Georgiana Jensen?" called the young man, pedaling the Schwinn.

"That's me!" she said, glancing around, but everyone looked as confused as she was—except Jordan, who sported a cocky grin.

"Delivery, here you go," the kid replied, passing her a small box.

"Who would send me something?" she asked.

"It's your bride's gift. Open it," Jordan answered, still wearing her garter over his eyes.

She lifted the lid and found a rose gold charm bracelet.

"What is it?" Becca asked.

Georgie lovingly touched the charms. "It's us."

One by one, Georgie ran her fingertips over the number eight, the number ten, a sweet little computer mouse, a tiny book, a miniature cookie, an adorable barbell, a Birkenstock sandal, and a dainty trowel.

Her heart felt as if it were close to bursting.

"When did you do this?"

"Hans helped me design it while you were still getting ready, and then he had a jeweler put it together. The reach of the Denver Wedding Frau has no limits," he added.

"I love it, Jordan," she said, then gasped. "But I didn't get a gift for you."

He gathered her into his arms. "Georgiana Jensen, in a matter of minutes, I'm going to take this damn garter off, and you're going to give me the best gift I could ever receive."

"And what's that?" she asked, forgetting the group gathered around them.

She stared up at this man, who'd changed everything for her. When she'd met him, their lives had collided like a tornado crashing into a tsunami. But no matter what life put in their path, they always found their way back to each other. The obstinate eight and the perfect ten, who once were ready to claw each other's eyes out, had found a love ready to last a lifetime.

He raised her hand to his lips and pressed a kiss to her palm.

"The most important thing. Something I'll guard and protect every day for the rest of our lives. Your heart, Georgiana. Your beautiful, caring, cardigan-wearing, sixty-nine-loving, vegan-chocolate-chip-cookie-eating, book-obsessed heart."

She could hear her mother and the rest of the group chattering away, reminding them they needed to get moving and that the guests were waiting.

But none of it mattered.

Not the cake or the flower arrangements or the twinkling lights.

While all that would certainly be wonderful, this would be the moment she'd carry with her for the rest of her life.

Here, on the sidewalk, standing next to a pest control van with her fiancé wearing her garter over his eyes. This was the location where she'd surrender her heart to the person who knew it best and loved it the most.

EPILOGUE
JORDAN

"The bride was a vision in white, dressed in a stunning ivory gown," Georgie read, glancing at her phone.

Jordan rolled over, took the device from her hand, and set it, face down, on the bedside table.

His gaze lingered on his wife's naked body. "I agree. You were a vision in white, but I'll take you like this over a dress any day."

She raised her hands over her head, presenting her beautiful breasts and lick-worthy torso as if it were his birthday.

Actually, it was better than his birthday. It was their honeymoon.

With the hypnotic ebb and flow of the ocean meeting the sun-kissed coast just a few feet from their private bungalow, two days after they wed, they'd traded the Colorado mountains for the stunning beaches of Fiji.

"I could get used to this," she said, then frowned.

"What is it?" he asked.

She glanced over at a plate of fruit. "I am a little hungry."

He reached over and plucked a piece of pineapple from the plate. "I can't believe you like this stuff now."

"It must be the island vibe," she answered before he placed the tropical bite of fruit into her mouth.

Georgie hummed her delight, and the sexy sound went straight to his cock.

After a whirlwind engagement, culminating in an unforgettable wedding ceremony, covered by CityBeat, viewed by millions around the world, and attended by all their friends and family—including at least five hundred of Georgie's mom's closest acquaintances, all he'd wanted was to be alone with his wife.

Wife!

He loved the sound of that.

And, clocking in at over six thousand miles away, a secluded beach house at an exclusive Fiji resort was just what they needed.

"I can't believe you didn't know your mom and Howard had this place," he said.

"There's a lot I didn't know about my mother and Howard, but I don't want to talk about my parents at the moment," she answered as her gaze hungrily traveled down his naked body and settled on his hard length.

That was the other thing. He might not have been wrong about making her out to be a sex maniac.

Honeymoon Georgie was downright ravenous—not that he was complaining.

After two weeks spent pining away for her, he was damn near ready to explode. Luckily, all that pent-up sexual energy wasn't going to waste.

She sat up and arched her back lazily like a satisfied cat.

"Do you know my favorite thing about lounging around all day in paradise?" she purred.

"All the pineapple you can eat?" he teased.

She shook her head, then reached for a strip of the sheer fabric hanging from the canopy bed. Slowly, she wrapped the lace curtain around her wrist.

"All the creative ways we can *fuck* without even leaving the house," she answered.

Yep, Honeymoon Georgie had a dirty, dirty mouth when it came to getting down and dirty.

He reached over toward the other side of the bed and pulled another sheer strip of fabric over. He brushed the lace across her torso before wrapping it once, then twice around her other wrist.

"I've got you right where I want you," he said, prowling the length of her body and dropping kisses between her breasts.

With the lace wrapped around her wrists and her body glistening in the sun-dappled light cascading in through the bungalow's open windows, Georgiana Jensen-Marks looked good enough to eat.

He worked his way down, licking a heated trail from her breasts to her navel before settling between her thighs. Georgie writhed beneath his touch and cried out as his tongue found her most sensitive place. He gripped her ass, pressing his fingers into her soft skin, then gazed down at his beautiful wife.

He'd never tire of this view.

He tightened his grip on the perfect globes of her ass, then glanced up and met her gaze. "Are you ready for an earth-shattering orgasm, *wife*?"

"Are you up to the task, *husband*?" she asked with a sexy as sin smirk.

"You tell me," he breathed against her tight bundle of nerves.

She gasped as he feasted on her sweet center, working her with his mouth and setting a seductively slow rhythm.

Georgie's chest heaved with each breath as he set a pace to drive her wild. This wasn't going to be a quick fuck—not that there was anything wrong with a quick roll in the proverbial hay. They'd started the day with a little yoga on the beach that quickly turned into an erotic downward-facing doggy-style sexual melee. But this sexcapade was not going to end in a matter of minutes.

Georgie moaned, and a surge of possessive desire coursed through his body. With her arms restrained, he had complete access. He was in charge of making every cell in her body beg for his touch.

He dialed up the pace, savoring her scent, her taste, and her heated, breathy cries.

"Jordan, I want you inside me. I need you now," she said, gasping for breath and balancing on the edge of oblivion.

Who was he to deny her?

Sweat coated their bodies as he slid his cock inside her and released a primal growl. He gripped the top of the mattress while his other hand tightened its hold on his wife's ass. With their bodies flush and his hard muscles meeting her soft curves, he captured her mouth in a scorching kiss.

"Jordan, please," Georgie pleaded against his lips.

She rolled her hips, and he couldn't hold back. The sultry scent of sex and steamy slap of skin on skin permeated the room as he rocked into her, filling her to the hilt with each thrust.

The coil within him tensed, growing taut as if he could explode at any moment.

Georgie tightened around him, calling out his name, and crashed into her release.

Pistoning his hips, he joined her, flying over the edge and soaring through an orgasmic cosmos where only the two of them existed. He couldn't tell where his pleasure stopped, and hers began. They were one, all sweaty limbs and heated breaths—all gentle caresses and sensual, lingering kisses.

She belonged to him. Her heart was his to guard, honor, and protect. As she gazed up at him with a sweet, sated expression, his heart was home.

"You get more beautiful every day, did you know that?" he asked, brushing a strand of hair from her face.

"Do I?" she replied through her lashes.

He drew his fingertips across her kiss-plump lips. "And every day, I find something new to love about you."

"What did you find today?" she asked on a sated sigh.

He kissed a line to her shoulder. "This freckle right here," he answered.

"It's a ticklish freckle," she replied with a giggle.

He reached over and unwrapped the lace curtains from her wrist. Georgie sank back into the pillows and stroked the back of her hand down the scruff of his jawline.

She gazed up at him. "I like you a little rough around the edges, *husband*."

He ran his hands through his hair, mussing his usually coiffed style. "We can't all have Brice-Casey-perfect hair all the time," he joked, and Georgie shook her head as her phone pinged.

She glanced over at her cell. "It could be Irene with a Mr. Tuesday update."

He pressed a kiss to her forehead. "Check it. I'll get us a snack," he said, hating to leave the cocoon of the bed but knowing she'd love an update on the sweet pup.

"Let's do chips and some of that amazing pineapple

salsa. I asked the resort concierge to send some over every day," she called.

He glanced at his wife, who was positively glowing.

"Pineapple salsa it is," he said, sauntering into the kitchen and procuring the snack staples.

"It is Irene," she said, holding out her phone to share a picture of Mr. Tuesday nestled in next to their friend's pregnant belly.

"How are they doing?" he asked, setting a bag of chips and the bowl of salsa onto a tray.

Georgie sat up and smoothed a spot for him to set their post-sex snacks, and he joined her back in bed.

"First, pineapple salsa," she said, loading a chip with more salsa than one would think humanly possible before crunching down on the sweet and salty treat.

"Wow!" he said, both amazed and a little intimidated.

She swallowed the bite. "Okay, Irene says Mr. Tuesday is doing well. He's very protective of her and loves her baby bump. And they got nine inches of snow last night," she finished, then typed out a message as her lips twisted into a naughty grin.

"What are you writing back?" he asked.

Georgie licked her lips. "I told her I got nine inches, but it has nothing to do with snow."

"Georgiana, what would your trifecta think?" he shot back, teasing his very naughty wife.

She gasped. "I don't know what's wrong with me! It's like I'm becoming a—"

"Sex maniac?" he mused.

"Yes," she answered, crunching into another pineapple salsa-laden chip.

He kissed her cheek. "You may also want to look into competitive eating."

"Oh, and look at this, Jordan!" she continued, ignoring his comment. "We have tons of posts on our blog, wishing us well on our honeymoon. Even the Belgian Waffle Princess sent us a message."

"How is her royal waffle-ness doing?" he asked, sinking into the pillows.

Georgie rested her head on his chest. "She says congratulations, and I quote, 'Georgie and Jordan's unorthodox courting and engagement has been a delight to read about. I can't wait to see what it's like when the two of them have a baby,'" she finished, then popped another chip into her mouth.

The breath caught in his throat.

Holy pineapple salsa!

He glanced around the bungalow. There were pineapples everywhere. She'd literally been eating pineapple nonstop since they'd arrived on the island. If it wasn't for all the sex, taking her away from indulging in the tropical fruit, she might have turned into one by now.

"Georgiana?"

"Yeah?"

"Do you want any vegan chocolate chip cookie dough? The staff stocked the fridge with about twenty tubes," he asked.

She shook her head. "It doesn't sound appealing."

He twisted a lock of her hair as his mind went into overdrive.

They'd been having lots of crazy, mind-blowing sex.

His wife now positively glowed as if she were part firefly.

And she suddenly loved pineapple more than anything —even, it seemed, more than her beloved cookie dough. And, slightly more concerning, she'd wolfed down those chips like a teenage boy hitting a growth spurt.

"A baby! Isn't that crazy? Can you even imagine, Jordan?" she said, reaching for another chip.

He smiled at his wife. If these signs meant what he thought, the Belgian Waffle Princess may not have long to wait.

ALSO BY KRISTA SANDOR

Sign up for my newsletter at **www.KristaSandor.com** to get all the up-to-date Krista Sandor Romance news!

Own the Eights Series

A delightfully sexy enemies to lovers series

Book One: Own the Eights

Book Two: Own the Eights Gets Married

Book Three: Own the Eights Maybe Baby

The Bergen Brothers Series

A steamy billionaire brothers romantic comedy series

Book One: Man Fast

Book Two: Man Feast

Book Three: Man Find

Bergen Brothers: The Complete Series+Bonus Short Story

The Langley Park Series

A suspenseful, sexy second-chance at love series

Book One: The Road Home

Book Two: The Sound of Home

Book Three: The Beginning of Home

Book Four: The Measure of Home

Book Five: The Story of Home

ACKNOWLEDGMENTS

There would be no shit shovel or dryer sheet hootenanny (I've always wanted to use this word) without Jessie and Becca. I love the outdoors, but I am not an outdoorsy gal and needed some help researching life in the wilderness.

I put out a call on Facebook, asking my friends to share their wilderness camping experiences, and thank my lucky, indoor-plumbing-loving heart, Jessie and Becca answered that call. Thank you for sharing your experiences!

Next, I have to thank the dream team of alpha-reading, editing, and proofreading: Tera, Courtney, Kendra, Michelle, and Marla. Whenever I write a book, I say to myself, this time, they won't find any edits! It's perfect! And every single time, I'm dead wrong. Thank you for using your eagle-eyes and editing knowledge to make my sweet little books sparkle and shine.

And what about this cover? Thank you, Marisa-rose Wesley from Cover Me Darling for always knocking it out of the park!

I must also thank my Book Babes Reader Group on Facebook. I adore you all! You brighten my life every day. You are my people, and I am so blessed to have you in my life.

Now, Ms. SE Rose, USA Today bestselling author, my partner in crime, and friend with a heart of gold. The day I found you on Twitter (yep, we met online), I knew we were going to be friends for life—whether you liked it or not! All kidding aside, I love you, my friend.

I cannot forget to thank the man of my dreams who just happens to be my husband. It's helpful when it works out like that. Thank you for being my person, for always supporting me and, most importantly, fixing my computer when I mess something up. I know you're rolling your eyes, but you still love me.

And you, dear reader. None of this is possible without your support and love. Thank you.

ABOUT THE AUTHOR

If there's one thing Krista Sandor knows for sure, it's that romance saved her.

After she was diagnosed with Multiple Sclerosis in 2015, her world turned upside down. During those difficult first days, her dear friend sent her a romance novel. That kind gesture provided the escape she needed and ignited her love of the genre.

Inspired by the strong heroines and happily ever afters, Krista decided to write her own romance novels.

Today, she's an MS Warrior and living life to the fullest. When she's not writing, you can find her running 5Ks with her handsome husband or chasing after her growing boys in Denver, Colorado.

Never miss a release, contest, or author event. Visit Krista's website at www.KristaSandor.com and sign up to receive book news updates.